C

Book One of the Protector Trilogy

Jack McCarthy

and

Brian Rathbone

DEDICATION

This book is dedicated to Velma, who has believed in me even when I couldn't do the same for myself.

And to Brian, for whom it can truly be said, "This book would not exist without him."

Special thanks to Andrea Howe, whose editing skills, keen insight, and attention to detail provided a much-needed finish to an otherwise rough draft. Blue Falcon forever!

ABOUT THE AUTHORS

Jack McCarthy was born and raised in Salem, New Jersey, and is a long-time resident of Cleveland, Ohio. His lifelong path to writer has included dishwasher, video store clerk, taekwondo instructor, factory assembly worker, telemarketer, casual letter carrier, office temp, door-to-door vacuum cleaner salesman, phone psychic, cashier, gas station manager, flight attendant, and software engineer. This combined skill set could belong to only one destined to write fantasy novels.

Brian Rathbone spends a little too much time in his own world, but this novel is proof he sometimes allows others to visit. Working with Jack McCarthy has been a longtime goal and dream. There will be more to come. In the meantime, Brian will be working on the fourth and final trilogy in the World of Godsland primary story line.

Chapter 1

Honor is the measure of a man: it defines his worth and gives weight to his words. Guard your honor as you would your life.
--Belond, headmaster of Scaleback Academy

* * *

Thick mist clung to the morning air. The sun, just above the horizon, fought to disperse the gray soup but was losing. Captain Torreg strained his eyes, peering into the murk, just able to make out the edge of the Jaga, demarcated by twisted and blackened trees, their barren branches resembling hands reaching for the sky in supplication.

As the sun rose, the landscape brightened and became somewhat visible, but the mist persisted. From his vantage point atop the hill, Torreg could make out the marshy, uneven ground that stood between the Jaga and himself. The previous night's rains had soaked the earth liberally; crossing the marsh would be treacherous on foot and impossible on horseback. Without turning to look, Torreg knew the same terrain stretched for miles behind, effectively cutting off any hope of escape.

It had taken two days of hard marching for his band of armed men to arrive at this location. The steady rain over several days made the swamp forbidding terrain. Exhaustion seeped from every soldier. Several coughed through their helmets--surely a sign of encroaching sickness. He had faith that his own men, all Royal Guardsmen, would hold up under these conditions, but the Midlanders accompanying him didn't inspire confidence. They were poorly trained and poorly equipped by his standards, but he felt gratitude for their numbers, despite those misgivings.

It presented bad circumstances for any battle, let alone facing an overwhelming enemy.

A discordant, shrill note originated from the twisted trees, shattering the morning quiet. The wait was over. Battle arrived regardless of how ill prepared his men might be. Those surrounding him clutched their weapons nervously.

Another note sounded from the Jaga in response. Figures began to emerge from the blackness, growing in size as they covered the ground to the defenders. Blood-curdling shrieks, like those of rabid animals, reached the ears of Torreg's little band of fighters. The ash-covered swamp men of the Jaga rushed across the marsh with surprising speed, waving their weapons wildly as they came. Even from this distance, Torreg thought he could see the whites of eyes widened with blood frenzy.

"Loose!" cried the captain.

The air filled with the sound of strumming and black-shafted arrows whipping away as the archers in Torreg's unit let loose the first volley. The savages of the swamp had not covered half the distance to them yet when the arrows descended upon them like a cloud of hungry insects. Many in the lead fell, but more spilled forth from the black forest. Even as the archers loosed a second volley, bringing down a swamp man with almost every shot, the ranks of the enemy continued to swell, and the first of the frenzied warriors reached the bottom of the hill.

The Royal Guardsmen formed the vanguard of the band, flanked on either side by Midlander footmen. The shining armor of the Guard stood in sharp contrast to the simple but sturdy leathers of the Midlanders. The Guard stood resolute as the frothing lunatics scrambled up the hill toward them. Torreg raised his sword in the air, and his men matched him. Their voices cried out in unison as the advancing line crashed into them.

"For the king!"

The swamp men fought savagely, without restraint. Their crude weapons clashed repeatedly against the shields of the Guardsmen, often breaking in two with the ferocity of the blows. Many fell to the guards' swords, for the attackers made no effort to protect themselves. Instead, the swamp dwellers seemed intent on shedding blood alone.

At first the formation held, and Torreg fought shoulder to shoulder with his men. But the onslaught, so chaotic and unpredictable, spread the fighting across the hillside, engulfing the Midlanders as well. Volleys of arrows flew from behind them, and the fallen littered the marshlands leading to the Jaga. However, the stream of invaders coming from the black forest seemed endless. The man on Torreg's right fell, and he turned to fend off an attacker, hacking the legs from underneath the savage before turning back to see the man on his left go down under the weight of two swamp men.

The hillside became a churning mudslide as more of the frenzied swamp men clambered up the slopes to reach them. Torreg's breathing came in labored gasps as he swung his sword again and again, driving the enemy back down the hill one step at a time. He found himself fighting side by side with a Midlander--a bear of a youth who dwarfed those around him. The Midlander fought fiercely, laying about with a heavy mace, a thick wooden shield strapped to his other arm. Torreg watched as the young warrior methodically blocked a clumsy thrust with his shield then crushed the attacker into the ground with a mighty downward blow. As another enemy rose in front of him, the fighter kicked the savage in the chest with a weighty boot, sending the ash-covered man tumbling down the hill.

A pair of savages adorned with black wolfskins set upon Torreg. The two dark figures displayed their brethren's barbarism but even more cunning. They attacked quickly and in tandem, one leaping out of reach while the other attacked, keeping Torreg off balance and unable to counter.

One exchange resulted in a flesh wound to Torreg's right calf. He stumbled backward, gritting his teeth with the pain, even as he drove the other wolfskin back with a savage chop of his own. The first dived back in, thinking Torreg undone, but the captain met his charge, despite the wound. The wolfskin ran into the point of Torreg's sword in mid leap, releasing a gurgling cry as the blade penetrated his throat.

The victory cost Torreg another wound, this time to his sword arm. His fingers went numb, and the sword dropped from his grasp, even as the wolfskin sent him to his back with a kick to the stomach. Torreg landed hard in the mud, gasping for breath, as the wolfskin raider launched at him with bloodlust in his eyes.

But the young warrior appeared in the raider's path. He shouldered the wolfskin aside with his shield and caught the unbalanced man with a strike from the mace. The savage crumpled and lay still, even as more of the ash-covered men converged on them.

"The captain is down! Rally on the captain!" cried Sergeant Bolg over the tumult. Torreg knew his men would not reach him in time.

The maceman looked around him, weighing his odds, as the raiders rushed forward. His gaze fell on Torreg momentarily, and his lack of years shocked the veteran captain. *Despite his size, he can't be any older than my daughter*, thought Torreg.

Torreg's surprise deepened when the lad raised his face to the sky and bellowed mightily before placing himself squarely between the raiders and the captain. He met the onslaught with a resounding crash, and one of the swamp dwellers fell in the initial exchange. However, two other warriors exploited the opening presented and drove the Midland fighter stumbling back until he almost stepped on Torreg. A third approached from the left, white froth spilling from the corners of his mouth.

The Midlander took a step back and planted his foot solidly in the muck, straddling the captain. He slammed his weapon into the crude shields of his opponents, driving them backward with his strength and ferocity. Torreg reached across to grasp his fallen sword with his left hand and rolled back just in time to fend off a clumsy attack from the flanking warrior then dispatched the raider with a desperate thrust.

The young warrior had made enough gains to step forward, but even as he did so, another wave of the ash-covered raiders joined the battle. Captain Torreg tried to gain his feet, but he slipped in the muck and remained prone.

With a shout, Sergeant Bolg rushed past the captain, taking up a position to the Midlander's right. They both fought mightily, refusing to give an inch to the Jagans. In short order, two more guards took position on the other side of the maceman, and the four broke the mad charge. Strong hands lifted Torreg from the quagmire, and he surveyed the landscape.

Surprisingly, more survived than not, but most carried wounds as well. The Midlanders had suffered more; almost half their number had fallen, and the rest looked to be in a sorry state. The archers had exhausted the arrow supply some time ago and had fallen to defending themselves hand to hand as the swamp warriors surged around the hill to the rear. Torreg's tiny band still held the hill but found themselves surrounded by quagmire and Jaga warriors.

More notes sounded from the black forest, hollow and booming. Torreg thought it must be some sort of horn, though the source remained hidden among the twisted branches. Immediately the frenzied pack of warriors began to withdraw. They left the perimeter of the hill and surged north, away from the marsh. At first, relief flooded through Torreg, but a chill set into his bones when he realized the implications of the enemy's withdrawal.

"No!" screamed Torreg. "They must not escape! We must stop them here!"

The men of the Jaga simply outnumbered them too much. If the enemy had pushed the attack, the defenders would have fallen. Instead, the swamp dwellers bypassed the hill entirely and moved on.

Torreg cursed his luck and began to contemplate his next move.

* * *

The business of tending the wounded proved difficult in the mud and slickness. Torreg saw to himself first, but before long he strode back and forth along the top of the hill, taking account of his ragtag bunch. His Guardsmen stood bloodied but unbroken, though some of the wounds looked to be problematic if left without treatment for long. Regardless, the men of the Guard didn't complain or even show discomfort. Torreg took pride in their hardiness and courage under such conditions.

The Midlanders fared much worse. They looked disheveled and spent, on the whole. The simple leathers comprising their armor did little to protect them from the biting blades of the Jaga raiders. Many had met death in battle, and from Torreg's estimation, most of the wounded would not survive the resulting infections. He felt for them; most were young, and it seemed such a waste to see them strewn about the hillside like so many broken toys. Of all the Midland forces, barely a third could stand on their own, let alone fight again if the need arose.

Torreg's eyes fell on the adolescent warrior sitting among his countrymen. He listened intently to a diminutive lad sitting next to him. The two looked almost comical when compared side by side.

Sergeant Bolg interrupted the captain's reverie with a grunt. The reliable man sported a fresh wound across his nose--soon to be an angry red scar, Torreg guessed. Bolg saluted sharply and spoke.

"The swamp rats have moved away from the river, by our scouts' reports. Instead, they've moved into the forest and seem to be heading east."

The news puzzled Torreg. Following the river would have led the raiders to Sparrowport. The trading center possessed considerable defenses, but the rewards would be enticing. Sparrowport rested on the trade winds, so large amounts of valuable cargo filled the town's warehouses. In addition to the trade that flowed up and down the river on Midland barges, the amount of commerce that flowed through Sparrowport was substantial. On any given day, a fortune in goods rested within the warehouses of the city.

But east, into the forest, made no sense. Nothing lay in their path except a remote lumber village named Lost Grove. Torreg had been there only once in his fifteen years of service in the Midlands. They would have nothing of value, not even significant food stores, just piles and piles of logs. Torreg bit his lip while lost in thought. The village contained nothing worth protecting, by the standards of the king, but the people of Lost Grove would be caught unaware and defenseless by the men of the Jaga. They would be slaughtered mercilessly ... or worse. It took him a few moments to realize that Bolg still stood at attention.

"Mobilize the men," said Torreg. "We set off as soon as we are ready."

"Where to?" asked the sergeant.

"I haven't decided yet. Get them ready."

Bolg saluted sharply and set to the task, barking out orders as he went.

* * *

In short order, the men packed their meager gear and gathered at the hill's base. Bodies, both friend and enemy, still littered the marsh around them. It pained Torreg to leave them lying in the fetid muck, but time did not permit proper burials.

The Royal Guardsmen stood behind Torreg, looking battered and worn but standing solid and resolute as statues. The remaining Midlanders gathered before him, looking bedraggled and exhausted, with hollow eyes and drawn faces. Their commander had died in the fray, and they looked uncertain and unorganized, not at all like an army at the moment. Torreg did not begrudge them, for what else could one expect from Midlanders? After all, they lacked the discipline and training soldiers received in the Heights. He couldn't possibly order them to accompany him--he simply did not have the right--but he frankly needed every man.

"Men of the Midlands, you will return to Sparrowport," said the captain. "Take the wounded there, and resume posts guarding the town. My men and I will continue to Lost Grove to face the enemy there. You've fought hard already. Most of you come from Sparrowport, so I cannot order you to follow me to Lost Grove. Return to your homes."

Torreg paused momentarily as he considered his next words.

"I cannot order you to come, but I can ask," he continued. "You know the enemy we face, and we are outnumbered and fatigued. But I must continue. I cannot leave the people of Lost Grove to the fate awaiting them. If any among you have the courage and strength to accompany us--"

Without a moment's hesitation, the broad-shouldered warrior took a stride toward Torreg.

"Step forward now," concluded Torreg, rather lamely. He locked eyes with the young man. Fire and determination lay within them. After a second, the young warrior's diminutive companion joined him. Then, in twos and threes, more than half of the Midlanders stepped forward.

Torreg looked at the force before him. Bedraggled, dirty, and battered, they looked fine enough to him at the moment.

"We leave immediately. Send runners ahead to fetch mounts for us. Without them, we have no hope of reaching Lost Grove before the enemy."

As the men began to move out, Torreg caught the eye of the bearish Midlander and beckoned him forward.

"You fought well," said Torreg. "I am pleased you've decided to come with us. What is your name?"

"Onin, sir," said the barrel-chested young man. "My name is Onin."

Chapter 2

The powerful have a responsibility to protect the powerless. An honorable man will never take advantage of those who cannot defend themselves and should cast the harshest rebukes at those who do.

--Belond, headmaster of Scaleback Academy

* * *

The trek through the marsh was taxing on the best of days; to the exhausted men following Captain Torreg, it became brutal. Onin ached all over his body, and he felt fatigue like never before in his life. Onin couldn't imagine a simple village of woodsmen and their families facing the nightmarish raiders from the Jaga. *Not while I breathe,* he thought. *Not if I can do something about it.*

He stubbornly placed one foot in front of the other, refusing to let his pace slacken.

"By all the dragons in the sky, I'm tired," said Flea. Onin shot a glance over his shoulder. The little man stumbled as his foot slipped in the ubiquitous mud of the marsh. "I'm going to sleep for a week once we get home."

"As if Janda will allow it," replied Onin with a crooked grin. "Can you imagine what condition the stable will be in by then? Your first week will be mucking, not sleeping."

"Maybe they'll need us for long, boring stints of guard duty out in the middle of nowhere," said Flea. He made a disdainful face. "Someplace my stepmother won't be able to find me."

Onin laughed. Janda might be kind enough to Flea, but she always overworked the boy. She seemed to have an aversion to paying for labor, so she assigned as many duties as possible to her stepson. Since he lived at her inn, with nowhere else to go, Flea had little choice but to shoulder the work.

"Are you kidding? After this, we'll be appointed to the Royal Guard and have to move to the Heights!" said Onin. "Before you know it, we'll be riding on the back of a dragon, on our way to meet the king."

"And there you go with the dragons again. I swear you're going to marry one."

"It would be an expensive dress," Onin said. Flea laughed and so did Onin. The mirth felt good and lessened the sense of fatigue at least. After a moment, however, they both remembered the destination and their purpose. Suddenly the joviality seemed out of place. The boys fell silent as they contemplated what awaited them in the coming hours.

The march continued through the rest of the day. As the sun set, the band of fighters reached the boundary of the marsh and the way station storing the supplies. Without stopping to rest, the group split into two. The wounded and few who had no will to fight departed for Sparrowport, while Torreg's Guard and the Midland volunteers saddled the horses to make for Lost Grove.

"Make haste!" shouted Captain Torreg. "If we leave immediately, we can reach the village by dawn!"

The men, Onin and Flea included, redoubled their efforts. Within minutes, the horses were saddled and remaining supplies were packed in the saddlebags.

They set off at a canter, setting a pace intended to eat up the distance but preserve the horses as long as possible. Onin had much more experience saddling horses than riding them. Each trotting step sent shudders through his body. Before long Onin felt a terrible ache in his thighs.

Several hours passed before they reached the forest boundary. The rising moon resembled a happy crescent of silver dangling in the sky like a woman's earring. It soon disappeared behind the dark canopy of branches and leaves as they continued into the woods.

Complete darkness soon enveloped them. Patches of night sky peeked through the blackness, but Onin couldn't see anything around him. He had no idea how the horses could see well enough to maintain the current pace but they did. Despite the horse's jostling beneath him, Onin found his eyelids drooping, and his hands felt numb on the reins.

The warmth of the day faded completely, and a deep, wet chill settled over the woods. Steam rose from the mouths of man and horse as the steeds continued to churn along steadily to their destination. The shadows streaked past, and forest sounds echoed in Onin's ears, only to fade behind him. Hunger gnawed at his belly, and he chewed on some jerky he fetched from his meager supplies.

The horses slowed down as the band reached a stream. Taking it slowly, the horses crossed the stream, splashing through to the other side. The cold water shocked Onin to wakefulness, at least for a time, and the horses resumed their canter.

The first hints of daybreak made themselves apparent when the village of Lost Grove came into sight. Onin let out a great sigh of relief, even as his teeth chattered. He desperately wanted to get off his horse and sit next to a fire. By the time he reached the village square with the rest of the soldiers, Torreg had already dismounted and called the locals out of their beds.

A barrel-chested man with an equally large and flowing beard approached the soldiers. He wore his night clothing but carried a wide-bladed woodsman's ax with a well-worn handle. Other villagers, also armed with axes, converged on them.

The captain and the village headman conversed hurriedly. Other woodsmen joined the conversation, but Onin couldn't wait to see more as the soldiers dismounted and began to take stock of the town's defenses.

* * *

Torreg wasted no time and, after a perfunctory greeting, started his explanation before even hearing the bearded woodsman's name.

"Jagan raiders are on their way here. They cannot be more than two hours behind us. Rouse every able-bodied person and arm them. Send the children and elderly into hiding."

The woodsman looked stunned and more than a little skeptical. "Why would raiders be coming here? We are far away from the swamps and have nothing of value."

"I do not know the answer," said the captain, shaking his head. "But they can have no other destination in mind, unless their plan is to wander the woods aimlessly. I doubt that is the case."

The woodsman had been joined by several neighbors, and they conferred hurriedly among themselves. After a short discourse, the first woodsman spoke again.

"We have nothing to offer. We cannot afford your protection. Leave our village now. We'll see to our own safety, like we always do."

Torreg gritted his teeth. While he understood the sentiment, he had no time to convince these hardy folk of his good intentions. He wanted to scream at the gathered men in frustration, denouncing them as fools, but then an alternate tack sprang to mind.

"Very well, we shall depart immediately," said Torreg. "But before I leave, may I inquire as to your funerary preferences?"

"What? Funerary preferences? What are you getting at?"

"Your preferences--as in, would you rather be buried or have your corpses burned? Will there be a need for individual graves, or will a single mass grave suffice? There can't be more than a hundred people in this village, so a ditch of appropriate size could be dug within hours. Then again, with all the logs available here, we may opt for a funeral pyre."

The collected woodsmen looked angry but fearful at his words. They took turns looking at one another but said nothing. The spokesman for the village recovered first.

"By what you say, we could easily take it to mean you will kill us if we do not accept your generous offer of protection from these savages."

"If I intended harm to you or your families, I would have ordered my men to attack the moment we arrived. You were all asleep and unprepared.

This village would be in flames by now." Torreg softened his voice. "Please, do as I say. For the sake of your families, heed me. Each minute is precious."

The woodsmen shared another set of glances and seemed to arrive at a silent consensus.

"All right, we will listen to you," the bearded man said. "But what if these savage bandits never come here?"

"It's my sincerest hope they don't."

* * *

"Here I am, sitting on a stump in the middle of the forest, and it's the most comfortable I've been in days," complained Flea. He wasn't so much sitting as reclining across the stump. His bedroll served as a pillow, while his legs dangled over the edge, resting his feet on the ground.

Onin reached up and yanked the bedroll away. Flea's head landed on the stump with a hollow-sounding thud. Onin laughed as Flea yelped with the sudden pain.

"Your head even *sounds* empty."

"Not all of us can be blessed with a solid rock like the one you have perched on your shoulders." Flea turned to give Onin a disapproving look. "You know I crack walnuts on your forehead when you're sleeping, don't you?"

"That would explain the shells surrounding my bed in the morning." Onin chewed on a knuckle thoughtfully. He took a few steps closer to the forest, staring into the darkness. "How far out do you think they are? Are they really coming this way?" he wondered aloud.

"The captain seems sure of it. I don't know about you, but I'm inclined to listen to him." Flea sat up, his posture pensive and tense. Onin could sense their jokes served to hide the concerns they shared.

"By the gods, there's a lot of them." Flea shuddered with the memory. "When they came from the swamp earlier, I could feel my knees giving way. It was all I could do to keep from running the other way."

"But you didn't," said Onin. He cast a meaningful look on Flea then turned his gaze back to the dark forest. "You stayed and fought as bravely as any of us."

"But I don't know if I can do it again!" he whispered harshly. "What am I doing here? I'm no fighter! I barely know which end of a sword to hold. Any sane man in my position would have gone back with the wounded."

Onin reached out and grasped the front of Flea's tunic. He pulled his friend closer until they were face-to-face.

"You are here because you know it's the right thing. Look around you."

Shocked at his friend's intensity, Flea turned his head to both sides in compliance.

"These people are at the mercy of those devils, and we both know the swampy bastards have none to give," Onin continued. "You were scared before, but you fought anyway. You'll do it again because you know it's the right thing. It's why you chose to come along instead of returning with the wounded."

Onin released his grip. Flea's hands trembled but he set his jaw.

* * *

The preparations were almost complete. The women and children were away, sequestered in nearby caves. Torreg had watched them file past, most in nightclothes with blankets thrown over shoulders. Their eyes were wide with fright at the sudden flight into darkness. Wives pleaded with husbands, children clung to fathers, but the men of the village ushered their families away with reassuring words. After the last of them had moved from sight, the hearty logging folk took up the positions designated by Torreg.

Sergeant Bolg, as always, stood near Torreg. "The women and children are gone. I hear the caves have plenty of space in them. One might wonder why we aren't joining them."

Torreg kept his gaze ahead. "These men seem to understand the need to stay."

"Every man wants to defend his home, of course. But they don't understand the odds like we do. We should lead them to the caves, save as many lives as possible."

"And let the raiders have this village? Then what? This village will be in shambles, and raiders will still be roaming the countryside. No, this ends here."

"What harm can they do? There's not another settlement within days of here. You said so yourself. What are they even doing out here?"

"Only the Founders know the answer. But I am sure it isn't good. Every community, no matter how humble, is under the king's protection. I will not leave Jagans to ravage as they please. As for the odds, they are significant, but we can win this battle. We both know that."

Torreg shot his sergeant a sidelong glance. Bolg nodded reluctantly.

"We end it here. It's our duty." Torreg's tone carried finality.

* * *

By the time the marauders launched the attack, less than an hour had elapsed since the arrival of Torreg's men. The men of the Jaga came streaming from the forest and up the trail, screaming wildly. Most of them still had blood on their weapons from the previous day's battle. The forest echoed with the sound of their approach.

The attackers entered Lost Grove uncontested, and at first impression, the village seemed empty. After the Jagans entered the village square, however, armed men appeared from the doorways, and arrows began to rain down on the savages from the rooftops. The raiders along the trail took the brunt of the archery, and many fell with feathered shafts sprouting from them. More soot-blackened figures emerged from the forest to clash with the defenders on the ground.

Torreg's Guard formed at the far end of the village thoroughfare and advanced on the main body of the enemy. The tight formation of interlocked shields allowed the Guardsmen to thrust their swords over the edges to great effect. The Jaga raiders came at them in a mob, and the stream of savages crashed against the formation and fell away, like crockery being dashed against a boulder. At first Torreg and his men seemed unstoppable, but in a short time, the greater number of attackers began to take its toll. One Guard fell to an attack from a flanking raider, which left an opening in the formation. The raiders pushed into the breach, and two more Guards became casualties. The advance came to a halt as the raiders pressed in from the front and flanks of the Guardsmen.

The Midlanders and ax-wielding woodsmen of Lost Grove had concealed themselves with the log homes of the villagers. In accordance with Torreg's hastily contrived plan, they fell in behind the formation of Guardsmen advancing down the thoroughfare, finishing off the stragglers left in their wake. However, the advance stopped, and the Midlanders and men of Lost Grove gathered into a cluster behind the Guard. More frenzied barbarians spilled forth from the trees, and several hoisted themselves onto the cabin roofs to attack the archers.

Onin found himself at the rear of the group, hard pressed by the encroaching raiders. He smashed at them mightily, driving the enemies within reach away or down to the ground with crashes. Flea fought beside him tenaciously, any hint of his earlier fear having faded away. The large wooden shield fairly covered his entire body, allowing Flea to lash out with quick strikes or stab around the edge, while barely exposing himself to harm.

Onin felt his lungs burn as he heaved about with his mace. Blood flowed from gashes across his arms. A Midland soldier fell to his left, and he moved that way to lend aid. His efforts came too late, however, as a raider stood on the man's sword arm while another ran him through. With a hoarse cry, Onin crashed into them shield-first, sending both sprawling. Still more took their place, and Onin fought on.

Onin's heavy wooden shield, already splintering at the edges, finally gave under the punishment. A chunk sheared away from the top, and the enemy's blade bit into Onin's shoulder. Even as blood flowed from the wound, Onin gritted his teeth and pushed his way forward. He shattered the attacker's sword arm with a follow-up strike then finished him with a backhanded swing to the soot-covered head. Onin's vision grew blurry.

Onin stumbled over the body of a woodsman as he struggled to clear his eyes. Screams of the wounded and enraged filled his ears, but he pressed on, attacking fiercely even though his arms felt leaden with fatigue. He found himself near Flea once again, just in time to see his friend get bowled down by a burly raider. The two rolled over one another, each struggling for an advantage. They came to a stop with the raider on top, his hands clenched around Flea's throat. Onin reached the spot just in time and laid the savage low.

Wordlessly Onin helped his friend back to his feet. Flea shot him a look of gratitude, but neither could spare the breath for words. The pair found themselves in a lull on the battlefield, and Onin used the opportunity to take stock of the situation.

Near the outskirts of the village, the battle still raged. Captain Torreg and his men stood resolutely in the center of the road, their ranks bolstered by the remaining Midland fighters. The enemy swarmed about them, a disorganized rabble, but their chaotic attacks struck home far too often.

Fighting had broken out on most of the rooftops in the village. The archers had long since given up the bow in favor of melee weapons as the savage warriors clambered onto the log dwellings to get at them.

A disturbance at the other edge of the village pulled their attention. The high-pitched screams of children pierced the cacophony of battle, and some tiny forms darted from one of the houses with a pair of raiders in pursuit. Onin would have sworn if he had the breath for it. All of Lost Grove's children had supposedly evacuated to a nearby cave along with the elderly.

Flea, closest to the fleeing children, sprinted forward. Onin pursued his friend but had a greater distance to cover. Raiders joined the chase, seemingly excited by the prospect of easy prey.

Flea collided with the first Jagan just as the fleeing children reached the tree line. The impact sent Flea to the ground, as the enemy outweighed him substantially. However, the savage reeled from the blow and could not effectively counterattack. From his prone position, Flea lashed out with his sword, scoring a deep wound in the leg of his foe. The man fell to one knee but left Flea vulnerable to the next attacker.

Onin willed his feet to move faster, but everything seemed to move slowly--too slowly. He watched in horror as the Jagan's blade entered Flea's gut. A visceral scream tore itself from Onin's throat, and the world exploded into motion, carrying Onin the rest of the distance to his fallen friend.

He smashed the savage with enough force to lift the man into the air. As the body landed in a crumpled heap, Onin spun, his own eyes wide with frenzy, and viciously crushed the knee of another swamp raider. The stout young warrior attacked with a savagery matching the enemy's. He felt a blade bite into his shoulder and another into his back, but there was no pain. His rage deadened him to any sensation. One by one, the marauders in his vicinity succumbed to his relentless assault.

Suddenly no enemy remained. Onin turned in each direction, looking, begging for someone to fight. Only the village defenders remained; the swamp raiders had all fallen or fled into the forest.

Dropping his weapon and shield, he rushed to Flea's side. He grasped the ailing man's hand in his own, but there was no answering grip. Onin looked into his friend's face, desperate for a sign of life. His eyes remained open but lifeless. Solemnly he closed them.

Hanging his head, Onin let the tears flow.

Chapter 3

Do not fear pain. Pain is the fire which tempers your inner steel.
--Prendor, teacher at Scaleback Academy

* * *

Onin lost all sense of time in his grief. He paid no heed to the world around him and gently rocked back and forth while clutching Flea's hand. He didn't become aware of his surroundings until he felt a grip on his shoulder.

He turned to find Captain Torreg regarding him with a sympathetic eye. Despite his red and puffy eyes, Onin scrambled to his feet to stand at attention.

"Nay, lad, there's no need for all that . . ." began the captain.

"I insist, sir," replied Onin. He straightened himself. "I'm not the only one who lost a friend today."

The officer's gaze fell on Flea's still form.

"I recognize him. What was his name?"

"Flea," said Onin.

Torreg laughed out loud. "How fitting." He looked at Onin abashedly. "I'm sorry. I don't mean to laugh at your pain, lad."

"I'm all right, Captain. I think he would have been happy you found it funny. His given name is Jarid, but everyone called him Flea, even his own father. He was my oldest friend."

No tears came but the pain shook his voice. Onin hoped Torreg didn't think less of him for his sentimentality. On the contrary, the captain seemed genuinely interested in learning about the young man.

"How old was he? What of his family?" asked Torreg.

"Fifteen last winter," said Onin. "His mother died when he was a baby, and his father, two winters ago. He only has his stepmother, and she owns the Mossy Scale Inn in Sparrowport."

Torreg nodded. "I know the place. The ale there is terrible. Mostly water."

"You're not the first to say that." Onin laughed.

Torreg looked seriously at Onin. "I saw what happened. I know what he did--what you both did--to save those children. I am honored to have served with Jarid." He turned his gaze on the still form for a long moment. He sighed deeply. "So young," he muttered. Then he turned back to Onin. "My condolences on your loss. I must take my leave of you now."

Onin watched the captain go. He had never heard of a commander taking such an interest in his men. His puzzlement must have been apparent as Sergeant Bolg addressed him next.

"He does the same for everyone. At least, when he can," said Bolg. An angry red wound stretched across his broad nose, marring his already-ugly face. "The captain always wants to know about any man or woman who dies under his command."

"Why?" asked Onin. "I've never heard of such a thing."

Bolg shrugged. "He considers it a matter of honor."

The sergeant turned and walked away. Onin could see the man, indeed, standing next to another fallen Midlander, asking the men around him what they knew about him. The survivors seemed nervous at first, as Onin had, but soon warmed to the task.

Based on the casualties Onin could see around the village, he thought the captain would have a long night.

* * *

It was a somber return trip, despite their victory. Many had been lost in the fighting, and the survivors felt they had lost something of themselves. Many Midlanders, in particular, looked hollow eyed and listless. Only the Guard seemed unperturbed.

Onin watched Captain Torreg closely while preparing for their departure. The stoic officer maintained an air of detachment, but Onin sensed sadness within him.

To his surprise, the captain sent word for Onin to join the front of the procession. The pace settled into something slow and leisurely, which suited Onin just fine after the past several days. As he approached, Torreg waved him forward until the young man rode alongside.

At first the captain said nothing to Onin, instead discussing logistical matters with Sergeant Bolg. Onin sorted through his own thoughts until he heard the captain say, "Would you agree, Onin?"

He reacted with a start. "What's that, sir? I wasn't listening."

"It sits ill with me to leave our fallen comrades in the muck of the marshes. We also have many wounded men who need care sooner rather than later. Do we stop at the marshes to see to the dead there or press on directly to Sparrowport for the sake of the wounded?"

Onin had never been asked his opinion on something so serious. After opening and closing his mouth a few times, he finally spoke. "The dead are dead and can't be helped. The wounded may yet live. It's better to move for Sparrowport. We can return to the marshes to bury our fallen once the wounded have reached town."

"What of the families of the men left to fester in the Jaga?" interrupted Sergeant Bolg. The ugly Guardsmen cast an eye on Onin. "What do you say to the widows and orphans of those men?"

Onin was not a callous lad, but the thought of widows and orphans as an outcome of battle had not really occurred to him.

"I . . . I would tell them we are going back to retrieve them right away and they sacrificed themselves for a worthy cause."

"A worthy cause by your standards, perhaps," interjected Bolg. "I'll wager the women and children of Sparrowport would rather have their men home safely."

Onin's anger rose at the jibe. "And what of the people of Lost Grove? Are their lives worthless?"

"No, course not," said Captain Torreg. "But a poor widow with hungry children will take scant comfort from knowing a few woodsmen survived due to her husband's death."

"But . . . but the ones who went volunteered! I was there! I saw them!" Onin struggled with the conflict between his empathy and his ideals.

"Still, that knowledge will not fill empty bellies come winter," said Torreg coolly. He fixed Onin with an intense stare. "Why did you volunteer to go? Do you have family in Lost Grove? You've the frame of a woodsman."

"No. No family there." Onin grew increasingly uncomfortable with these difficult questions. "I just couldn't bear the thought of defenseless people having to face those . . . things. I don't think any of them would have survived without our help. Who could abandon all those children?"

Torreg pressed on. "If we had this to do over again, would you still volunteer?"

Onin nodded vigorously, without hesitation.

"Even knowing your friend might still be alive?"

This gave Onin pause. A catch rose in his throat as he tried to reply, and he only coughed. After a few moments of clearing his throat, he composed himself enough to say, "Flea knew what he was getting into, and he knew it was right. Neither of us could have lived with ourselves knowing we had left those poor villagers to die."

Try as he might to fight them off, tears blurred his vision. Torreg gave no indication he noticed them, which suited Onin just fine. The officers exchanged a meaningful glance, which Onin missed, and they fell silent for a while as the forest slid gently past.

* * *

Later in the day, they stopped for an afternoon meal. Onin took care of his horse first, tying off then unsaddling the mare to give her a little time to graze. He rummaged around his saddlebags for something to eat, but Sergeant Bolg interrupted him.

"The captain says to come eat with him."

This puzzled Onin more, but he made no protest as Bolg led him to the shaded spot where the captain sat. Torreg stirred an iron pot over a campfire, and steam issued from within. He lifted the spoon to his mouth and tasted it, licking his lips afterward. Nodding in satisfaction, Torreg sprinkled a pinch of herbs into the mixture.

Onin's stomach rumbled loudly as the aroma reached him. The two Guards obviously heard the noise. They both looked at the young man with mock surprise then laughed.

"Better feed the lad before he eats us." Bolg laughed.

"I've heard a dragon's stomach growl before, and it wasn't much noisier," replied Torreg. He began spooning out the stew into tin bowls he had beside the cooking pot.

Onin wasted no time digging in and ate with gusto.

The captain chuckled at Onin's clear enjoyment of the food. "Could use some more onions, and some saffron wouldn't have gone badly," he said, "but thank you all the same. Not bad for trail rations, I suppose."

"Be careful, lad," said Bolg with a smile. "Many a Guardsmen will be jealous you got to eat the captain's cooking. It's been said Torreg is as at home with a ladle in his hand as a sword."

"Aye, and I'm happier with a ladle in my hand too, if truth be told about it," said Torreg between mouthfuls of stew.

Onin nodded in assent.

The little iron pot held a surprising amount, as each man received three healthy servings of the succulent dish. With the stew gone, each man leaned back in satisfaction. Torreg and Bolg produced pipes and pouches of tobacco. Within minutes, both were sending smoke ringlets wafting into the branches of the tree above them.

"An army travels on its stomach," said Torreg. "After enough years of eating dried beef and stale biscuits on the march, one learns to make use of whatever is around." He patted a pouch at his belt. "I've also learned to keep a selection of herbs and spices on hand. A well-cooked meal can do much to raise the spirits of soldiers in the worst possible conditions. Granted, I haven't enough for everyone here. I wish I did. The Founders know they've earned a good meal today."

"Aye, like that winter in Saltgrave," interjected Bolg. He turned to Onin and explained. "We spent two months guarding the salt mines there, but the enemy never came. By the time we realized they weren't coming, we were stuck in the gods-forsaken place for the entire winter. Weeks crammed into the mine's entrance, could barely move without stepping on another soldier. If it weren't for the captain's stock of spices, I think we would have turned on each other before spring."

Onin had heard of Saltgrave before, but he only knew it lay far in the north of the Midlands. Barges loaded with salt would arrive in Sparrowport, and the seasoning would be transferred onto special cargo containers shaped rather like giant baskets. Then they were swooped up by the verdant dragons and carried to the Heights.

Onin stifled a yawn. The warmth of the food had worked its way throughout his body, and the fatigue from the past few days settled on him like a blanket. He felt he could lie back under the shade and fall asleep right there.

Before he could drift off, though, Torreg tapped the ash from his pipe and rose to his feet. Bolg did likewise.

"Time for us to be moving. Get the men ready."

Bolg hurried off to give the order while Onin scrambled to his feet. He wasn't sure if the captain intended for him to ride at the front of the procession again, so he waited before moving there himself. After a short time of overseeing the preparations, Torreg indicated with a wave Onin should once again join him in the lead.

* * *

It wasn't long before the band of men broke out of the forest into open air. The trail turned into a dirt road before them, and the rolling hills bordering the forest stretched away, lustrous and green. The afternoon sun shone brightly, the warmth welcome.

In the sky overhead and far away, Onin could barely see the form of a gigantic verdant dragon. Straining his eyes, he could make out a cargo basket carried in the beast's claws. Onin couldn't help but stare at the dragons in the sky.

As he watched, another verdant came into view, flying in the opposite direction, presumably destined for Sparrowport. The dragons could be seen on any given day, ferrying trade between the Midlands and the Heights.

"Ever seen one up close?" asked Captain Torreg. Onin looked over to see the captain also watching the dragons in the sky.

"Not really," said Onin as he shook his head. "The closest I've been is when they swoop down to grab a cargo basket from Sparrowport." Onin remembered how the wake of their flight would send leaves tumbling down the streets during the autumn. Occasionally the dragon would roar as it went by, shaking the ground.

"Wait until you have to fly on one of those big bastards." Bolg laughed. "Most faint the first time they have a look over the edge of the tierre. Not me, though . . . I just threw up."

Onin laughed in spite of himself. He tried to imagine the view from the back of a dragon. He had been in the mountains before; he thought it must be similar to the view from a sheer cliff.

"I can't imagine why I would need to fly on a dragon, but that sure sounds like something."

"You never know," chimed in Captain Torreg.

* * *

As the city gates drew near, a modest procession came forth to meet the returning victors. The lady mayor and her various hangers-on as well as persons of note from Sparrowport's high-class families comprised the dignitaries. One in particular caught his eye: Zorot Durantis, the trade ambassador. Torreg had never met the man in person, but he was clearly from the Heights, judging by his look and dress. Zorot was known as one of the wealthiest men in Sparrowport, and he held vast influence over the city's trade.

Torreg smiled, though he tried his best to hide it. Everything was going according to plan . . . so far.

"Isn't he the one?" said Bolg in a harsh whisper, indicating Zorot with a sideways glance.

"That's him. He could be our passage back to the Heights."

As a captain of the guard, Torreg was no stranger to court politics, trade agreements, and petty gossip. Far too often, he had been the victim of the first and the last, as his career-long assignment to the Midlands demonstrated.

The captain dismounted to receive his official welcome from the mayor and her gaggle of city officials. Bolg took up position on Torreg's right side, and indicated for Onin to do likewise on the left. Onin did as he was bidden, but with a confused look.

The greetings expressed sincere warmth and gratitude, even from the mayor herself. Her followers issued the usual chain of compliments showered upon the victorious commander: his bravery, strength, cunning, heroism. Torreg received them each with a polite nod.

After the last of the officials had congratulated him, Torreg saw Zorot approaching. He fervently hoped, for once, his deeds had made some sort of impact. He cast about for some way to get a meeting with this man. Politics had never been his strong point.

Before his mind produced a suitable introduction, Zorot stepped right past him and embraced Onin. Onin returned it warmly. Torreg and Bolg looked at one another.

"Captain Torreg, my congratulations to you," said Zorot. "I see you have met my son."

Chapter 4

Family is more than blood and lineage. A true family is bonded through trust and love.

--Zorot Durantis, trade ambassador to Sparrowport

* * *

"The servants found him as a baby, floating in a basket on the river," explained Zorot. The official welcoming ceremony had concluded, and Zorot had graciously invited Torreg to his home for a meal and a talk. Torreg had, of course, jumped at the opportunity. Onin departed shortly after arriving at the Durantis manor, claiming to have other business in town.

"We had just lost our own infant son to fever," continued Zorot. "When the servants brought him to us, we took it as a sign from the gods and adopted him as our own. Onin was so tiny as an infant, I never guessed he would turn into such a bear of a man!"

Torreg nodded. Zorot was not of the Great Families, so adopting a Midland child would not have run counter to his breeding and lineage. Zorot clearly adored his son, adopted or not--his broad smile proof.

"I can say he has done your family proud. He has a moral certainty that makes quite an impression." Torreg went on to describe how Onin volunteered to aid the village of Lost Grove against the Jagan raiders and his valor in battle. Zorot seemed surprised by the story.

"Onin has never been reckless, but he has always been stubborn when he thinks he is in the right. On more than a few occasions, I've had to sort out situations brought about by his sense of ethics.

"But I am surprised by his battle prowess. He has received rudimentary training from the town's militia but has never been in a real battle before this excursion. Truthfully, as he departed, I feared I would never see him again."

Torreg was amazed. Many men could barely stand their ground the first time in battle; Onin had fought like a seasoned veteran. Torreg found himself once again reevaluating the young man and his capabilities. He thought of a way he could curry favor with Zorot while benefiting Onin.

"Zorot, what plans does your son have for his future?" asked the captain with a sly grin.

* * *

When Onin delivered the news of Flea's passing, Janda reacted much as he expected. She made a great show of grief, sobbing loudly and pulling her hair while cursing the gods for taking her "sweet, innocent Jarid" away from her. The display sickened Onin; he couldn't recall Janda having referred to him so affectionately.

Still, he could not bring himself to voice his feelings. Real or not, Onin would not trivialize her grief.

"I am undone!" cried Janda piteously. Her sobs wracked her body, but her eyes were surprisingly free of tears. "What is an old widow to do? How will I manage with all the additional work? The stables alone will be the death of me!"

Onin stifled a snort of derision. He'd never seen Janda so much as lift a broom in her own inn, let alone muck out the stables. He suppressed a smile when one of the patrons spoke out.

"I suppose you'll just have to pay someone to do it, like every other innkeeper in the world."

Janda scowled in the direction of the voice. The speaker, perhaps wisely, decided not to identify himself. Several other patrons covered their faces with their hands, suppressing mirth. Onin had no patience for humor. Though her only relative, blood or otherwise, had died, her first thoughts were of the increased workload for herself. His disgust turned to righteous anger.

Onin left the Mossy Scale Inn and turned to look upon it one last time, knowing he would never return. Onin wiped moisture from his eyes as he hurried away.

He spent some time wandering the streets of Sparrowport, lost in his own dark thoughts. He had spoken his convictions truthfully to the captain and sergeant and truly believed even Flea would do it all over again. He still struggled to accept the empty place his friend's absence left in his heart. He felt responsible for Flea's presence on the field as the two friends had joined the militia together. Onin doubted Flea would have been on the battlefield at all if he hadn't been there.

But in the heat of the moment, Flea had acted courageously and without hesitation. Onin was certain those children lived today because of his friend's quick action.

Many locals greeted Onin as he walked; being the son of the richest man in town had that effect on people. One of the primary reasons Onin had valued Flea so highly was he had been one of the few people who never sought to curry favor with Zorot through his son. He waved or nodded politely at each greeting or congratulatory statement, but he never stopped to talk. He simply had no words to share and no patience for platitudes.

It was not long before his strides carried him toward his home. He had nowhere else to go in Sparrowport. He had no friends among the wealthy families of the town. In fact, he held nothing but disdain for the scions of the rich as he found them arrogant and frivolous. When the militia had been rallied and sent to the marshes bordering the Jaga, no wealthy scions joined them. Onin knew all of them trained in arms and armor, possessing superior equipment and quality steeds, yet none of them would lower themselves enough to serve in the militia.

Onin passed one such house as these thoughts crossed his mind. The Blankenfort family owned a great number of warehouses within the city and made a fortune buying foodstuffs from the local farmers and shipping them to the Heights inside the dragon-borne cargo baskets. He could hear the sounds of thumping and cracking, punctuated with an occasional pained cry, coming from the garden behind the house. Curious and yearning for a distraction from his morbid thoughts, Onin went to investigate.

The gate to the garden stood open, and Onin could see a group of young men inside. He knew them all, the sons of the wealthy playing at being knights. The Blankenfort heir, Roddin, stood in the practice yard, adorned in his beautifully crafted and shined armor, armed with a wooden practice sword. As Onin watched, Roddin mercilessly beat his opponent, a younger boy whom Onin recognized as Carus Wheeler. The shorter boy stumbled under every blow, even if he managed to get his shield in the way, and each time the practice sword got through his guard, Carus would let out one of the yelps that Onin had previously heard. Roddin clearly possessed greater strength and skill, yet he showed no mercy for Carus. Eventually Roddin struck him a ringing blow to the helmet, and the slight boy fell to all fours, dropping his wooden armaments. With a contemptuous sneer, Roddin kicked Carus hard in the ribs, sending the boy tumbling over and gasping for breath.

"Only a coward hits a defenseless opponent," said Onin. The words came from his lips before he could stop himself. But he felt the anger growing within him. Onin's inner wounds were quite raw yet. Seeing someone reminiscent of Flea being beaten so remorselessly rankled.

Roddin turned his sneer upon Onin. "So the mighty militia man returns! You must have the most interesting stories about digging ditches and scratching fleas!" Roddin paused to allow his cronies to laugh, which they did obligingly.

"We've heard about the great victory over the savages. Why don't you tell us all about your part in the battle, Onin, or did you just run away like a spooked deer? I'll bet you didn't do anything at all except make a mess of your trousers." Another round of mocking laughter escaped the cronies.

Onin stepped into the garden and lifted Carus to his feet. He led the boy to a bench at one end of the garden and deposited him there then returned to fetch his wooden sword and shield. Roddin continued with his haranguing, undeterred.

"You can't really be blamed for your uselessness, though," said the arrogant heir. "After all, you haven't had the benefit of fine training like we've had here. If only we would have been there; then you would have seen something!" Roddin raised his wooden blade in salute to himself, and his friends did likewise with a hearty yell.

After retrieving sword and shield, Onin headed back to Carus, still quite rattled from the beating at Roddin's hand, and placed the shield there. But he kept a hold of the practice sword. The stout young man then returned to the center and squared off with Roddin, wooden blade in hand.

"Come on, then," said Onin coldly. "Let's see if you're worth anything."

Roddin looked shocked then enraged. With a fierce cry, he leaped for Onin, swinging his wooden sword in a vicious arc. Onin raised his own weapon to parry, almost casually. Roddin's wooden sword scored a glancing blow, opening a small cut above Onin's right eye. Onin didn't flinch, a trickle of blood flowed from his scalp down his cheek.

Onin took a step forward and knocked the sword from Roddin's hand with a single blow. The wooden blade went flying clear over the wall of the garden. Onin then reached forward with his left hand and grasped the rim of Roddin's shield and yanked it from his grasp as well. The sudden assault left Roddin stunned and off balance.

Suddenly disarmed, Roddin could do nothing to protect himself from the rain of blows that followed. He tried to cover himself with his arms, tried to retreat, but Onin would not be stopped. Each blow connected with a painful thud, and he followed Roddin around the garden with deliberate, unrelenting steps, giving him no quarter and no respite.

Finally Onin swung his mightiest blow yet, striking Roddin squarely on the helmet. The wooden sword fairly exploded with the impact, sending a shower of splinters cascading through the air. Roddin collapsed onto his back, his armor clattering like so many cook pots. Dents and dirt marred the once-shiny armor.

"How dare you--!" began one of the cronies, but Onin fixed him with an icy glare that clamped his mouth shut, rebuke unspoken. Onin's glare ensured continued silence.

Onin tossed the hilt of the broken practice sword on the ground in contempt. He gave the gathered cronies one last glare then spun and stomped away.

* * *

Without conscious thought, Onin's footsteps carried him to his home. Beating Roddin had taken the edge from his anger. He took satisfaction in knowing Flea hated Roddin and would have cheered Onin on had he been there.

Onin crossed the threshold, lost in his misery. A manservant approached to say his father had called for him. Onin indicated for the servant to lead the way, and the servant looked at him with a puzzled expression, though Onin didn't know why. Dutifully Onin followed to his father's library, where the older man preferred to spend the majority of his time.

To Onin's surprise, Captain Torreg was there as well, sipping a goblet of wine. The remains of a lavish meal sat on a nearby platter with two empty decanters. Onin found this odd as his father rarely drank wine and never during the day. Both men had been indulging, though. Onin could tell by the rosiness of their cheeks.

"Yes, Father?" asked Onin. He stood straight and tall.

"What in the world happened to you, my son?" exclaimed Zorot. He stared at Onin's head. "You're bleeding!"

Onin looked at him in confusion then ran his hand over his scalp. His fingers came away sticky with blood. He had completely forgotten about the blow to his head.

"It's nothing, Father," said Onin. "I had a . . . practice session. Didn't realize I'd been cut."

Zorot motioned a servant over and ordered clean water and a dressing be brought to the library. After the servant scurried away, Zorot waved Onin to one of the lavishly comfortable chairs that resided in the library. Onin sat, being careful not to get any blood on the chair.

"A practice session?" commented Torreg, draining his goblet with a final gulp. "Must have been some bout to have given you such a cut under your helmet."

Onin shrugged. "I wasn't wearing a helmet."

Zorot raised his eyes to the heavens. Torreg looked about to say something when the servant returned with the water and dressing. Without pause, the servant began to clean and stitch the wound on Onin's scalp. Torreg watched as the servant went about the task with practiced hands.

"Do all of your servants know how to tend wounds and make such clean stitches?" he asked of Zorot, and the trade ambassador returned a wry look.

"They all do now," said Zorot. "Each member of my staff has had a chance to minister to my son on multiple occasions. They get good at it after a while. The longer you know him, the more you realize you'd better have a supply of bandages on hand."

Both men laughed, a little too loudly. The wine seemed to be having its way with them. Onin grew a little annoyed at them for talking as if he weren't there. To his surprise, his father poured a goblet of wine and handed it to him.

This also made Onin a little nervous. His father rarely drank during the day, but for him to give Onin wine was unthinkable. He had a mad, momentary thought this must be an impostor, sent here to impersonate his father. He pushed the thought away and accepted the wine nonetheless, while his father refilled the two other goblets.

"We toast!" exclaimed Zorot, and all three men lifted their drinks to their lips. The wine had a strong flavor, almost sour. Onin wasn't sure he liked it, but relaxing warmth spread throughout his belly after imbibing. He barely noticed the prick of the needle in his scalp as the stitching continued.

"Um . . . Father," began Onin. "What are we toasting?"

"You! We are toasting you, my son!" said his father with a wide grin. Zorot's enthusiasm clearly ran away with him, no doubt fueled by the uncharacteristic wine. But he seemed to notice his son's melancholy and adopted a somber expression.

"Yes, I forget." His eyes softened in sympathy. "You are grieving for Jarid, and rightly so." The sound of the name gave Onin a pang; Zorot insisted on using Flea's given name. Zorot's expression spread into a grin again.

"But I know your friend would not begrudge you," said the trade ambassador. "He would cheer your success and wish you the best!"

Captain Torreg smiled in smug anticipation. He belched lightly as Onin glanced over at him.

"I've long wondered what you would do with your life, Onin," continued Zorot. "In your younger years, I entertained the hope you would take over the family business. As you've grown, it has become apparent to me trade and diplomacy hold no fascination for you."

Onin could only nod. He had no patience for the negotiation, gilded words, and social niceties both fields required.

"I then supposed you would devote yourself to Sparrowport's militia," said Zorot. "You know my opinions about such a thing. A soldier's life is low on coin and high on risk, but it does suit your temperament."

Onin nodded again. He had joined the militia over his father's protests.

"Now," said Zorot. His grin widened to a point Onin thought it must surely hurt. "A true opportunity has come to you, my son."

Onin finally spoke up. "What in the world are you talking about, Father?"

Torreg interjected a question. "Have you ever considered joining the

Royal Guard, Onin?"

Onin looked at the captain but could think of nothing to say at first. He would have laughed at the notion but was too unsettled by recent events and his current strange situation.

"Every child does," he said. "But it's just a dream."

Tales of the Guard slaying dragons single-handed were the stuff of fireside tales and bedtime stories. But only those from the Heights could join the elite order. Torreg might as well have asked him if he had ever considered being king.

"No, not just a dream," said Torreg. "Your father and I have had a long and fruitful discussion about many things. We have come to an arrangement which will allow me to sponsor you to Scaleback Academy."

"But . . . I'm a Midlander," stammered the young man. His stature, dark hair and ruddy complexion all attested to his non-Heights heritage.

"But, adopted or not, you are the son of a man of the Heights," interrupted the captain. "While not one of the Great Families, the Durantis line is quite respectable, and your father, a man of no trivial influence. This will allow me to sponsor you for the academy."

Onin felt slightly giddy. He wondered if the wine had gone to his head but then looked down to realize he hadn't taken more than the first sip.

"Being a Guard is being a soldier, Onin. Your father is right about his views; it's no road to wealth or prominence," continued Torreg. "But it is a path of dignity, honor, and duty. We've fought together, and I see the makings of a Guardsman in you, make no mistake. More than your strength in arms, the Guard requires strength of character. Everything I've seen so far says you have that in abundance.

"So, Onin . . . will you join the Guard and serve your king?"

Without hesitation, Onin hoisted his goblet. "To the king!" he cried and drained it with a single gulp.

The two other men rejoiced as well and raised their own goblets in salute.

* * *

Onin had the dream again, stronger than it had been in years. Dragons filled the sky, all flying in the same direction. Their numbers stretched from one end of the horizon to the other. Behind them, Onin could see the shape of a shooting star, a giant comet brightening the night sky with its luminescence. He could hear their mighty roars, from a great distance, and the landscape beneath them burned. Fires raged everywhere his eye wandered, and smoke rose to the heavens until even the endless stream of dragons was obscured by it.

As it always did, an amber glow grabbed at his attention from the top of a great mountain. Without even willing it, he had the sensation of passing over miles and miles in the blink of an eye, until he found himself looking into what appeared to be a nest dug out of solid rock. Inside, the shells of sizable eggs littered the area. In the middle rested a single, lonely egg, its shell dappled in the colors of stone and sand. Glints of metal sparkled over its surface. As Onin stared, an apparition of two eyes superimposed itself over the egg. One eye was amber, the other sparkled like blue gemstone.

Chapter 5

A life in service is a life well spent. To be part of something greater than yourself is to strive for virtue, and the gods smile upon the virtuous.
--Prendor, teacher at Scaleback Academy

* * *

Within a few days, Onin found himself at the dragon pier with Torreg and Bolg. The cargo baskets looked different up close. When carried by a dragon in the distance, they looked fragile and thin. Up close, Onin could see the thick timbers and sturdy lashings, like what they used on the barges that carried cargo along the river. In the center and above the basket, a log thick enough to be a ship's mainmast ran parallel to the ground, providing a claw-hold for the dragon as it flew past.

The dragon appeared as a dot near the horizon, at first obscured by the view of the Heights behind it. It grew and eventually took shape, looking magnificent as it glided smoothly through the air, its four legs dangling lazily underneath it. As always, the apparent grace of the huge creatures impressed.

As it drew nearer, Onin felt his knees weaken. The verdant dragon's true scale became apparent to him, and he had second thoughts. The reptilian head was so huge, he thought it could swallow a horse whole. It could crush an entire cottage within a single massive claw. Onin had always believed the stories of dragons hollowing out entire mountains for nests to be fables. In the moment of the dragon's approach, he believed the fables. Even a mountain couldn't resist such a beast.

For the first time, Onin wondered why this had seemed like such a good idea.

"Cargo, ready!" came the cry of the cargo master from her perch on the loading dock set to the side of the cargo basket. In response to her cry, passengers double-checked the ropes securing them in place. Each man had a rope tied around the waist and attached to the hull of the cargo basket. The knots had been tied for them by the cargo master's crew--a slipknot made to release with a single pull.

"Best you sit down now, lad," cried Bolg. The ugly sergeant sat on his posterior, as did Torreg. Onin let his own knees buckle and virtually collapsed where he stood.

"You look a bit peaked, my boy." Torreg laughed.

Onin tried to think of a witty retort but could only gulp.

Turning back, Onin looked at the approaching dragon. Darkness invaded as its shadow fell over them. He heard the whoosh of air passing over the dragon's sleek form and the rasping crunch of the claw as it grabbed the pole of the basket. Onin felt himself pressed to the wood beneath as his stomach dropped away. His hair whipped about with the sudden wind, and the breath escaped his lungs for a moment.

Then, as abruptly as it began, the chaos ended. There was still a strong breeze, but the cargo basket settled into a gentle sway, not unlike the rocking of a boat.

"Ha!" cried Bolg. "Didn't even throw up this time!"

"Thank the gods for small favors," said Torreg over the wind. Both men stood and pulled the release on their safety ropes. After catching his breath for a moment, Onin did likewise. The high walls blocked their view, so they clambered atop the crates on board to peer over the edge.

Bright blue sky and surrounding landscape stunned Onin with its beauty. His entire homeland spread out before him, a vast expanse of green and brown, of pastures and fields and structures and people, but they looked miniature, like wooden toys from his childhood. The sky stretched away, pale and blue, in all directions, an endless, open expanse. Onin marveled at the true size of the world. To the south, he could see the miles of marsh and even make out the dark expanse of the Jaga. To the west, he could see their destination, the Heights, the city within a great hollow mountain, surrounded at its base by the Cloud Forest, itself a land of legendary dangers. Onin's anxiety melted into excitement then exultation.

The voices of men shouting from above called his attention. As he looked up at the majestic form of the dragon, he could make out the shapes of men, dragon riders, clambering down the beast's leg and onto the claw that held the cargo basket. Onin squinted and noticed a rope mesh winding its way down the dragon's leg, providing a sort of ladder for the last part of the climb.

The first dragon rider had reached the claw and lowered a rope for the men. Torreg went first, climbing hand over hand until he grasped the outstretched hand offered to him. In moments, he continued over the dragon's claw to climb the foreleg.

"You're next, lad," cried Bolg.

Onin grabbed the rope and began his ascent. He kept his pace measured and careful and made steady progress. His strength didn't fail him. Soon he grasped an outstretched hand and clambered onto the back of the dragon's claw. The scaly dragon hide was slick like mossy stone. Onin was thankful for the ropes serving as handholds.

Torreg had already climbed halfway up the foreleg along the rope harness. The wind was strong but nothing to be feared, and Onin was already beginning to feel more relaxed. He climbed along the foreleg and risked a look down. The ground was so far below him, he could no longer judge the distance. The once toylike figures and structures became dark specks on a patchwork tapestry of green and brown. His stomach quailed at the sight, but it was more excitement than fear.

He climbed the rest of the distance, without rushing, carefully picking his handholds as he went. There was one moment where the wind gusted and threatened to pull him away from the ropes, but his tight grip held him in place. After a deep breath, he resumed his ascent.

When he reached the base of the tierre, another dragonrider awaited him, hand outstretched. He accepted the hand gratefully and was hoisted over the edge to land in a heap. The tierre was arranged with chairs, about twenty in all, bolted to the floorboards. Each seat sported a pair of ropes. Torreg sat nearby and the ropes secured him in place with a simple knot across the midsection. Onin clambered to his feet and tied himself into the seat next to the captain. The tierre was empty, except for the half dozen dragon riders serving as crew.

Torreg offered a flask to Onin. The young man accepted it wordlessly and took a long draw from it. Onin immediately descended into a coughing fit but refused to relinquish the flask to Torreg until the fit had subsided and he'd had a second drink.

Bolg arrived a few minutes later. He rose to his feet and strapped himself in then accepted the flask from Torreg and finished it in one swig. "Best settle in for the long flight, my friends. There'll be no stopovers. If by chance we end up in the swamp, chances are that's where we'll remain.

"It's a wonder more people don't travel by dragon," commented Torreg.

* * *

The flight on the verdant dragon was more glorious than any of Onin's childhood imaginings. Once the warmth from the contents of the flask had spread throughout his body, he relaxed, and he felt soothed by the wind in his face, despite the tears gathered in the corners of his eyes. The ride was surprisingly smooth, and Onin felt secure with the rope holding him to the seat, even when the dragon turned sharply to one side as it swung about gracefully to avoid a bank of clouds. Onin's heart felt as light as the clouds they passed on either side.

Bolg and Torreg looked much less comfortable, Onin noticed. Bolg had produced his own flask, and the two old comrades passed it back and forth between them. Onin politely declined when offered the flask, as he still felt the effects of his previous indulgence. Bolg and Torreg continued to talk, mostly about places they planned on visiting in the Heights, but Onin hardly paid attention. Lost in the wonder of the experience, he alternated between watching the clouds scroll past and peering over the edge to see the landscape below. It was a fairy tale come true for him--flying on the back of a dragon on his way to the Heights to enroll in Scaleback Academy and one day join the Guard.

Onin thought once again of his friend, but it was more than sadness and regret; there was a sense Flea would have been proud of him. He silently promised Flea's spirit he would continue to strive and live up to this opportunity.

Onin lost track of time, his mind drifting as they soared, but the sun was low in the sky by the time they reached the destination. Onin watched it grow over a long time, the mountain beginning to dominate his view. Blue sky beyond was visible through the massive holes carved in the mountain. Other dragons flew about, following right behind one another as they entered or left the hollow mountain through one of the enormous chambers. It was not unlike a giant beehive, thought Onin, as he took in the sight on their approach.

The dragon they rode upon swooped in majestically, furling its wings slightly to slow itself as it entered the interior of the mountain. Onin noticed how the wind was strong inside the mountain, and to his amazement, the giant verdant came to a complete but gentle stop, allowing the currents of air under its wings to keep it aloft. Long wooden docks protruded from the mountain's cavernous interior, and the dragon came to a rest beside one of them.

A pier extended to the tierre, and the dragon riders ushered them across to the waiting dock after they hurriedly untied themselves. Looking about, Onin could see other dragons hovering in place near other docks, and a long wooden arm with two immense iron hooks attached to it extended from beneath the dock they stood upon. The dragon, with a casual, almost offhand air, hung the cargo basket on the iron hooks. The thick log it held in its claw fit neatly inside the two hooks, and the wooden arm creaked and bowed slightly as the weight of the cargo basket settled on it. The arm slowly retracted to its space below the dock, along with the cargo basket. The other docks had similar cargo platforms and arms, and Onin could see they alternated between receiving cargo baskets from the arriving dragons and presenting outgoing baskets for dragons about to exit the mountain.

The Heights were as magnificent as any description Onin had heard. Whereas Sparrowport contained sturdy wooden structures and the occasional stone building, the Heights were carved from the stone itself. The smooth walls displayed decorative stencils but followed the mountain's natural contours. Wide steps, pavilions, and staircases allowed for movement up and down, while the streets flowed like rivers of cobbled stone, only running with people and animals, instead of water. But water wasn't absent; on the contrary, it appeared in abundance with a system of channels and fountains fed by the mountain peaks. Several lakes could be seen, each with palatial dwellings ringing the shore. The place smelled clean, as the mountain breeze constantly cleared away the stink of unwashed bodies and animal refuse he associated with towns in the Midlands.

Onin took in everything he could as they walked, trying to look everywhere at once. He almost got separated from the two Guardsmen twice in the press of bodies, but after the second close call, he became more mindful of following in their wake. They stopped for a meal at a well-appointed tavern, finer than any in Sparrowport. Onin had been so enthralled by the sights and sounds of the Heights, he hadn't realized how famished he was until food was in front of him. He greedily ate the dish of cold lamb, cheese, and bread. Even the foods here tasted different than what he was accustomed to in the Midlands.

After the meal, Torreg led them down another series of cobbled streets and into a tunnel that descended into the depths of the mountain. It was like being lost in a catacomb. The wide corridors served as streets with dwellings on either side. Families went about the daily business of cooking and cleaning. The passages often opened into wide halls with tall ceilings. Street vendors hawked their wares at blatantly inflated prices. The life of the city spilled into these corridors and halls and continued unabated, despite the lack of sunlight.

Walking the corridors of the city for an hour or more, they eventually came to an expansive round chamber with a fountain in the center. Two other corridors led away from the room, but on the fourth side was a tall archway. Hanging over the archway was a stone placard with ornate letters filled in with gold filigree carved into it.

Scaleback Academy, the sign read. Onin could hardly believe the fact of his presence. Not for the first time, he wondered if this entire experience was an elaborate dream.

They crossed the threshold of the arch and entered the academy's reception area. A flamboyantly carved table stood in the center of the room, and two circular staircases rose from the left and right sides to merge into a balcony that held a set of double doors, apparently constructed of thick oak and stained so dark as to be almost black. There was a second door below the landing where the two staircases came together, similar in style and construction to the double doors above. Two guards stood at the base of each staircase, resplendent in shining breastplate and holding well-polished halberds.

Seated behind the table was an old, white-haired man dressed in simple but clean and well-maintained robes. He scribbled on a parchment with a quill, an inkpot within reach. Stacks of parchments rested on either side of him, and as they watched, he finished with the document in front of him, placed it in the pile to his right, and picked up the top sheet from the left pile. His movements were meticulous and neat, and his fingers were clean and free of ink; he never seemed to need the ink blotter resting to one side. His eyes did not rise from his work as they entered and approached him.

"Honored scribe," said Torreg by way of greeting.

The old man looked up and squinted at the captain. His eyes lit up with surprised recognition. A grin split the wrinkled face, showing many missing teeth.

"Torreg!" cried the scribe. "I thought you were stationed in the Midlands. What brings you here?" The old man rose creakily to his feet and extended a hand, which Torreg grasped warmly.

"I am here to sponsor a student into the academy," said Torreg, indicating Onin. "I was only just released from my duties in the Midlands and appointed here. It's good to be home, I can tell you that."

The old man squinted at Onin, looking him up and down, and frowned.

"Midlander," he said with a grimace but extended his hand to the lad all the same. Despite his age and frailty, Onin was surprised at his firm grip.

"Not exactly," said Torreg. "Or not completely. Is Headmaster Belond present today?"

"Oh, yes," cackled the old scribe. He picked up the pile on his right and leafed through them, finally holding one up to his face to squint at the writing on it. "He has his schedule filled with meetings. Most of them are with nonexistent dignitaries and officials. It's how he makes time for his poetry. Let's see . . . We'll just shift the appointment with the cobblestone guildmaster to next week. Since he is one of the imaginary, then he will hopefully not be offended by the delay." The old man scribbled a note on the parchment. "Just got transferred back, you say? That didn't take long. Only took what? Ten years?"

"Fifteen," corrected Torreg.

"My, time rushes by faster at my age," muttered the old man. "Seems like only yesterday that you and this miscreant"--the old scribe pointed at Bolg, who looked at the ceiling innocently--"bribed me with sugared nuts so that you could sneak back into the academy at night. You didn't happen to bring any sugared nuts today?" The old man looked at them slyly.

Torreg began to mumble an apology and excuses, but Bolg produced a simple cloth pouch and handed it to the old man.

"I'd never forget those, honored scribe," said the ugly sergeant with obvious but subdued affection.

"Ah, my favorite rascals never fail me," cackled the old man as he stuffed some of the sweets into his toothless maw. "Can't crunch like I used to, so I just suck on them now. I've never understood why the students most keen to break the rules were always so reliable when it came to bribes." Torreg and Bolg cast sidelong glances at Onin, looking more than a little sheepish. Onin couldn't help but smile, picturing these two as adolescent troublemakers. It wasn't really difficult to imagine.

"Let's go see the headmaster, then," said the old scribe.

* * *

The headmaster's office was opulent while managing to be understated. The stone walls and floors appeared to be frequently scrubbed, and the room was lit by a chandelier of candles hanging above, as well as some oil lamps on the solid wooden desk that dominated the chamber.

Headmaster Belond sat behind the table, and just like the old scribe, bent over a parchment with quill in hand, his brow furrowed in deep concentration. Again, just like the old scribe, he didn't look up when they first entered the room. However, unlike the scribe, Belond was broad shouldered and thick fingered. The headmaster was as stout as Onin, if not quite as tall. His age showed through graying beard and lines about the eyes, but he was strong and vibrant looking. Onin could easily picture him in full battle regalia.

"And to the autumn leaves, I pledge," the headmaster said loud in a well-defined cadence, "when the summer comes again, live again, you will, you will . . ."

The headmaster then put the quill down and lifted the page up to his eyes, judging the words written there. His bearded face was set in a frown.

"By the gods," said Belond. "That's the worst poetry I've ever heard. It's simply dreadful."

With a sigh, the headmaster put the parchment down and put his face in his hands, elbows propped up on the table, as if a great weight rested on his shoulders. It seemed to dawn on him that he wasn't alone, and he wearily peered over his hands at them.

"How did you get in here? Did that desiccated husk of a scribe bring you?" demanded the headmaster. Onin turned to look where the old man had just been standing, none stood there.

"Pardon the interruption, Headmaster," said Torreg. "I am Torreg, a graduate of Scaleback--"

"I remember you," said Belond, cutting the captain off with a wave of his hand. "You graduated in one of the early years I assumed my position. Quite disappointed about your deployment to the Midlands." The headmaster looked at Bolg. "I remember you too. That face is unforgettable." The sergeant managed to look pleased with himself. The headmaster's eyes fell on Onin next and looked him up and down with a critical eye.

"A Midlander," snorted the headmaster. Then he turned his gaze back to Torreg. "So what brings you here, Captain?"

"I am here to sponsor this lad. His name is Onin. He deserves a place here."

"Midlanders can't be accepted into the academies. You know that. Or have you forgotten your lessons so soon?" said Belond. The headmaster stood, showing he was massive, even by Onin's standards. He was thick bodied but also tall, standing a full hand over Onin, despite his earlier impression.

"I have forgotten nothing, Headmaster," Torreg said, looking slightly offended at the statement. "This young man is the son of Zorot Durantis, trade ambassador to Sparrowport. Durantis is not one of the Great Families, but they are in good standing nonetheless, and can enter the academy with the patronage of one of the Great Families. I will sponsor this lad."

The headmaster stroked his beard and walked around the table. He stood before Onin, inspecting him like a prize piece of horseflesh. Belond stopped in front of the young man and looked him directly in the eyes, holding the stare for many long moments. Onin met his gaze as evenly as he could, but he found the older man's stare unsettling. The headmaster spoke again, but his gaze never left Onin's eyes.

"Is he capable?" asked the gray-haired man.

Onin felt distinctly left out of the conversation.

"He has fought with my men in battle," said the captain. "It is why I've brought him here. My sergeant will attest to his abilities."

"Aye," chimed in Bolg. "Right tough lad he is, mind and body both."

Seemingly satisfied by what he found there, Belond finally broke the locked gaze. Onin breathed a sigh of relief, though he hadn't realized he had been holding his breath. The headmaster turned back to Torreg.

"Just returned from the Midlands, and you want to sponsor this Midland lad into the academies?" asked the headmaster skeptically. "Did you enjoy your time there so much, you want to go back immediately?"

"No offense to the boy's homeland, but I've no intention of ever returning there," said Torreg. "Still, I must do what I think is right. I have seen the measure of this boy--no, this man--and I tell you he will make a fine Guard. To do anything else would be to waste his potential."

"You have ever been a slave to what you think is right, eh, Torreg?" asked Belond. Before waiting for a reply, though, he relented. "Fine."

Belond turned to Onin.

"Onin, son of Zorot Durantis, you are hereby accepted into Scaleback Academy. Long live the king."

Chapter 6

Many men have made their careers on the battlefield and then lost them at the dinner table. Be sure to study the use of cutlery as much as the use of the sword.
--Doren, teacher at Scaleback Academy

* * *

Life at the academy was strict, regimented, and highly disciplined. The days began before dawn and continued to well after sunset. The mornings always began with the chores: bundle the bedroll, sweep the sleeping quarters, and put away any personal items from the previous night. Soon after rising, the students assembled in the meal hall for breakfast. The usually simple but hearty fare was devoured in relative silence under the watchful eye of the headmaster and other teachers. Once breakfast concluded, the students attended the morning lessons.

Morning lessons provided arms training for the younger students, those in their first and second years at the academy, with the afternoons dedicated to academic lessons. The third- and fourth-year students reversed the schedule. Onin learned, to his chagrin, the headmaster valued scholastic progress as much as skill at arms.

Ostensibly students could spend the evening hours as desired. In practice, finishing the day's academic assignments consumed most evenings, although many students spent time in additional arms training as well. Onin liked to do so himself, whenever possible. The younger students got few opportunities to work with the older students on combat skills.

Once the sun would no longer allow for mock battles or further writing, then the business of evening chores began. Most chores involved the kitchen in some form or another--the struggle to feed several hundred hungry adolescents was monumental, so best to make them do most of the work themselves. Onin had never scrubbed so many dishes in his life.

But it wasn't all drudgery and work. The first friend Onin made was the young man who shared his sleeping quarters. He introduced himself as Fargin Whistlewind. He was stocky and strong, though not as big as Onin, with a shy smile. He wasn't the talkative sort, which suited Onin just fine; a chatterbox for a roommate would have driven him mad. He found Fargin had a sense of humor underneath his meek demeanor when Onin's undergarments turned up missing one morning. Onin looked all about the cell they shared, with Fargin's help, but to no avail, and Onin became more and more impatient. When Fargin suggested that they expand the search to the gardens outside the sleeping quarters, Onin became suspicious. Soon after, he found his undergarments hanging from a tree. Several nearby students stifled laughter as Onin came out in his bedclothes to get them. By the time Onin had retrieved them and gone back to the cell, Fargin was rolling on his cot in hysterics.

Hangric Anover was another new friend, the only first-year student bigger than Onin. They had been matched together on one of the first days of arms training. Their initial clash drew spectators from all over the yard. The match wasn't completed until each had broken the practice sword on the other. They fought hard but fairly and developed mutual respect. Before long, they took all of their meals together.

But Rabbash Kurz made his way most firmly into Onin's heart. Short and skinny, Rabbash possessed a keen wit. He stood out to Onin not because of strength of arms but because of scholastic excellence. Onin struggled with the academic side of their studies, and Rabbash had apparently noticed. Whenever Onin foundered with a concept or idea, he could rely on Rabbash to explain it to him in terms he would understand. Onin had never met someone so intelligent.

Teacher Prendor oversaw the arms lessons. His strict methods demanded more from his students on a daily basis than they really felt they could give. But give they did; somehow the dour-faced man with scant praise could motivate them to ever greater feats. Over and over again, a student would be soundly thrashed or collapse on hands and knees in exhaustion, seemingly unable to continue. Prendor would kneel down, whispering advice and encouragement, somehow demanding the would-be Guardsman stand up and do the exercise again. He cajoled, he threatened, he dared, he insulted; Prendor would do whatever it took to keep them striving.

He also required strict behavior from his students. He brooked no arguments or discourtesy among them. He demanded the utmost in respectable manners and speech. He rebuked them for angry outbursts or bouts of impatience. Most important, he had no tolerance for those who took unfair advantage of a weaker student.

Teacher Doren, on the other hand, focused on their academic advancement. If anything, he demanded more of his students than Prendor. Prendor would make allowances for students based on their capabilities, such as limited muscular strength or a lack of agility. Where Prendor would guide students in ways to work around their shortcomings, Doren refused to acknowledge the failings of the students. He demanded critical thinking, accuracy, and retention from them all. Mastering the morning lessons consumed many hours of the students' evenings, each lesson building on the one before.

Despite his demanding nature, Doren displayed a nurturing attitude toward the students. Many of the boys grew homesick or despondent during their time at the academy, and Doren would be the one to console them, encourage them, and make them feel better. During the time at the academy, Prendor acted as father, and Doren became their mother.

Under the dual tutelage, the students advanced in ways they had never imagined. Onin had always been a stumbling reader, but over time found himself able to quote whole sections of poems. Despite his strength and stamina, his agility failed him, and many drills and exercises from Teacher Prendor had him balancing on thin beams, climbing tree branches with no hands, or walking while balancing a bowl of water on his head. All of the students learned repeatedly to test their capabilities and grew in their abilities as a consequence.

But beyond even the practical skills they learned, the teachers tried to instill in them the principles that made the Guard distinct from other soldiers. Terms such as "honor," "loyalty," "sacrifice," and "chivalry" became part of their daily intake, just as much as food or water or air. Lessons came through stories and fables, but also through a series of leading questions, ones designed to bring the student to the desired conclusion.

"How do you know when an action is honorable?" asked Doren one day.

"When we are doing our duty," offered one student.

"What if you are ordered to kill an unarmed man?"

"Loyalty demands we obey," said Fargin, though he looked uncertain.

"Is obedience the sum of loyalty?" asked the teacher.

"No," said Onin. "Question the order first. Ask why the man has to die."

"Bold," stated Doren. "But why?"

"Because it is our duty to protect our charge's honor as well," replied Onin. "We would be remiss to allow the ones above us to mistakenly damage their honor forever."

"Unless the unarmed man poses a danger to the protected," countered Hangric. "An unarmed man is not necessarily harmless."

"Good, good," said Doren. "Never forget your first duty is to the protected. Sometimes disobedience is required to guard them properly, not just their bodies but their reputations."

One day during arms practice, Prendor deliberately mismatched them, pairing the smallest students with the largest. He ran them through a series of brutal drills that involved trading a series of blows, with the partner parrying with the weapon and sometimes with the shield. The intensity of the exercise increased with each repetition. Before long, the yard plunged into chaos as the outmatched students inevitably gave under the onslaught. Onin was paired with Rabbash, and his slight friend had a hard time remaining on his feet as the lesson progressed. Onin held back, but Prendor was on him in an instant.

"No quarter!" the teacher screamed. "Full power on each and every blow!" Onin redoubled his efforts in response.

The next blow sent Rabbash reeling to the ground. He struggled to his feet, but immediately stumbled and fell again. Onin raised his weapon and gritted his teeth, silently begging his friend to stay down.

"Hold!" cried Prendor. The fighting came to a stop. All of the students seemed relieved the exercise was over, regardless of whether they had been giving or receiving the beating. Prendor glared at them all.

"So what do you think that was all about?" he said smoothly. "Do you think it unfair and churlish of me to make such unbalanced pairings?"

"It hardly seems honorable, sir," said Hangric. Prendor glared at him for a long moment, and Hangric withered noticeably.

"Life is not fair," said the arms teacher. "Neither is battle. You'll not have the leisure of pairing yourself with someone your own size. Larger or smaller, the enemy is bent on killing you, plain and simple. This goes just as much for you other students; underestimating your opponent because you are bigger will lay you low.

"Now form up!" Prendor shouted. "The parries I see lack precision. Remember whether the attack misses you by a foot or a hair's breadth, it is still a miss. There's no need to exaggerate your movements! Keep your shield tight to your body!"

And so the drills continued.

* * *

The year progressed. The seasons turned. By Onin's first winter, his life in the Heights was so full, he almost forgot his previous existence as a wealthy man's son in Sparrowport. No longer was he mingling with those who sought to use him for advantage due to his relations; everyone at the academy came from a good family. It was easy to relax around his new circle of friends, which was a new experience for him.

Good friends they made too. All of them were at an age that required them to act like men, but they still had the impulses of the boys within. The number of pranks and shenanigans that played out in the barracks of the early students would have driven most parents to fits, but the teachers took it all in stride, seemingly used to certain excesses from rowdy young men. Still, though, being caught in the act meant discipline, which usually arrived in the form of scullery duty. It was an effective deterrent, as scullery duty was the most likely to cut into the student's free time. The idea of losing some of the precious little time afforded them unthinkable, they kept their gags reined in for the most part.

Despite their boyish tendencies, the sensibilities of budding men became apparent. This manifested itself in a variety of ways, but none more so than a fascination with the fairer sex.

"Why don't we have any girls at academy?" asked Fargin over breakfast one day. "I'd give just about anything to see a pretty girl once in a while."

"Me too," added Hangric. "Not even a kitchen maid here."

The others muttered their agreement. Onin couldn't remember the last time he'd seen a girl, and he wished he had really taken a long look when he did. Onin had never thought much about girls until he had none in his daily life; he now missed them deeply, though he would have been hard pressed to say exactly why. Contemplating the question made him slightly uncomfortable.

"Maybe girls aren't cut out to be Guards," said Fargin. "Maybe the training is too difficult. Most of the boys I know couldn't hold up under the arms practice. I can't imagine a girl who could do it."

"You've never met my sister." Hangric laughed.

"It's for our own sakes," chimed in Rabbash, talking around a mouthful of gruel. "If we had girls here to look at, we'd never get anything done. It would ruin our ability to concentrate on our lessons."

The others scoffed.

"We wouldn't be distracted," said Hangric. Even seated at the table, his head towered over the rest of them. "I mean, girls are nice and everything, but I would be more concerned about keeping my head attached to my shoulders."

"You say that now," countered Rabbash. "But tell me, what do you spend most of your time thinking about now?"

Hangric considered for a moment. "Girls!" he answered.

"Exactly," said Rabbash. "Imagine girls all over the place. Speaking of which, there's a girl now!"

Rabbash pointed over Hangric's shoulder, and each of the boys turned to look. Once Hangric faced the opposite direction, Rabbash struck him soundly on the crown of the head with his spoon. It made a hollow, tinny *thunk* as it impacted Hangric's thick noggin and left a clump of gruel in the husky boy's hair.

"Too easy," said Rabbash with a smile.

* * *

It was a wholesome, self-contained world they lived within. Each day they worked and trained in the ideals that made the Heights great, by some accounts. Notions such as honor, duty, and chivalry carried greater meaning than mere words, describing virtues to cultivate. The teachers fed them on parables and sweat, philosophies and stew. They grew in mind and body, and each piece given to them by their teachers became a brick in their internal castles, built on principles from days past.

Not all in the academy aspired to join the Guard, however. Some few students, perhaps a dozen or so, attended strictly for the academic lessons and did not participate in the lessons-in-arms, so they would never be eligible to join the order. However, many wealthy and powerful families would pay handsomely to have their children attend. The "academics" lived alongside the fighting students, largely unnoticed. The lack of visibility was reinforced by a lack of proximity, as the academics lodged in their own chambers, away from the others.

During the afternoon arms practice, the academics spent their extra time in additional studies or pursuing art- or craft-related endeavors. On one such afternoon, two academics, twin brothers, sat near a window while reading from historic texts. Tall but slight of frame, both possessed light blond hair and striking blue eyes. The seats they occupied afforded them a view of the fighting students at work. They would glance up from their text from time to time to observe the arms students. The gaze never lingered, however, and they inevitably returned to reading in apparent boredom.

A pudgy boy with pasty skin entered the hall with a ponderous text in his hands. He approached the twins, pointedly looking at one, then the other. Each met his gaze without a change of expression. The fat boy held the book to the twin on his left.

"Here it is, Altavus," said the chubby boy in a whiny voice. "Just as you asked, *Magics of the Ancients*."

"Thank you, Sensi," said the twin to his right. "But I am Altavus."

Sensi looked him right in the eye, and after a slight pause answered, "Except you are not, Lornavus."

The twins shared a brief but inscrutable glance. Sensi wondered if they somehow spoke in each other's mind. They almost never spoke to one another yet seemed to know what the other was thinking. Sensi was the only person who could identify them consistently--even the teachers couldn't tell them apart. Sensi himself was unsure how he did it, except that it had something to do with the eyes.

The twin on his left reached out and accepted the book, proving he indeed was Altavus. Uncharacteristically, Lornavus gave a slight smile, his lips turning up at the corners. The smile didn't reach his eyes; it never did. Sensi found himself drawn to those pale blue orbs, like staring into cold, reptilian eyes.

"I'll need that book back next week. Librarian Togg is planning on doing an inventory of the classic tomes. I'll need to have it back by then," said Sensi. "The old goat will have my hide if he catches me removing such an old book from the library."

"It will be returned in time," said Altavus, his speech clipped and precise, each syllable enunciated clearly. He thumbed through the book, stopping every few pages to study an inscription or examine snippets of text. The book was filled with the archaic High Script, a language Sensi himself didn't understand. Most of the truly great works of learning and culture had long ago been translated into contemporary language, so there wasn't much need for the ancient tongue.

But over and over, Sensi would get requests from them for this or that obscure manuscript, usually in High Script. Not for the first time, Sensi wondered what interest these moldy tomes could hold for Altavus and Lornavus. His thoughts were interrupted when Lornavus produced a pouch from the folds of his robe and tossed it to him.

"Your finder's fee," said Lornavus.

The pouch clinked as it landed in his hands. Sensi squirreled it away and left the twins to their book.

Chapter 7

Honor and law are not the same thing. If a man adheres to the law, it does not make him honorable in thought or deed, but the honorable man must sometimes break the law to do what is right.

--Torreg, captain of the Royal Guard

* * *

"If it's meant to be our day of rest, why do we have to dress in all this?" asked Onin as Fargin and he approached the temple's entrance. "This collar is so stiff, it makes my neck itch like nothing else."

"Look, it's only once a week. We dress in our best as a sign of respect for the Founders."

"Yes, I get that. It's just sort of strange to me. Back home, we had temples, but the priests weren't so . . . involved in everything."

"What's wrong with that?" asked Fargin. He reached out and straightened Onin's collar, but the big lad immediately shrugged it back to its disheveled form.

"Don't do that, it only makes the itching worse. I find it hard to believe the Founders are going to be at all impressed with these clothes. Wouldn't they rather see us comfortable and smiling at service?"

"Maybe it's just the sacrifice they ask of us. A little itching to show as a sign of faith."

"Somehow I don't think that's going to impress them either."

The boys entered the temple and moved to occupy one of the many stone benches. The sacred chamber had high ceilings, and the voices of the choir echoed through the air. Onin found the song mournful and solemn, and it made his mood worse.

"These benches are ludicrous too," whispered Onin as they settled onto the hard, cold surface. "Is this another sacrifice of comfort? Why would the Founders even begin to care about that? I don't understand this at all."

"That's obvious," hissed Fargin through clenched teeth. "Now shut up."

Onin resolved to keep his complaints to himself for the rest of the service. The priest arrived in short order to deliver the weekly sermon. Onin restrained a groan as a frail-looking old man teetered his way to the front. He remembered the old man from a previous sermon, a long and boring one. He didn't necessarily mind all of the sermons, but most concerned the genealogy of the Great Families. Onin felt slightly put upon. Why should it matter to him?

Perhaps it wouldn't be so bad if the priests didn't insinuate themselves into every aspect of daily life. The prayers preceded every meal. Minor altars and shrines to sundry semi-historical figures littered the streets and byways of the Heights. Every aspect of life somehow involved the church.

Though it seemed interminably long, the sermon came to an end in due time. Onin's stomach had started grumbling noisily near the conclusion. It struck him as odd that he could work up such an appetite just by sitting on a stone bench all morning.

Onin drove his fist into his stomach to quiet it down while he listened to the list of names being intoned by the priest. Each sermon ended with a dedication to a Founder, followed by a litany of genealogy tracing to modern days. The list came in the form of a long string of "son of" or "daughter of" declarations until it culminated with the current head of a Great Family, thereby drawing a direct line of descent to the Founders themselves.

Onin found the thought of Founders slightly dubious, though he took care in what company he shared the thought. While the records kept by the Great Families were no doubt accurate, they seemed like nothing more than ordinary people to Onin. They had their strengths, their weaknesses, and their petty issues, much the same as the Midlanders. He saw no cause for the seeming arrogance of being descended from gods. If the Great Families were truly scions of the divine, then Onin honestly hoped for much more than the High Folk represented.

The thought preoccupied him throughout the rest of the old priest's words, and he remained quiet as the congregation rose to leave. He followed Fargin out into the street while the minstrels played in the background. Many of the congregation drifted outside the temple and chatted in groups, but the young men avoided them and made their way down the street.

"Fargin," he said as the two walked back to their barracks. "Do you believe in the teachings? Are the Great Families really descended from the gods?"

Fargin looked surprised at the question. "I suppose it must be. Why else would they teach it?"

"But doesn't that seem far-fetched? What makes the Great Families different from other folks?"

"Same as always: ancestry. It only makes sense. Could you imagine what it would be like if anyone could become king, not just the Great Families? It would be crazy." Fargin laughed at the thought.

Onin, however, kept his opinion to himself.

* * *

The library could be musty on the driest of days, but after a week's worth of soaking rain, the air in the closed space was downright murky. The librarian seemed not to notice and refused Sensi's suggestion to burn incense to counteract the odor.

"Nonsense," said the crinkled old man. "Have you any idea how much damage smoke would do to these volumes? Completely out of the question!"

So Sensi endured the smell for days on end. It clung to his clothes when he left the library for his private quarters, and even bathing seemed to do little to remove it. Sensi had a great fondness for books but thought at times he would be happy to never see another one if it meant being rid of the smell of mold. But he had no recourse, and his discomfort made him irritable.

As he went about dusting the shelves, he looked once again to the twins. The stack of books surrounding them seemed innocuous enough--simple texts on literature and mathematics, arousing no suspicions.

From time to time, another student would sit down with the two for a whispered conversation. It never lasted long, and usually the visitor looked quite nervous in the presence of the icy calm the twins exuded. Sometimes the visitor left a pouch behind, which one of the twins would casually pick up and tuck away within billowing robes.

Many visitors rose and departed without another word. Most seemed eager to get out of the presence of the twins. Sensi could understand the urgency, given his own experiences with the rail-thin pair. They were never angry in any sort of visible sense, which was unsettling.

On this occasion, the visitor, one of the arms students, rose to leave, only to be stopped by a soft word from one of the two. Sensi strained to hear while being careful not to be seen. However, the distance was too great. He could hear voices but not make out any words. The tone of the visitor was certainly tense, almost pleading.

Unable to resist the temptation, Sensi went around to the other side of the bookcase nearest to the twins. A casual glance in both directions showed he was alone in the aisle. He moved silently across the stone floor and stopped at a gap in the books, allowing him to peer through to the other side. He found himself looking over the shoulder of the twin on the left. He couldn't tell which from behind, but thought it was Lornavus. As he came to a halt, the words being whispered became discernible.

"That's preposterous," said the visitor. A big, burly lad, he leaned forward menacingly. "I didn't agree to take on that kind of debt. It's almost twice what I borrowed from you."

The twins, at least the one Sensi could see from his vantage, weren't the least bit perturbed. The whispered reply was calm, even patronizing.

"Ah, but you did," said the twin before Sensi. "We have your signature, and it is legally binding. The document is clear on the specifics of interest and missed payments. The amount is correct, and we will take you before a magistrate if you do not pay."

"A magistrate?" the arms student asked. His expression spoke of alarm.

"Yes, a magistrate," chimed in the other twin, still in a whisper. "The full proceedings with a clerk and witnesses present. It's bound to bring up all sorts of questions about why you needed money in the first place."

The boy's expression went from alarm to fear before settling into resignation. "I shall pay," he whispered. His tone carried his defeat clearly. "When do you expect the next payment?"

"A similar amount, a month from now," said the twin in front of Sensi.

The would-be Guardsman paled visibly and clenched his fists until the knuckles turned white.

"A similar amount?" he asked in disbelief.

"One month from now," came the cool reply.

The student left the table, his shoulders slumped in despair. Sensi watched him walk away for a long moment, wondering what in the world the lad would do to make the next payment.

His gaze returned to the twin before him, and ice ran down his spine as he realized it was Lornavus. He could tell by the eyes looking back at him through the gap in the books.

"It's all right, Sensi," said the twin. "Come around."

Sensi did so dutifully, feeling like a scolded child caught being naughty. He stood before the twins, waiting for chastisement. They seemed amused, however.

"You've not witnessed anything inappropriate," said Altavus, now sitting on Sensi's left. "We have him bound fully and legally. Appearing before a magistrate will cause us no embarrassment."

"What did he need the money for?" asked Sensi.

"An illegitimate child," said Lornavus. "A former serving girl of his house is the mother. He needed the money to send them away to the Midlands."

Any sympathy Sensi might have felt for the lad evaporated. Just another privileged lout throwing money at a problem to make it disappear. In this case, Sensi derived comfort knowing the problem became much more expensive in the long run than anticipated.

* * *

Onin had grown up as a Midlander and, as such, possessed an awareness of the general disdain the High Folk had for his kind. Still he was unprepared for the reality that would confront him living in the Heights.

The study and work routine of the academy was rigorous, but Onin settled into it soon enough. He never was one overly blessed with social acumen, so he took no notice at first of the little jibes about his heritage and relative intelligence. After all, he had heard enough of such insults even in Sparrowport. With time, however, he began to feel the true but subtle venom fueling harsh words uttered behind his back--or sometimes to his face.

Onin engaged in free practice with Fargin. Both wore the simple but effective armor they used for training drills and were armed with wooden practice swords. Prendor had introduced them to a complicated series of attacks and corresponding defenses meant to increase their skill with the blade. Both young men had been confounded by the intricacy of the movements and decided some time would be well spent practicing in the evening. As usual, similar activities crowded the practice yard. From pairs to small groups, a flurry of activity existed throughout the space.

"There it is!" exclaimed Fargin as he landed a ringing blow on Onin's helmet. "Remember to withdraw your blade to a ready position after a low strike. I keep seeing an opening." Fargin had landed several such blows already. Onin's ears rang inside his helmet.

Onin raised his hand to call a halt to the exercise and wearily pulled his helmet off. The ringing persisted in his ears, and Onin shook his head several times to clear it. He almost didn't hear the snide comment over his shoulder.

"The Devalt Exchange! As if a Mudlander could master such a maneuver. Might as well teach arithmetic to a dog."

Onin turned to see who had spoken, and his eyes fell on a fellow student--a fourth-year, by the looks of his uniform. His hair was long and blond, and he sported a rough, stubbly beard. He was not as big as Onin but didn't miss the mark by much. Onin had seen the lad before, during other free practice sessions, but had never spoken to him. This wasn't shaping up to be a fruitful first conversation.

"I've a long way to go before I master it, I'll grant you. That's why I'm here practicing," Onin said.

"Well, that'll do for the day, then," said the older student. His own practice blade rested nonchalantly on his shoulder. "You can practice some other time. My friends and I need this space for our own use."

"You can't do that," blurted Fargin. As everyone's gaze fell on him, Fargin suddenly looked as if he wished he had remained silent. "The rules state that no one can have their practice space taken from them during the free time. Once you have the space, it's yours until you're done with it."

"That rule doesn't apply to Mudlanders," said the blond student. He looked straight at Onin while he said it. "Since you've no chance to master the Exchange, then you should yield the space to someone who might get something from practice."

"I'm a student here too," said Onin, his temper flaring. "I'm from the Durantis family."

"Adopted, I've heard," the older student said. "But you are clearly not of the High Folk. You shouldn't fret yourself about it. It's not your fault, so there's no need to worry about letting anyone down. No one expects anything of you."

"You," Fargin said then paused to gulp. "You still can't force him out of his spot."

The blond student looked thoughtfully at Fargin for a moment. "I suppose you're right. The solution is obvious. The Mudlander can simply choose to give it up. No one is forcing him." He turned his gaze back to Onin. "What do you say, ox? Will you go away willingly?"

"No," said Onin without hesitation. He kept a grip on himself, but his blood boiled.

"Then allow me to practice with you," said the older lad. "It's been some time since I worked on the Devalt Exchange. I may be a bit rusty. A refresher would be good for me."

The blond student had a gaggle of friends close by. They enjoyed the cat-and-mouse game extensively. Onin could sense he had been tricked but couldn't resist the chance to smash his smug face.

"All right," said Onin. "Come and spar with me." He held his practice sword in a salute.

The blond lad wasted no time on formalities and went directly into the attack routine of the Devalt Exchange. His movements were swift and precise. His blows landed with power. Onin blocked the first two but took a sharp blow to the knee on the third. He stumbled back a step, but before he could recover, his opponent had continued with the routine, hitting Onin repeatedly with painful blows, despite the practice armor. Abandoning the routine altogether, Onin tried desperately to deflect the incoming strikes but with little success. After finishing with a ringing blow to the helmet, the older student stepped back with his practice sword in a ready position.

"Your defense is pathetic, as I expected," said the smug young man. "See, you are not letting me down. You are exactly meeting my expectations! Now show me the attack routine. Assuming you can remember it."

"Gladly," said Onin through clenched teeth, and he went on the offensive.

He stuck to the routine, paying attention to all the details stressed during practice: footing, balance, hand position, angle of attack. Each of his strikes met with a graceful, effortless parry, as dictated by the Devalt Exchange. When Onin reached the end of the series, however, he continued to attack, lashing out at the taunting lad with every bit of strength he possessed. His efforts drew nothing more from his adversary, each attack deflected with the same ease. Onin paused, breathing heavily, while the older lad had yet to break a sweat.

"Also pathetic," he said with a sneer. "Probably more so. Try that again, ape. Your attack routine needs quite a bit of work." Onin had no breath for a retort but refused to give up. He launched himself into the attack routine once again.

This time he didn't get far before the older lad sidestepped his ponderously slow downward slash and struck Onin's wrist hard, knocking his sword from his grasp. The older lad smashed his other hand into Onin's helmeted face, sending him sprawling backward in the dirt.

When Onin's vision cleared, he stared up at the sneer of contempt on the blond youth's face.

"I could go like this all night," said the older lad. "What do you say, Mudlander? Will you choose to stay and practice?"

Onin could see he was bested. Despite his inclinations otherwise, he finally said, "No."

Onin withdrew from the field, hurt pride and all. The cronies of his opponent gave catcalls in his wake and taunted him with ape sounds. Fargin fell into step beside him loyally but quietly. But another voice cut through the mocking din.

"Stop right there!"

The voice belonged to Prendor. The mocking boys fell silent, and all turned to see the teacher striding purposefully toward them, his face livid. He addressed Onin's opponent first.

"Sandus! What have I told you about these displays of bravado?"

The fourth-year shot an ugly look at Onin, clearly blaming him for the teacher's untimely appearance. "But, sir, we were merely practicing, and he couldn't keep up."

"Indeed. I saw that. I saw quite a bit, actually." The anger had dissipated from Prendor's voice, but his eyes remained steely. "What was it you said in the beginning? Something about being rusty at the Devalt Exchange, I recall."

Prendor pulled his own practice sword from his belt. Sandus took a step backward, his eyes wide.

"I concur with your estimation, young man." Prendor smiled. "It simply won't do at all. Put your sword in your hand, Sandus. It's time to practice."

Sandus paled visibly. His cronies backed away, but Prendor jabbed at them with his weapon.

"Hold, you lot! I'm sure you all need practice as well. I'm suddenly feeling quite vigorous."

Prendor turned to Onin and Fargin.

"Thank you for willingly giving up the field, Onin. I'll make sure the time is well spent. Move along now."

Onin and Fargin were crestfallen to be dismissed at that moment but dared not hesitate in the face of the teacher's ire. Despite the disappointment, Onin grinned from ear to ear as they returned to the student quarters.

Chapter 8

There is no such thing as dishonor in battle; do whatever it takes to win. Nothing honors the king more than victory.
--Luros, teacher at Dragonbane Academy

* * *

The seasons touched the Heights with a light hand, coming and going quietly with few theatrics. Onin wondered if the altitude had something to do with it. The sun created delicious summers with abundant cool breezes. Cold and snow accompanied winter but held no comparison to the soul-crushing experiences called winter in the Midlands. Spring, by far, was the best. A variety of flowers, grown in pots and stone planters, released breathtaking colors in the various blooms.

Every spring the sleepy quiet of winter gave way to a sudden bustle of activity with the first thaw. While the melting snow swelled the ducts and pipes throughout the city, people emerged from their homes, like bears out of hibernation, and began the many preparations for the spring festival. The major celebration of the year, to honor the new growing season, hosted every manner of diversion made available to the people of the Heights. From confections to specialty sausages, marionettes to grand theatrical performances, everyone in the city had something that stirred anticipation.

With the festival came the tournament. Each year, the academies selected the most promising last-year students to test one another in martial contests from jousting to swordsmanship. The contests culminated in a mock battle between the eldest students of the three academies. The popular event filled the stadium to capacity.

The years passed at their own pace, until Onin and his friends found themselves in a flurry of last-minute preparations for the tournament. Last-year students participated, though not all would see the field. Rabbash was clever but lacked the stature to contend with the best warriors. Onin and Hangric were obvious competitors, due to imposing size.

Fargin also seemed a natural choice. The soft-spoken young man was skilled in combat; he took the patient approach in any challenge. His quiet nature led him to keep his composure while in the thick of things.

Despite his own disqualification, Rabbash showed equal excitement for his friends. He continued to drill with them and used his cunning mind to devise strategies and defenses for them, help them shore up their weaknesses, and take best advantage of their strengths.

The tournament was the highlight of the festival, the culmination of the day's events. Most of the Great Families would be attending. The rest of the seats would go to those who could afford the cost of admission.

While several lesser events were held before and after the tournament, the grand melee had the most bragging rights attributed to it. There was no official prize or winner's purse associated, and no academy benefited from it outside of perceived reputation. The matter of victory didn't hold much weight for anyone but the academies themselves, but that did not deter the institutes from striving to outdo one another, and the crowd enjoyed the spectacle.

As the afternoon began to draw to a close, and the shadows lengthened, the peal of horns rang from the high walls of the arena.

At long last, the time for the tournament had arrived.

* * *

They were all tense and fidgety in anticipation of the coming competition. Onin absently paced back and forth over a strip of dirt outside the arena. His comrades stood ready, each one preparing themselves in some manner for the contest ahead.

"Keep shield formations tight," came Rabbash's voice from the darkness to the rear. "Fill in behind the van as it progresses through the enemy ranks." The slight lad had been indispensable in planning the strategies they employed. While preparing for the contest, Rabbash had become a sort of honorary captain for the team. He understood their strengths and how to use them effectively. His ideas formed the backbone of their strategy. "The van will assault the enemy formation where they are tightly packed."

Rabbash strode up and down the three-score ranks of the Scaleback students. He next indicated the group to the back, about a dozen fighters led by Fargin. Each wore light armor and carried sword and shield as armament.

"Skirmishers," said Rabbash. "Stay back from the main body, we will need you to guard against assault from the other enemy." All three academies would be fielding a force. Onin knew from stories told by the teachers, poor choices from commanders had led two of the teams to cause heavy casualties to one another, only to allow the third, unscathed team to swoop in and claim victory with ease by wiping out the two weakened armies. This usually led to a period of stalemate, where each team waited for the others to make the first move, and hence the first mistake.

Rabbash studied the written accounts of previous years' contests. Each team from Scaleback wrote detailed accounts of each battle afterward, and Rabbash had used them to come up with a sound strategy. Rabbash seemed about to go on but horns interrupted.

So it began.

The door before Onin opened, and the sudden light blinded him. His ears were met by a cheering crowd. He blinked several times to adjust his vision, and the arena came into focus around him. They were in a circular stone pit, perhaps thirty yards in diameter, with a sand floor. Encircling the pit were towering stone walls topped with sets of bleachers filled with High Folk.

Onin and Hangric stepped through the door side by side; they formed the vanguard. They set themselves shield to shield, and the rest of the Scaleback fighters poured out of the entrance to form up on either side of them. The lightly armored skirmishers formed a line in the rear.

Across the arena, the two other academies, Gemtooth and Stoneclaw, fell into formation as well. As he had in previous years, as a spectator in the stands, Onin noticed a fourth door to the arena left unused. The unused door was to the right of the Scalebacks, placing Gemtooth directly across the field and Stoneclaw to their left. Officials in black robes were scattered about the arena, ready to call out when a warrior was struck a mortal blow and removed from the contest.

Onin and Hangric led an immediate charge to the left, heading directly for the center of the Stoneclaw formation. The ranks fell in behind them, and in seemingly just a few strides, the Scalebacks clashed against the Stoneclaw students. The crowd let out a roar as the initial exchanges were made and the first casualties inflicted. The Stoneclaws were tough but unable to hold up under the onslaught by Onin and Hangric. The formation neatly split in two, and the Scalebacks filled in behind them, keeping the Stoneclaw force divided.

As soon as the Gemtooth fighters realized what had happened, they attacked the Stoneclaws from the opposite direction. Early into the fight, the Stoneclaws found themselves split into two groups and fighting on two fronts. The spectators in favor of Stoneclaw vented their outrage, while the fans of Gemtooth and Scaleback were exultant. The Stoneclaws fought heroically, never giving an inch, but their numbers dwindled. As tournament rules dictated, the fallen contestants dropped where they stood and lay still.

While the Scaleback vanguard executed the frontal assault, the skirmish line moved to flank the Gemtooth fighters. Fargin and the other skirmishers were on them in an instant, covering the intervening distance with long strides made easy by the light armor they wore. The Gemtooth force melted under the attack at first, and many of their fighters fell, but the force recovered quickly, driving the skirmishers back. The noise of the crowd escalated with the strikes, and the Scalebacks fell back to regroup. The Gemtooth fighters followed, disrupting their attempts to form a defensible line.

Onin found himself driving the Stoneclaws before him into the waiting arms of the Gemtooth line. The divided Stoneclaw force suffered heavy casualties from both sides, and the group caught in the vise fared the worst. Onin pressed the attack, and before long, there were no Stoneclaws left in front of him; he was directly engaged with the Gemtooths now.

He smashed at them, hammering away at their shields mercilessly. Many of the students on the receiving end of his blows stumbled even when struck on the shield. When his attack breached the guard of a Gemtooth, the target went down in a heap, only to be called out by the judges. In the chaos, he lost all sense of his allies' locations.

The Gemtooth formation proved solid and hard to breach, the line of shields like the wall of a citadel as they continued to advance, driving the Scalebacks and remnants of the Stoneclaws up against the wall of the arena.

Finding themselves sudden allies, the Stoneclaws and Scalebacks formed a line with one another to hold back the assault of the Gemtooth fighters. The attack was highly disciplined and relentless. Man after man fell as the defenders were pushed against the wall; only a few were Gemtooths.

Onin found himself once again side by side with Hangric, and the two strong young men strove to beat back the Gemtooth fighters. Their blows were telling, sending opponents stumbling backward or down to one knee, but the Gemtooth men gave as good as they received. The Gemtooths were not just disciplined fighters; they struck with terrific force. The blows were so strong, Onin thought his shield would fly into pieces under them. Hangric went down, felled by a resounding blow to the helmet.

Something snapped within Onin, seeing his friend fall. Unbidden memories of blood and pain, of lost friends and helplessness, swept over him, and his vision swam with red at the edges. With a roar, he rushed forward, shield first, his rage and bulk sending the fighters in his path scattering like toy figurines. He lashed about with his sword, making no note of his targets, just smashing armored figures with every ounce of strength he could muster. He burst through the Gemtooth formation to find himself among Fargin and the remaining skirmishers.

Onin, his vision still red with rage, fleetingly met eyes with Fargin, and both young men turned and plunged back into the enemy lines with determination. The rest of the Scalebacks were not far behind, and the remaining Stoneclaws joined in the counterattack. Working in concert, they had the Gemtooths surrounded. The crowd cheered the exciting turnabout.

Still the Gemtooths were vicious, and their blows, powerful. The light armor of the skirmishers had the Scalebacks at a disadvantage, and one by one, they succumbed under the mighty strikes of the Gemtooths. Onin paid no heed to the casualties and continued to press the attack with all his strength. He received multiple hits but never flinched, immune to the pain. His own attacks were not so easily ignored, and he felled Gemtooth after Gemtooth as they squared up against him.

Suddenly no men stood before him. The battle ended and with it,

Onin's rage. He drew deep breaths as he looked about for his companions, but none were left standing. The arena was littered with bodies, and all of the Gemtooth fighters were eliminated. Besides Onin, only a half dozen fighters remained--all Stoneclaws. The crowd screamed, swept away with imaginary bloodlust.

Onin stepped to the center of the arena, one of the few clear spaces remaining since so much of the battle had happened near the high stone walls. Fatigue gripped Onin and his arms felt heavy. He wanted so much to lay his sword and shield down and just rest. But instead he set his jaw and saluted the six Stoneclaw fighters.

The crowd went wild. Onin had no chance. It would be easy for them to surround him and strike him down.

The six made no move to do so, however. Instead, they looked at each other, and something passed between them. They all nodded in consensus, and turned to face Onin again.

The Stoneclaw closest to him stepped forward and returned the salute. He attacked Onin while the other five remained disengaged. The crowd applauded uproariously to show their approval. Onin met his attacker head-on and struck him down with the first exchange.

The next Stoneclaw stepped forward and saluted. Onin returned the salute wearily. They circled one another for a moment, each probing for an opening. Onin found his first, driving home a short, quick strike that removed the opponent from the tournament.

The next fighter engaged Onin immediately, forgoing the salute. Onin retreated several steps before striking a lucky blow to his opponent's helmet, sending him to the ground. A nearby judge called the Stoneclaw out.

The final three looked at one another again, rethinking their honorable approach. Onin neared the limits of his endurance. His shield sagged with fatigue, and he struggled to keep it raised. He had to choose his attacks carefully and make the most of the strength left in his limbs. He could only hope the remaining Stoneclaws were as tired as he.

One of the Stoneclaws stepped forward to salute. Apparently honor had won out among them. Onin traded several blows with his adversary. He felled his opponent with a powerful overhand chop, although he took a painful shot to the knee in the process.

Now limping, Onin wasted no time before engaging the next fighter. He lurched forward, slamming his shield against the Stoneclaw, sending him reeling back. Onin's follow-up strike knocked the lad's helmet sideways. Behind him, a judge cried, "Out!"

The last Stoneclaw squared off with Onin. The crowd alternated between screaming and cheering. Onin took a deep breath and focused all of his attention on his opponent. The sounds of the crowd grew distant in his mind. His opponent closed the distance in a sudden rush, and their shields collided with a crash.

Onin cried out with the pain as his knee buckled under the weight of his adversary. Twisting to the side to divert the charge, Onin dropped his sword and smashed his gauntlet-covered fist into his opponent's helmet. The ferocious blow clanged against the Stoneclaw's helmet and brought him to one knee. Before he could recover his footing, Onin's fist sent him to his back with a crash.

A judge cried, "Out!" As one, the crowd rose, roaring with applause. Flowers rained down into the arena as the spectators cast them out in handfuls.

Onin, limping painfully, saluted all four directions of the arena. The rest of the contestants, done playing dead, came to their feet and did likewise. In a show of sportsmanship, the students clasped hands with one another and offered congratulations. They then walked or limped to the doors they had entered from. As Onin approached, Rabbash poked his head through the door.

"Hey! Grab that sword!" said Rabbash, trying to whisper and shout at the same time. Onin looked where he pointed and saw a practice sword with the Gemtooth symbol on it. He gave Rabbash a puzzled look.

"Just get it! I'll explain later."

Onin stooped to grab the weapon and limped through the door.

* * *

Not everyone was riveted by the spectacle of the tournament. While the prospective Guards were testing their mettle against one another, sharp minds conspired in the silent halls of Scaleback Academy.

Sensi rushed from the library with a stack of scrolls in his arms. The scrolls he had put in their place were a set of old recipes, on similarly aged parchment, so they should pass a cursory inspection. Getting them out proved easy since the halls of the academy were virtually empty on festival day. Returning them to the correct place unnoticed would be more challenging, especially with recent developments.

Still, he had no choice. For his own reasons, he needed the coin provided, wherever the twins got it from. Over their years at the academy, Sensi had been able to see the financial accounts tracking the allowances of the students bequeathed by their parents. The twins indeed came from a wealthy family, but the amount of coin the two spent far exceeded their allotment. Sensi had received a fair portion himself, and most of the other academic students were paid for some service or another, and the twins had passed coin to numerous arms students as well. Sensi had no idea what they could be up to with their old books and clandestine meetings or where they secured the money they were using so lavishly.

Sensi found them in their customary seats in the student hall. As usual, they sat quietly, thumbing through various texts or scrolls and scribbling the occasional note on a nearby parchment. The twins always covered what they were researching when Sensi approached, slamming books shut or piling items to conceal parchments, but this time he seemed to have caught them off guard. Sensi caught a glimpse of the book Altavus studied, and the page contained a picture of a woman dressed in robes holding two scales in her hands. He knew which books and scrolls he fetched from under the librarian's nose, and he always pored over the contents of the ones he could read but discovered nothing useful. If the twins had a goal in mind, Sensi couldn't fathom it.

Sensi dropped the pile of scrolls unceremoniously in front of them. They hardly looked up and seemed completely disinclined to speak to him. Once it became apparent Sensi wasn't going to leave, Lornavus broke the silence.

"Is there something else?"

"Yes, there is," said Sensi. He felt about to step onto ice that may be thin. "That little fighter named Rabbash was poking around in the antiquities department. He was looking for some text on a historic battle, and he noticed one of the books he wanted was missing: *Testament of the Augur.*"

"Why does an ox want the *Testament?*" asked Altavus. Both of the twins always referred to the fighting students as oxen. "There are no accounts of historic battles; it is a book of prophecy."

"Who knows?" said Sensi with a shrug. "But he has raised the text's disappearance with the librarian, who is now searching all over for it. If it doesn't reappear soon, suspicion will fall on me in due time. That is, if it hasn't already."

The twins shared a long glance.

"We have what we can glean from it," said Altavus. "We need the original, not this modern translation." Sensi puzzled over the comment. The manuscript was rumored to be more than a thousand years old.

"I am still concerned why an ox would want it," said Lornavus. "I'm surprised they even know the text exists. I can't imagine why he would need to study it himself."

Sensi shrugged again. "Perhaps he's a follower of the Old Faith."

The twins looked at one another again then at Sensi. It was disconcerting to have the full attention of both of them at the same time. After a long moment, Lornavus fished a pouch from inside his robes, and it made the familiar tinkling sound as he tossed it to Sensi. Altavus produced the *Testament* from the pile of books they hoarded and gave it back to Sensi.

"After this has been returned, we've another task for you, Sensi . . ."

Chapter 9

Men of honor represent the pinnacle of civilized behavior and the warrior ideal. Warriors without cultivated ideals succumb to base thoughts and become marauders and barbarians. Men of education but no skill of arms make poor generals and cannot protect anyone.
--Belond, headmaster of Scaleback Academy

* * *

At Scaleback hall, the wine flowed, the music boomed, and the feast unfolded. Tray after tray of mouthwatering dishes came from the kitchens; barrels of wine and ale were rolled into the great hall. Minstrels played with wild abandon, and flagons were raised, emptied, filled, and raised yet again. Laughter permeated the hall as the day's contestants told and retold the tales of daring and recounted each move of the battle with exaggerated motions and ridiculous pantomimes.

Zorot watched his adopted son from a short distance away. The parents and other adults attending the celebration were seated at their own table. Onin had not grown much taller in his four years at the academy, but he had filled out across the shoulders. He cut a truly imposing figure of a man, and he had looked magnificent on the field in his battle regalia. Zorot couldn't have been more proud.

Torreg, sitting next to Zorot, seemed to be enjoying the celebration as much as any of the students. He asked for his goblet to be refilled time after time, and his nose and cheeks were tinted with a rosy blush. He grabbed a haunch of mutton from the banquet table and tore into it with his teeth, pulling away strips of succulent meat.

"A good contest," said Torreg. "He did as well as I had hoped."

"Indeed," said Zorot. "I had my reservations about this life for him. But I can see it suits him well." As he watched, a tall young man poured a tankard of ale over Onin's head. Onin reacted with mock anger and made like he would wrestle his friend to the ground but stopped short as another student thrust a full tankard into his hand. Onin tossed his head back and drank deeply, and the boys roared with merriment.

"He'll be done with his studies soon and assume the mantle of a Guard." Torreg belched. "Then his life can truly begin."

"Speaking of his life beginning," said Zorot. "How are the preparations coming?"

"Slowly," said Torreg with a look of distaste. "I really don't have the head for these things; I'm glad my daughter is able to do them. I don't know how she manages to run our household and keep the hatchery operating smoothly."

"So things are improving? I've heard all the hatcheries have been struggling these last few years," said Zorot. He tossed a copper coin to a passing minstrel.

Torreg's expression sobered. "Well, no, not really," said Torreg. "Each year we are seeing less eggs, and fewer of those produce a viable hatchling. Many that do hatch are runts or deformed or both and need to be put down straight away."

"A tricky business, breeding dragons." Zorot nodded sagely. "Animal husbandry has never been my strong suit." His attention wandered back to Onin. A pretty girl, one of the festival dancers, sat on the lad's lap. Onin's cheeks flamed red--from the ale or something else, Zorot could only guess. The girl leaned over and whispered something into his ear, and Onin flushed even deeper. She giggled at his obvious discomfort. Zorot laughed.

"He's always been a tough boy," said the trade ambassador. "But terribly shy around girls. I wonder if he gets it from me. I must say, though, he looks fairly at ease, considering what awaits him a few months from now."

"That's because he doesn't know," said Torreg with a bit of a slur.

Zorot looked at him incredulously. "He doesn't know?" he exclaimed. "How can he not know?"

Torreg shrugged. "Haven't found the right time to tell him."

"Right time?" Zorot said, his pitch jumping up a notch. "You've had four years!"

"Well," said Torreg sheepishly. "The lessons do consume so much of the students' time, and I didn't want to distract him from his studies . . ." Torreg trailed off as Zorot gave him a withering look.

"Four years," repeated Zorot. His tone dripped reproach.

"I'll tell him tonight," came Torreg's reply. The captain drained his flagon once again and beckoned for a refill.

* * *

The bowels of the mountain contained seemingly endless passageways and halls, forming a vast complex never touched by the light of day. The darkness wasn't empty; the laments of the poverty-stricken and the stench of unwashed bodies filled it. Sensi hated every time he had to make these trips, which were becoming more frequent.

Sensi's hand rested nervously on the handle of the dagger concealed in his robes. It had been some time since he'd needed to brandish it, but hard experience taught him the underbelly was no place to be without some form of protection.

The corridors were narrow and cramped; in places it seemed every square inch of floor had some poor wretch curled up on it. He found his way barred by a shapeless mass of dirty clothing. Sensi kicked the pile forcefully until it grumbled and rolled aside.

His disgust for the underbelly continued to grow--not just the place itself, but the hypocrisy it represented. For all the grandeur of the city above, resplendent in the sunlight and open air, the corridors below epitomized the cesspool that held everything the people of the Heights would wash away and refuse to acknowledge about themselves. The poor, the sick, the low class; all made their way to the underbelly to eke out a meager existence from the scraps discarded by those above. The most unfortunate souls were born and raised in the subterranean slum; stories whispered in taverns said some of the inhabitants of the underbelly had never seen the sun or open sky.

Sensi pushed himself against the wall as a pair of watchmen passed by, dragging a protesting ruffian between them. The Heights may not recognize the existence of the underbelly publicly, but they made sure their authority stretched there. The city watch were a frequent sight in the filthy tunnels, and when assigned a quarry, they pursued it doggedly, whether it be a thief, a murderer, or some other undesirable. Any who would get in the way were beaten or even killed. The watch did so with impunity. Who would protest in the great courts in the city above? Anyone with friends above would be with them instead of huddling in the underbelly. The watch acted without repercussions and would accept bribes, extort the inhabitants for protection, and take advantage any number of ways.

Sensi continued along the winding corridors, taking care to keep the worst of the filth off his clothing. He arrived at his destination, a flophouse of sorts. A stone staircase led to a short hallway filled with doors, perhaps about a dozen. Many of them were open, and rutting animal sounds issued from within. As he passed them, Sensi glanced through the door to see painted ladies plying the oldest of trades. The watch frequented this place as well, whether spending their own coin or looking for someone.

Sensi arrived at the last door on the left. It remained closed and probably locked, as always. The rotund young man knocked delicately and waited a few moments. Finally, a voice came from within.

"Who is it?"

"It's me, Mother," said Sensi with a hint of exasperation. "Who else comes to see you?"

A clicking sound came from the other side of the door, and it opened to reveal a dingy room with a cot on one side and a table on the other. The cot was piled high with thick but dirty blankets. The table contained an oil lamp, currently the only source of light, and a framed picture of a man. Next to the picture rested a pair of dice, the common type used in games of chance. A limited assortment of iron pots and pans, including a teakettle, were clumsily stacked under the table.

Sensi wrinkled his nose as the putrid air of his mother's cell assaulted him. She never left this room anymore, as far as he knew. It must have been years since she had seen sunlight, like many other denizens of the underbelly.

His mother made a frightful sight. Gnarled and matted hair hung from her head, and her fingers were caked with grime. Her tattered clothes were filthy. Sensi sighed. He had brought the dress a month ago, and he wondered how it was already in such poor condition. She was wracked with a coughing fit as he entered the room.

"Ah, my son," she said and pulled him closer to kiss him. He really wished she wouldn't but held his breath and allowed her cracked lips to touch his cheek. "My sweet boy."

Lacking any other available seat, Sensi sat gingerly on the cot. He set his satchel on the ground and produced a hard round of cheese, some dried beef, and a fresh loaf of bread. He set them out on the table, and his mother hungrily dug in to the meager fare.

While she ate, Sensi refilled the oil lamp from the flask he'd brought with him. He admonished her to use the lamp sparingly, as he always did. He fetched an iron grate on thin legs and the teakettle from the stack under the table and placed them over the lamp's flame to boil water, which Sensi had also brought along. He placed medicinal leaves in the water to steep.

Sensi sat quietly while the water came to a boil. He felt the need to speak, if just to fill the silence, but could think of nothing to say to her. It had all been said before and didn't bear repeating. As it usually did, his gaze came to rest on the picture occupying a place on the table. The man in the painting was handsome, tall and regal looking. His mien bespoke nobility, as did his extravagant clothes. Even the picture frame looked expensive. Sensi had tried to get her to sell it many times in the past but she refused. On one occasion he had tried to take it forcefully, but she wailed and clutched it to her chest. She bit him when he tried to pry her fingers away from it.

"You look just like him," she said. "Spitting image, you are." Sensi knew differently. No one who looked at him would think he bore any resemblance to the man in the picture.

"He would be so proud of you," she continued. "Attending academy, taking care of your mother, making important friends. When he learns of it, he's going to raise you up to sit at his right hand. Then you'll be important too." She lifted the picture from the table and cradled it in her arms lovingly.

"He won't ever know," said Sensi. "Even if he did, he'll never do anything for us."

His mother's eyes flashed wild and angry. "That's not true. He loves us! He'll come for us!"

Her vehemence caused her a fit of coughing. Sensi took the picture from her hand and placed it gently on the table then guided her to sit next to him on the cot. Despite his gentle actions, Sensi's voice grew harsh.

"He'll not come and he doesn't love us," he said. "You were his parlor maid, not his lover. I am his bastard son, and he will never recognize me. He has no use for us, and you'll never see him again." He didn't know why he bothered saying these things to her; they never sank in. Anger often clouded his reason.

Her coughing fit subsided and Sensi made her drink her tea. Her consumption was getting worse, he could tell, and the medicine he needed to treat it was expensive. He brought her as much as he could afford, as often as he could, but it wasn't enough. She rested her head on his shoulder and wiped her mouth with the back of her hand. Sensi could see blood on her sleeve.

"You'll see," she said. "When he hears about how clever you are, he'll come for us."

* * *

"Weighted," said Rabbash smugly. "I knew something didn't look right about them."

The words didn't fully register on Onin for a moment or two. Rabbash had hurriedly pulled the circle of friends away from the celebration. They had left reluctantly, but Rabbash's insistence swayed them. They gathered in the passageway outside the feast hall to listen.

"What are you talking about?" said Onin. His words were slightly slurred from the ale. Rabbash held what appeared to be a wooden stick in front of him. After a blank look, Onin realized he held the Gemtooth practice blade. The tip of the wooden sword was split, revealing a strip of metal protruding from the end. Rabbash tapped it with his finger.

"Lead," he explained. "The wooden shaft of the blade has been hollowed out and filled with molten lead. Think about today's fight. They were skilled, no doubt, but have you ever been hit so hard? I'll bet all the Gemtooth weapons were weighted."

Onin shared angry looks with Fargin and Hangric. All three wore painful reminders of the day's contest. Fargin even had his right arm in a sling. The students were addled by the alcohol, but the implications were sinking in.

"What difference does it make, though?" asked Hangric. "They cheated but we still won. That just makes our victory even better, doesn't it?"

"What of the principle?" countered Rabbash. "We won but by the most narrow of margins. It literally couldn't have been any closer for us. And what of the injuries inflicted? Fargin will be unable to train or go on duty for as long as his arm needs to heal.

"And what about next year? We won this bout because of Onin and Hangric. Next year will the Gemtooth students do the same thing, ensuring their victory? For another matter, how do we know they didn't do it last year, and the year before, and so on?"

The implications began to sink in for the other three. It made no sense to Onin. There was no prize or reward associated with the tournament. Why bother to cheat at all? It was only a matter of pride, and no one seemed to care who had won the tournament within a couple of months. He couldn't ignore Rabbash, though. Whether it made sense or not, cheating in such a way was underhanded.

"So what do we do about it?" said Onin.

* * *

When Onin and his friends returned to the feast hall, his father and Captain Torreg were waiting for him. Zorot walked steadily while Torreg had obviously been enjoying libations. His red-nosed face beamed in a wide smile as he clapped Onin on the shoulder heartily.

"Well fought today, lad!" exclaimed Torreg. He had already congratulated Onin. Twice. For some reason, he was more unsettled by Torreg's attention than when the girls were taking turns sitting in his lap and batting eyelashes at him. Torreg didn't seem to notice and continued unabashedly. "Never have I seen such a display! The tournaments are usually fairly boring, despite the interest from the festival-goers."

"Well," replied Onin. "I fought as hard as I could, which is all I could do. It really wasn't anything." He noticed some of the lasses from earlier looked in his direction. Onin didn't have much experience with women, but he anticipated gaining some.

"Nonsense, my son," said Zorot. His eyes shone with pride. "Every man out there today did the same, but you were the one still standing at the end of it all."

Onin shook his head in response. "If the remaining Stoneclaws had attacked me all at once, I wouldn't have been," said Onin. "We owe our victory to Stoneclaw honor as much as our own efforts."

"A gracious victor as well," continued Torreg.

Onin began to suspect the drunken captain enjoyed making him uncomfortable. The girls Onin had noticed earlier moved within earshot, and he found himself hoping they could hear Torreg's words, despite himself.

"You've the makings of a great hero, Onin."

Torreg seemed to notice the young women lingering in Onin's vicinity. His expression became that of a man who found himself surrounded by sharks in deep water. With sideways glances, Torreg grasped Onin by the arm and led him back to the table. Zorot followed, stifling a laugh.

"Yes, a great hero," said Zorot. His father's mirth contagious, Onin found himself smiling. Torreg placed a filled tankard in his hand then raised his own in a salute.

"To the future!"

All three drank deeply.

"To family!" said Torreg.

Onin could only agree, and all three drank again.

"To grandchildren!" said Zorot.

Onin was not so sure about that one but drank anyway.

"To marriage!" said Torreg.

Onin stopped his tankard halfway to his mouth and looked at the captain suspiciously.

"What are we toasting exactly?" said Onin.

Torreg looked momentarily embarrassed but then split his face with a wide grin. "Onin, my boy," said Torreg. "Congratulations on your betrothal. You're to be married a month from now. To my daughter."

Chapter 10

The king is no blood of man, but the chosen one of the gods. Each king shall find his successor among the great ones and cherish the successor, for that is where the future rests.
--excerpt from *Testament of the Augur*

* * *

The next month found Onin at the Chapel of Bonding, dressed in finery, awaiting his bride. The robes adorning him were made of the finest silks, and a velvet cape hung from his shoulders. His father stood beside him, representing Onin's family, and his friends occupied the foremost stone pew. Onin took comfort in their presence, although the sight of Hangric, Fargin, and Rabbash dressed in formal attire would have made him laugh out loud under normal circumstances. The air remained cool in the vaulted chapel, but Onin sweat nevertheless. He absently wiped his forehead with his sleeve.

"Stop that," his father whispered. "You'll stain the fabric. You'll want to make the best possible impression."

"I still wish we could have met before the wedding," said Onin, probably for the hundredth time. "This is an uncomfortable way to meet anyone, let alone your soon-to-be wife."

"Tradition, my boy, tradition," said Zorot sagely. "Common wisdom holds that if the newlyweds never meet before the wedding day, then the marriage truly starts with a clean slate." Onin had heard this many times already, but it did nothing to help him relax.

"What if she hates me?" said Onin. "What if she wants to talk to me? Do I have to talk to her? Is that expected of a husband?" His eyes looked a little wild.

"Yes, conversation is a must," said his father. "But I think you'll be fine. Remember, she is meeting you for the first time as well."

"That's what I'm afraid of," said Onin. "She has no idea what she's getting into."

His friends gestured to get his attention. When Onin looked in their direction, all wore expressions of mock seriousness. Rabbash tugged at his left ear in an exaggerated fashion--the signal they had worked out earlier. If Onin were to tug on his own ear, it would be a sign they were to flee from the chapel and find someplace to hide. It had been a joke they contrived to assuage Onin's fears, he knew, but he gave the idea serious consideration.

The chapel was filled to capacity for the blessed event. The guests ranged from fellow Guardsmen--old friends of Torreg's, as well as a few new friends of Onin's--to representatives of each of the Great Families.

Onin understood their presence but didn't like it. A marriage among their peers was a significant event, and none among the social elite wanted to miss out on something so gossip worthy. Onin wished it were otherwise, but his father explained the necessity of it since he married into one of the Great Families. Still, it disturbed him that so many guests were complete strangers.

"Who is the lady in the hideous purple hat?" whispered Onin. "Is that supposed to be a bird?"

"That's Atriva Golence, the minister of investitures," came the reply. "I've no idea what the hat is supposed to be."

"What about the bald man with the splotches on his head?"

"Jutnel Holgrim, minister of trade," said his father. "He gave me my appointment as trade ambassador to Sparrowport."

"What about the pock-faced fop? The tall, skinny one? I don't like how he's looking at me."

"I don't know him," said Zorot. "But the young lady sitting next to him is about to be your cousin by marriage. Pock-face is probably her husband."

"She's awfully pretty," Onin said, hoping the characteristic ran throughout other branches of the family. "How did she get saddled with such a wretch?"

"Through an arranged marriage, in all likelihood," said his father with a chuckle. "It's the way things are done among the Great Families. Not everyone can be beautiful."

Onin considered the implications of the statement.

When the music began to play, the assembled crowd hushed, and the lilting sound of flutes echoed across the vaulted ceiling. A figure, actually two figures, stood silhouetted by the sunlight in the entrance. They became distinct as they entered the chapel, and Onin recognized Torreg, his soon-to-be father-in-law, escorting a petite, feminine form through the entrance. She looked resplendent in ornate white robes with a jeweled tiara nestled in her raven hair. Her skin was pale and soft, and her beauty took Onin's breath away.

Her father guided her to the altar, each step full of grace and poise. Her delicate feet seemed to glide along the marble stones of the floor. Onin stared self-consciously, feeling the sweat bead on his brow. He almost wiped with his sleeve again but stopped himself.

She never lifted her eyes as she walked to her waiting groom. Onin doubted shyness on her part; she walked with too much confidence to be nervous. He looked into her face as she grew near. Her features were delicate with thin, dark eyebrows and an alluring blush to her cheeks. Onin could feel his heart pounding in his chest with each step she took until she finally stood at the altar. Only then did she lift her eyes and meet his gaze.

Onin nearly recoiled. There was no love in her eyes, no shyness or uncertainty, just anger and resentment. Her lips were pulled tight in a grimace, and she refused to smile, even as Onin gave his own nervous grin as an offering of good will.

Great, he thought. *I haven't even spoken to her yet, and already I'm in trouble. Married life is going to be easy.*

* * *

The conclusion of the ceremony rested on pomp and circumstance. The bride and groom clasped hands with one another, while the attending priestess wrapped a white ribbon around their forearms, tying them together. It was the first touch they exchanged, and Onin would remember it forever. Her hand felt tiny and delicate in his, but warm and inviting. Torreg and Zorot concluded the ceremony, each making a short speech about the promise of the future and budding love, but Onin wasn't really listening. His attention remained fixed on his new wife.

After the initial brief, but hostile, glance, she refused to look at him further. Onin wondered what bothered her. Had he somehow managed to offend her, or did she just hate him on sight? The soft skin of her hand made him want to brave that withering look once again.

Once the ritual had concluded, and the ceremonial knot untied, the newlyweds were bundled into a luxurious carriage drawn by two magnificent white horses. The interior was cramped but richly decorated, with two cushioned seats situated opposite one another. His wife climbed aboard, aided by the attending footman, who gave Onin a smile and a wink. Onin climbed into the seat opposite his wife, her icy glare unchanged. He looked pleadingly at the footman as the carriage door shut, leaving them alone for the first time.

They stared at each other for a long moment. She gave no indication she intended to speak, so Onin decided to take the initiative. He opened his mouth, but his dry throat released only a croak at first. Onin swallowed hard to recover himself.

"I'm Onin . . . I'm your . . . um, husband," he muttered lamely, not knowing what else to say.

She rolled her eyes to the heavens in response. "I'm Yolan."

At least he had learned her name.

Onin decided their first conversation qualified as a success and left it at that. The rest of the carriage ride passed in silence, even as the calls of well-wishers reached their ears through the carriage windows. Yolan ignored them and merely stared out the window without changing her expression.

After what seemed like hours, they arrived outside of an elegant manor located on one of the highest tiers of the Heights. The grand exterior, finely carved from the stone of the mountain, had sculptures and water fixtures incorporated into the building. Fountains tinkled merrily, and the courtyard was spacious enough for a battalion of soldiers to stand in formation. Many servants in the finest livery scurried about. No sooner had the carriage come to a rest than the door opened and a footman extended his hand for Yolan. She climbed from the carriage with the same smooth grace she had displayed in the chapel. Onin could watch her move all day and never tire of it.

Torreg and Zorot were already present. Onin hadn't seen them leave the chapel and absently wondered how they managed to arrive before the newlyweds. Both men looked absolutely cheery and showed wine had already been imbibed that day. Onin was grateful to see a friendly face, and his father clapped both hands on his shoulders warmly.

Meanwhile, Torreg extended his arms to embrace his daughter, but Yolan walked past, ignoring him. Torreg watched her stride away with defiance and opened his mouth to speak but then seemed to think better of it.

"I really thought she'd have come around by now," said the captain after she had crossed the threshold of the manor.

"She needs more time," said Zorot. While he spoke to Torreg, he looked directly into Onin's eyes. Onin knew the words were meant for him more than Torreg. "It is a difficult adjustment for everyone."

Torreg seemed lost in thought for a moment, staring after his daughter, then shook himself. "Well, no use standing out here. The feast awaits!" he exclaimed. Torreg led Onin and his father inside the manor. The entryway was ornate to the point of opulence. Magnificent marble staircases led up and away to another level, and numerous elaborate doors dotted the walls at regular intervals. Torreg led them to the only open door.

Beyond it waited the grandest feast hall Onin had ever seen. Stout wooden tables and stools were arranged throughout the room, and a head table lay at the opposite end. Yolan was already there, her sullen look in place. High stone walls blocked most of the sunlight, save what entered through narrow windows set directly into the roof. It was the walls that commanded attention, however.

The walls were a celebration of color, covered with paintings from floor to ceiling. Numerous scenes, both historical and mythical, were depicted in a rolling, continuous piece of work wrapping the entire hall. Onin recognized the Heights itself depicted in the work, and the primary theme seemed to be dragons. Verdants of all types and colors adorned the art: flying, nesting, fighting, and one image showed two dragons with necks and tails entwined. He was fairly sure he knew what that one depicted.

Torreg took notice of Onin's incredulous look as he gaped all around the room.

"Well, what do you think, lad?" he exclaimed. "Or should I say, 'my son'?"

"This is amazing," said Onin with sincerity. "What is this place?"

"You don't know?" said Zorot. He turned to address Torreg. "You don't tell this boy anything."

Torreg only spread his arms wide and shrugged before speaking to Onin again. "This is Manespike Manor," Torreg proclaimed proudly. "This is your new home. Unless, of course, you have arranged for better accommodations elsewhere."

Onin wondered how many times he would be rendered utterly speechless by this man.

"My father's right," he said. "You don't tell me anything. This is your home? I had no idea. I imagined only the king would live in a place like this."

"The years have been kind to my family, for certain," said Torreg. "Like I said, it's now *your* home too." His smile faded to concern as he looked around at the murals. He seemed to forget the others were present in his preoccupation. He gave a slight start when Zorot directed a question at him.

"These murals are depictions of the family business, aren't they?" he asked, indicating the art-covered walls.

Torreg smiled again. "Yes, most of these are generations old," said Torreg. "But they tell the stories of some of our earliest successes."

"What business is that?" asked Onin. He felt foolish--he'd married into one of the most prominent families of the Heights, and he didn't even know about the family business, let alone its exact nature.

"Dragon breeding!" said Torreg. The same troubled look passed across Torreg's features, but only for an instant. The young man thought no more of it, as the nature of the family business sank in.

"Dragon breeding?" Onin repeated to no one in particular. He took a long, slow look around the hall at the murals, and this time the images made much more sense to him. He realized the mural, when viewed end to end, provided a pictorial history of the Manespike family.

"Indeed," continued Torreg. "Our family has produced some of the finest stock ever to grace the skies."

"That was true at one time," came a voice from a short distance away. The voice belonged to a tall, almost statuesque woman. Her face was thin and pointed, her features birdlike, and her finery marked her as a member of a Great Family. "The Manespikes haven't produced a viable clutch in several years."

The captain's face became dark as a storm cloud. Torreg smiled at her, but no hint of warmth or friendship was conveyed in the expression.

"The problem isn't isolated to us, Lady Vestrimol," he countered. "If memory serves, your own stock has seen some trouble these past few seasons."

"The Vestrimols produce good dragons each and every season," said the lady haughtily, her nostrils flaring. "The dragon riders give us a ringing endorsement every year, which is more than some can claim." She spun and stalked away stiffly. Onin wondered if the dress she wore caused her to walk that way or if it was natural.

"A competitor?" Zorot asked after she had gone.

"A pretender, more like," said Torreg in disgust. "Her fledglings are little more than runts, the lot of them. Imagine the nerve, casting aspersions like that . . . on my daughter's wedding day, no less."

"So there's no truth to what she said?" Onin inquired.

Torreg looked worried once again. "Well, I cannot dispute it, in truth," said Torreg. But then his expression brightened. "This is no day for such talk. Let us celebrate the union of our families." Onin found the sudden joviality dubious but made no protests as they took seats at the head table.

Once again Onin found himself unable to take his eyes from Yolan, and she seemed unwilling to even look at him. A plate of food and a full goblet sat before her, but she hardly touched either, her delicate hands primly folded in her lap. Onin wanted to hold her hand again, to feel its softness and warmth against his own skin. He wanted to speak to her, but no words came to mind. Her full lips made the most adorable pout, and Onin found himself pondering what it would feel like to kiss them. He had to resist the urge to wipe his forehead with his sleeve again; he could feel the sweat starting to bead and wished it were cooler in the feast hall.

Onin's attention was pulled away when his friends arrived at the feast. A sense of relief followed the sight of familiar faces, and he immediately rose to meet them. They each vigorously clasped hands with him, offering up congratulations, except for Hangric, who lifted Onin from the floor in a bearlike embrace.

"Oh, but she's a beauty!" exclaimed Fargin. "What a catch!"

"What is she like?" asked Rabbash, his eyes twinkling.

"I don't know, really," said Onin, rubbing his beard thoughtfully. "She's . . . intense, I guess."

"What did you talk about in the carriage ride? Or was there no time for talking?" asked Fargin while throwing him a naughty wink.

"Nothing. She wouldn't talk to me," said Onin with a slight blush. "There was certainly none of that going on either," he said to Fargin pointedly. All three friends laughed at his discomfort.

"I'm glad you're all so amused," he said sarcastically. He turned back to look at his young wife. Already, she presented a complete enigma to him. He wondered what the next few months would be like. Despite his reservations, the thought of waking up next to Yolan every morning was inviting.

"Take heart, my friend," said Rabbash. "It's not long before we all succumb to the wiles of matrimony. There will be plenty of time to poke fun at us later."

"No doubt," said Hangric, his expression somber. "My betrothed has a face like a horse."

All three laughed at that.

* * *

The days following the wedding passed, and Onin soon found himself engaged in another formal but important function. His induction into the Guard had come, and he, along with his friends, assumed a place of honor within the elite order.

Each arrived in full ceremonial dress, with brightly polished breastplates; shining helmets; and rich, red capes draped over the shoulders. The graduates of each academy attended, and it felt odd to be shoulder to shoulder with the same young men he had battled in the tournament not so long ago.

The young men were arranged in formation within the Grand Hall. This same hall had been used countless times before, not only for inducting new Guards, but for any formal function the order engaged in.

The induction was performed by none other than the Guardmaster, the head of the order. Guardmaster Strull was an old man, balding, but stood tall and strong, unbent by his advanced years. His resonant voice carried through the hall with ease.

"On this day you leave your old lives behind," Guardmaster Strull said officiously. "This is the day you put aside the name of your family to enter the service of the kingdom. Since the inception of this order, all Guardsmen have put aside their familial obligations to serve our true purpose--the protection of the king . . . and the successor.

"The king is more than a man, but the personification of the Heights. As he lives, so do the Heights live, and each king finds his successor to continue the chain of rulership and ensure the ascendancy of our kingdom.

"I welcome you into this order and task you all with preserving the honor, integrity, and lives of the king and successor."

Chapter 11

When it comes right down to it, eggs are eggs.
--Polgrin, master incubator

* * *

Dragons filled the sky. The scaled forms stretched from one end of the horizon to the other. They numbered in the hundreds--the thousands. They all flew in the same direction: toward the setting sun, fleeing the night. Behind them, dispelling the darkness, came a multitude of comets. Like arrows from the gods, the comets traversed the sky, leaving golden trails behind them.

Dragons began to die. In growing numbers, they simply stopped flapping their wings and plummeted from the sky until it seemed to be raining dragons.

The eggs. There were eggs nearby in a nest scraped from the stone by immense claws. The shells were gray like stone but flecked with gold and silver. Other striations of brown and black wrapped over and around the shells. A strange pattern adorned the foremost egg, one resembling a birthmark. The marking took the shape of a shield.

Two ghostly eyes appeared superimposed over the egg. One bright yellow, the other sparkling blue like a gemstone. The shield-marked egg cracked, and the earth trembled.

Onin awoke with a start. The morning sun streamed through the open window of his bedchamber. The bed was empty next to him. As usual, Yolan had arisen before he and would be gone for the day or, more likely, had not yet returned from the previous night's escapades. It was just as well; he was in no mood for her prickliness. In the months since their wedding, she had thawed toward him considerably, he had to admit. But she still relished vexing him on a daily basis. Staying out all night bothered Onin the most, so she did it frequently.

Unable to shake the visions from his sleep, Onin swung his feet to the floor. It was the first time the dream had visited itself upon him since coming to the Heights, but it was more vivid than ever. He remembered more of it as well. He had no idea what it could mean, if anything, or why it would leave him feeling so uneasy. In particular, the ghostly eyes haunted him and refused to relinquish their hold on his thoughts.

* * *

The summer day started out hot and dry. The persistent breeze permeating the Heights provided the only relief from the glaring sun, but high-turreted walls surrounding the trial field denied that comfort to the magistrate's court. The king's champion stood in the center of the field, resplendently armed. The champion was a veteran warrior named Wrent. Onin and Fargin stood on either side of the magistrate, sweating profusely in full battle regalia.

The day's petitioners stood in a line across the trial field. A group of fighting men, wearing the colors of House Strandor, faced them. Despite the sweat streaming down their faces, their expressions were set in determination.

The magistrate sat perched in a small balcony near the center of the field to better officiate the proceedings. A cloth awning and a pair of fan-wielding servants spared the graying man the worst discomfort. Even so, the heat wilted him. The magistrate rose to speak in a clear voice.

"House Strandor has petitioned His Majesty for expanded mineral rights in the mines of the northern slope. The king has refused, and Strandor has claimed the right of trial by combat to prove its case. We are assembled today to test the mettle of the fighting men of Strandor with the Royal Guard. If Strandor achieves victory, the king shall grant their petition.

"In accordance with our traditions, before the contest takes place, we shall read out the full accounting of the events preceding the contest . . ."

"Oh, for the sake of the gods, get on with it," Fargin muttered with exasperation. "We all know this part; it's always the same."

"I think the magistrate gets paid by the word when it comes to his pronouncements," said Onin. "Have you ever noticed it takes him ten minutes to say 'the people you see here want something, and they're going to have to fight to get it'? It hardly requires skill in prose."

The reading of accounts ended soon enough, despite their grumbling, and the contest began. The challengers from House Strandor would pit their strength against the king's champion, a veteran warrior from the ranks of the Guard. Onin and Fargin, fresh out of the academy, lacked the rank to represent the king in battle. Instead the two served as honor guards, whose sole duty was to broil in the sun and look impressive. According to the magistrate's ruling, each victory gained by the fighters of Strandor would secure one-third of the desired mineral rights. If denied a single victory, Strandor would leave empty-handed.

The first challenger took the field against the champion. The largest of the three, the Strandor man stood a half foot taller than Wrent. The champion fixed a steely gaze on his opponent, unperturbed by the size difference. Onin saw the glint of sweat on the champion's brow but no other sign the heat was affecting Wrent.

The fighters donned helmets and saluted one another, and the contest began. Onin was momentarily dazzled by the bright sun reflecting from their blades. The petition bouts were fought with real weapons, so the danger was significant. Deaths during contests were rare but not unheard of.

The Strandor man trusted in his size and strength, charging ahead with a hoarse shout. The champion sidestepped the overheard swing and delivered a slash to the back of the challenger's thighs. The battle cry turned to a yelp, and the Strandor fighter fell on his face in the hot sand. The man struggled to rise, but the cuts were deep, and he withdrew from the field instead. The first bout was over as quickly as it had begun.

"That's impressive," said Fargin. "I'm not sure I could fight at all in this heat. The champion seems to be in top form."

"I'd have trouble just seeing my opponent," replied Onin, wiping sweat from his face. Onin nodded in appreciation of Wrent's prowess, not only out of respect for the skill itself, but that the remaining bouts would also see quick resolution.

Mercifully, this proved to be the case. The Strandor men, while respectable fighters, proved to be no match for the king's champion. Wrent dispatched them with ease, giving each man a painful wound but no more. Within minutes, the magistrate was making the final pronouncement. Onin knew his time in the blazing sun neared its end.

". . . and so, having failed to prove their worth on the field of battle, House Strandor shall leave with no additional mineral rights and shall be required to pay the costs associated with today's contest. Long live the king, and glory to the Heights."

As the wizened magistrate made his way out of the proving grounds, the champion approached Onin.

"Ye gods, that sun is brutal." The champion removed his helmet, his hair dripping with sweat. "Pass me that waterskin, will you?"

"Glad to oblige." Onin pulled the sloshing bag over his shoulder and tossed it to the veteran Guard. Wrent tipped his head back, drinking deeply from the skin.

Fargin approached the two of them. "Well fought, Champion. Onin and I were just saying we doubted our ability to fight in this heat, let alone win against three opponents."

"Like anything else, it takes practice. After some time in the field, you'll be able to endure as much," said Wrent. He passed the skin back to Onin. "Onin here I have heard about. We don't have so many Midlander Guards, especially this big. I don't know you, however . . ."

"I am Fargin. The two of us are classmates from Scaleback."

"Been deployed yet?"

Fargin shook his head. "No. We are both set to go in a few months. Until then, we will continue to serve as honor guards." Fargin's tone betrayed his disappointment.

Wrent chuckled and laid a hand on Fargin's shoulder. "When you're out there, you'll begin to long wistfully for these days of standing around, even with this heat."

"I've heard stories," interjected Onin. "Torreg once told me about spending an entire winter in Saltgrave waiting for an enemy that never came."

"How is that rascal?" asked Wrent with a smile. "I hear he is back, but I haven't caught up with him."

Onin shrugged. "I don't see him much myself, frankly. He seems to spend most of his time at headquarters, meeting with people. He does seem happy to be home after such a long time away."

"Well, hopefully he's learned his lesson. He's a man of conviction and a fine officer, but sometimes he doesn't know when to leave well enough alone."

"Forgive me, Wrent. But what exactly did Torreg do to be stationed in the Midlands so long?"

The champion looked shocked. "You don't know? Perhaps I've said too much, then. Suffice it to say his words--not his deeds--landed him in hot water." Wrent paused to wipe sweat from his brow again. "And speaking of heat, I am ready to get out of this sun."

Without another word, the king's champion turned and strode from the field. Onin and Fargin were quick to follow his lead and retire to cooler places shaded from the unforgiving sun.

* * *

"This is utter blackmail," said Sergeant Noreth. Sensi could tell the Guardsman teetered on the edge of a conniption. Veins were bulging on the man's thick head. Sensi could measure the sergeant's pulse by them.

"I find your terms unacceptable," said Lornavus in an even tone. The tall, thin man sat behind a simple wooden desk, armed only with writing implements. The Guard's outburst did not disturb him in any noticeable way. "It is as simple as that."

Sensi had trouble adjusting to a lone brother's presence. They had been inseparable for as long as he had known them. He kept looking around, expecting the other twin to be nearby.

"What you're demanding will ruin me," said Noreth. His anger took on a pleading tone. "My family can't handle the debt. It will bring too much attention to me."

"Your problems with the Traders' Guild are just that," remarked the twin with the hint of a sneer, "your problems, not mine. I am only asking you to repay the debt you rightfully owe me."

"When we made that arrangement, I never dreamed it would come to so much," spit the sergeant. "You knew it!"

"Again, your lack of foresight is not my problem," countered Lornavus. Noreth glared at him with murder in his eyes, but Lornavus met his gaze unflinchingly. "I will have what you owe me."

"What if I refuse?" said the sergeant. He thrust his jaw out, pulling his cape aside to expose the sword at his waist.

"You will not," stated the twin with irritation. Sensi started to sweat. He certainly didn't share the twin's confidence. "Because if you do, certain individuals with massive influence within your order will learn some uncomfortable details about your dealings, past and present. You think the paltry sum you owe will ruin your family? You have no idea what is in store for you should you defy me."

Noreth shook with rage, but his internal struggle came to an abrupt halt and his shoulders slumped in defeat. "I concede," he said with resentment. "You shall have your coin, Altavus." He left the cramped, poorly lit chamber in a hurry.

"What is he involved in to make him give up so easily?" asked Sensi.

"It is unimportant," said the twin. "Suffice it to say his lack of mathematical proficiency allowed him to take out a loan at a poor rate of interest. I am due to report to the lord chancellor. This will have to be quick."

Sensi spread his hands. "You called me here," said the chubby man. "I notice you didn't correct him on your name, Lornavus. Where is your brother these days? I haven't seen him in weeks."

"Altavus has secluded himself to go about his studies uninterrupted. We are at a critical juncture in our research, and the next months are crucial," said the twin.

"What is it about those old documents that obsesses you?" asked Sensi. He'd wanted to ask for years, having fetched text after text in their academy days. "What can you hope to gain from them?"

Lornavus looked him up and down. Sensi felt a chill when their eyes locked, and the twin held his gaze, unblinking.

"You would be surprised what the ancients have to offer us," said the twin. "It's more than the marvels from the legends, yet less than what the priesthood would have us believe."

Lornavus reached into a cabinet near his desk. He tossed Sensi a sizable pouch. It had the familiar clink of coin to it. By its weight, he guessed it to be gold.

"You have been granted an increase in your wages, scribe," said

Lornavus in response to his questioning look.

"I am gratified to be so recognized."

"There is no need for humility at this moment, Sensi," said the twin. For once, he gave Sensi a smile with a semblance of warmth. "You are intelligent, discreet, and cautious. You bargain with foresight and negotiate with patience. With this wage increase, I hope to ensure your loyalty as well."

Sensi only nodded, overwhelmed by such an expression from this normally cold-blooded man.

"I am loyal," he said. "I've kept your secrets for years."

"I have every confidence in you," said Lornavus. "I must report to the lord chancellor now, but meet me here at dusk. There are some people I'd like you to meet."

* * *

Instead of heading straight home to Manespike Manor, Onin went out of his way to visit the breeding pits. He spent his childhood dreaming of getting close enough to touch a verdant dragon; to be involved in raising them was a thrill.

The breeding pits were far from the manor, out of necessity. They nestled on the lower edge of the mountain's interior, where the dragons floated on the crosswinds that constantly flowed through the hollowed-out space. The mating pairs drifted in the air currents, intertwined by neck and tail. The impregnated females then floated to the lowest air currents in the mountain and waited to lay eggs.

As Onin arrived, a ready female gave a honking cry as her body expelled the fertilized eggs. The gray shells were slick with a mucuslike substance as they released, and they plummeted to a net suspended beneath the dragon. The eggs often struck one another but never broke. The common wisdom held dragons were bred to drop their eggs directly on the rocks of the mountain, so the shells had to be tough. Onin doubted the truth of that since that would make the nets unnecessary in the first place.

Seeing the eggs drop reminded Onin of his own excitement. A Manespike dragon dropped a clutch of eight eggs just a week ago. After inspection, the master incubator declared them low weight but otherwise healthy. The dark gray or brown striations, which were considered indications of an unhealthy egg, covered many. If the shell became too dark and developed too many striations during incubation, it generally resulted in flawed hatchlings.

The current clutch of Manespike eggs were clear with sparse coloration. The shells were flecked with gold and silver particles, considered a good sign, indicating the eggs contained enough minerals for the developing embryo. When Onin arrived in the incubation chamber, he immediately caught sight of Master Incubator Polgrin. The man's visage created unease in many people, as a milky eye and facial scar made him look sinister. Children would run away or hide behind their parents when he walked among them. However, Onin considered Polgrin to be about the most jovial person he had ever met and enjoyed the man's company immensely. A moment of carelessness with a hungry hatchling had resulted in the scar, and the master incubator had been born with the eye.

"Good day, Polgrin," he said by way of greeting.

"Good day, young master," came the reply. The tone was light, but Polgrin's expression betrayed his dismay.

"What's wrong?" said Onin. "Has something happened to the eggs?"

"The coloration has gone bad on one of them, m'lord." Polgrin indicated one of the incubating eggs. They rested nearby in an array of metal cups, heated from beneath. Onin leaned in to peer at the one indicated. He couldn't see what Polgrin meant at first but then noticed a set of thin, dark streaks emerging in the plain gray shell.

"It doesn't look so bad. You can hardly see the color," said Onin, but the master incubator shook his head.

"I've seen this enough times before," said Polgrin. "Those stripes will be darker than storm clouds in another week. We'll let it continue, of course, but if it hatches at all, I wouldn't expect a healthy dragon."

Any dragon breeder's reputation rested on having viable stock for the dragon riders. Onin bit his lip as he considered the implications. It had been some time, several years in fact, since the Manespikes produced worthy hatchlings.

"What can we do for them?"

"We continue to do what we always do," said Polgrin. He rubbed his chin thoughtfully. "Keep the temperatures stable while in the setting phase. Once we're seeing movement from the hatchling inside, we'll move it to the hatchery. It's warmer there, and we keep the shell soaked in water and steam to soften it, until it cracks open. After the shell softens, the hatchling will chip its way out."

"But if no movements come from the hatchling inside . . ." began Onin.

"They never make it to the hatchery," nodded Polgrin.

"What becomes of the unhatched eggs?" asked Onin.

"They get cracked open and . . . used," said Polgrin. His sour expression gave away his distaste for the practice. "Medicines, foods, and other luxury items made from dragon eggs are quite fashionable these days."

Onin didn't like it but could not form a solid argument to present to Yolan. Since the family hadn't sold a dragon in years, selling the unhatched eggs presented the only recourse.

Onin continued to be optimistic, despite the setback. He surveyed the eggs with more than a little pride. He was certain a good, healthy dragon would come from this batch, maybe more than one. He smiled and rubbed one of the stony shells.

Chapter 12

Always present the truth, no matter how difficult it may be to speak it. Except, perhaps, when your wife asks how she looks.
--Onin, Guardsman

* * *

Onin didn't return home until sunset. The long shadows throughout the city provided some relief from the heat of the summer day. As Onin crossed the threshold to Manespike Manor, the house steward, a man named Howle, met him at the door.

"Good day, m'lord," said Howle. The steward held a bowl of water in one hand and a towel draped over his other arm. Onin happily washed the sweat and grime from his face. He splashed the cool water over his head and rinsed his thick beard liberally, wiping himself dry with the towel afterward.

"Thank you," Onin muttered even though it was considered improper. He hadn't grown up with personal servants and was still getting used to being waited on. His childhood home had employed several retainers to maintain the estate and grounds and keep the horses, but his father thought hand servants to be an extravagance. The servants took his discomfort in good humor, however, and kept about their duties.

"Is m'lord ready for his dinner?"

"Shortly, Howle," Onin said then paused. He then asked tentatively, "Is Lady Manespike at home?" His face betrayed his mixed emotions.

"She has already eaten and retired to her chambers, m'lord," replied Howle. Torn between his appetite and his domestic obligations, Onin decided to talking with Yolan would likely spoil his hunger.

"I'll eat before I go up," said Onin. "Send word for her to expect me." It never ended well when he showed up at her chambers unannounced. She often refused to see him at all.

Torreg waited for him in the dining hall, the grizzled old captain his most common dining partner. When Yolan did eat at home, she usually did so in her own chambers at odd times. It rankled Onin that he had to chase down his own wife in his own home, but if he couldn't get along with Yolan, at least her father was good company.

Torreg stood and clasped his hand warmly, and both men took their seats.

"How goes it at headquarters?" asked Onin. Torreg spent most of his time with the order since his return to the Heights. The captain gave a distasteful expression in response.

"Still in over my head," said Torreg. "A lot has happened in fifteen years, and I'm still catching up. The number of raids coming from the Jaga has steadily increased over time. The king has a responsibility to support his allies in the Midlands, but the forces of the Guard are stretched thin. If the trend continues, all of the Guard divisions will be deployed to the Midlands instead of at home, doing their sacred duty."

"It's unthinkable," said Onin with a disapproving frown. "With all the Guardsmen occupied elsewhere, the successor will be vulnerable."

"Well, there's the argument, isn't it?" said Torreg. "It's unthinkable for us to leave the successor defenseless, but others ask what madman would kill the successor and doom the place he calls home. No one would, so many in the higher echelons of the order think our men are better used maintaining peace in the Midlands."

The servants had begun to place food on the dining table.

"So the Guardsmen are sworn to meet the king's obligations, while the fighting men of the Great Families stay here in their roosts? Hardly seems like the best use of those men," said Onin.

"We're not alone in thinking that way," said the captain. "However, those opinions are whispered, not shouted among our fellow Guards. The vocal ones end up being deployed to the Midlands for lengthy tours of duty." Onin narrowed his eyes, and Torreg gave him a bitter grin in response.

"That's how you ended up in the Midlands?"

"For being vocal in my opinions? Yes," said Torreg, pulling a leg from a roast chicken. He bit into it and continued speaking around a mouthful. "It has long been the same struggle--the Guard, instead of watching over our charges, enforce the king's will away from home. Meanwhile, the Great Families maintain that they need all of their men at home for defensive purposes."

"Defensive purposes?" Onin laughed. "Defense from what? Encroaching clouds?"

Torreg spread his hands helplessly. "Defense from each other, I imagine," he said. "The Great Families have long, intricate histories and some very long-running grudges between them. We've not had open conflict in generations, but the potential is there, I wager." The old Guard rubbed his temples wearily. Onin noticed his hair had thinned with age. "It feels like trying to row a boat up a waterfall at times."

The table was piled high by this time, and both men lapsed into silence while they ate. Torreg noted the other empty seat at the table. "Things are still difficult with Yolan?"

Onin shrugged. "Same as ever," he said around a mouthful of bread. "She hates me. Has since we met."

Torreg was visibly saddened by his words. "I never meant to make your life so unpleasant, Onin," he said sympathetically. "Yolan has always been a willful, even spiteful, girl. I hoped she would grow out of it over the years, but alas, she becomes more intractable with age, not less. Truly the jewel of the Manespike family, she is."

"I've been meaning to ask something," said Onin. "No disrespect, but, why me? Yolan is beautiful and wealthy and from a Great Family. Surely she had better suitors than an adopted Midlander from a common family?"

"Ah, you've caught me out, my son," said Torreg with a wry grin. "Firstly, you are correct on her beauty but not her wealth. The Manespike family is not as well off as you might suspect."

Onin gestured around himself vaguely. "But this household . . ." he began.

". . . is expensive to maintain, and we haven't sold a dragon in years," finished Torreg. "The other families know, and even if it wasn't common knowledge, you can bet the other breeders would be circulating that little tidbit. Despite our financial straits, though, there were suitors to be had-- good breeding, high standing, wealth. But Yolan would have none of them.

"Each of them had some flaw, real or perceived. Too tall, too short, too pale, bad complexion, bad manners, bad odor . . . you name it, she complained about it--loudly. Some of the suitors weren't easily dissuaded and would return multiple times to beseech her. Those were the ones she really treated badly. After one particular incident, the suitors stopped coming altogether."

"What happened?" Onin asked despite himself. Somehow it felt wrong to be gossiping about his own wife, but he couldn't help himself.

"She stabbed him," said Torreg uncomfortably. In response to Onin's shock, he added, "With a hairpin. Skewered his hand. When word got around, her prospects for a sound marriage were all but gone."

"I can imagine," said Onin with sarcasm. "How does it come down to me, though? I've no breeding or standing in the Heights, outside of my father's position."

"Ah, and there's my shame," said Torreg with a pained expression. "Your family has wealth aplenty. Zorot is a clever man who knows how to make the most of his investments. Your dowry has brought the Manespikes back from financial ruin."

"Wait," said Onin. "I came with a dowry?"

"Indeed," said Torreg. "There you were, one of the most gifted warriors I have ever seen, from a family with money and just enough standing to be socially acceptable. You would bring honor and wealth back into the Manespikes. It seemed like the answer to all my problems. Now it seems my wishful thinking has put you in an unenviable position. Forgive me, lad. I didn't realize what I was doing."

Onin sighed. This shed some light on what was going on in his house but didn't give him any clue on how to proceed.

"Why is Yolan so disagreeable all the time?" he said, his frustration coming to the fore. "She seems offended by my presence."

"I cannot really say," said Torreg. "I was dispatched to the Midlands when she was just a baby, and she grew up with only her mother to look after her. My Tulanda, may the gods watch over her soul, indulged our daughter to excess. She died during Yolan's twelfth year. I was still in the Midlands when I got the word the fever had taken her." A deep pain passed over Torreg's face. "I couldn't return home, and Yolan couldn't come to me. So she was raised by the servants afterwards.

"Yolan has spent her entire life going where she wants, when she wants, and doing as she pleases. She is not used to having strictures placed on her or taking orders. Maybe things would have been different if I had been able to be a true father to her, but this is the hand the gods dealt me. So I did the best thing I could and married her to you."

Onin rubbed at his beard, considering what he had just heard. A plan began to take shape in his mind. He drained the wine goblet in his hand and held it up for the servant to refill it. He would need several more to have the courage for what he was thinking.

* * *

Sensi arrived at the place designated by Lornavus shortly after nightfall. He dressed warmly for the summer evening, in a hooded cloak, but he desired the cover it would provide to him. He did not know this place well, which made him uncomfortable. He preferred a certain familiarity with a location's layout, should the need arise for a speedy exit.

The location, a back alley of modest dwellings, seemed deserted, however. Any of the locals were securely tucked away in their homes, sitting at their own hearths. No sound could be heard except the trickle of a nearby fountain and the whisper of the night breeze.

Sensi looked around often, searching for prying eyes. A tall, robed figure emerged from the shadows to stand next to him while he was looking the other way. He gave an abrupt start but recognized Lornavus and recovered himself. The twin nodded in greeting and motioned for Sensi to follow.

"I don't see the need for all this skullduggery," complained Sensi in a whisper. "Who do you want me to meet, exactly?"

"I cannot tell you," said Lornavus. "Because I do not know, exactly."

"You don't know?" said Sensi. "What do you mean?"

"Be patient," said the twin. "You'll understand soon."

At first, it seemed like they meant to enter one of the domiciles, but instead Lornavus led the way into another alley between two homes. The darkness engulfed them, and Lornavus produced a hooded lantern to light their way. A door waited at the back of the alley, tucked out of sight. The walls were high on either side. Sensi guessed the sun would never reach the place. Unless one knew where to look, the door would remain hidden, even during the day.

Lornavus halted at the door and rapped lightly. A few taps, then a pause, then a few more taps, followed by another pause and a final three taps. After a moment, Sensi could hear the sound of a bolt sliding, and the door opened. No light issued forth, the doorway was nothing but darkness. The thin man stepped inside without hesitation, and Sensi stayed right behind him. Sensi knew one thing for certain: the company of the twins would ensure the greatest safety. He had no reason to suspect them of wanting him dead; there were much easier methods than leading him off on some expedition like this. Still, the stealth and intrigue made Sensi nervous.

The lantern didn't illuminate the room much, but Sensi could tell they were in a storage cellar of some type. Crates were stacked about them, and another door stood on the opposite wall. The man who had let them enter likewise hid beneath a hooded cloak. Sensi didn't miss the sword in his hand, though. The mysterious doorman opened the opposing door and ushered them through, hastily closing it behind them.

Altavus awaited them in the darkened passage. The brothers exchanged a brief glance, all the greeting they required of each other, but Altavus politely inclined his head to Sensi.

"Pleasant evening, Sensi," Altavus said evenly. His tone sounded light, almost expectant.

"Greetings, Altavus," said Sensi. "It's been some time since anyone has seen you."

"I'm sure the rumors are rampant," said Altavus. "But my seclusion has been rewarding in the extreme. You are to share in the some of the fruits of my labor this evening."

"Meaning what?" said Sensi. "What is this all about, anyway?"

Wordlessly Altavus handed cloth-wrapped bundles to his brother and Sensi, reserving one for himself. The bundle had something light but solid in it, which felt like an oblong bowl. When the twins began to unwrap the bundles, Sensi did likewise. His confusion only compounded when he found himself holding a plain, simple mask, made from porcelain. The face was finely constructed, smooth but featureless, and had a pair of thongs for attaching it over the ears. The twins donned similar masks while he looked over the one in his hands, and realization dawned on him.

"So this is why you don't know 'exactly' who you're going to introduce me to," said Sensi with a grin. Sensi placed the mask over his face and tied the strings together behind his head.

"Exactly," said one of the twins. Sensi had lost track of which while putting on his own mask. It bothered him; they were indistinguishable at the moment. "We are introducing you to a collection of individuals who wish to remain anonymous to one another, and there is good reason for doing so. The masks allow us to gather and interact without being able to glean any identities."

"What is the nature of this group, then?" asked Sensi shrewdly. "Why is secrecy of the members so important?"

"Because we are the ones who seek to free our people from the yoke of religion," said one twin. Eerily, the other twin finished with, "We'll dispel the fog of superstition that holds us back from achieving what the ancients achieved before us."

* * *

Onin drank sufficient wine to feel warmth throughout his body. He strode through the corridors of the manor, steadily but purposefully, until he found himself outside Yolan's chambers. Only an occasional wobble marred the confidence of his stride.

A manservant guarded Yolan's door, mostly to keep away eavesdroppers. When Onin stopped outside the door, the servant had the look of a man who didn't know how to respond. Onin clearly intimidated him; he stood a full head above the man and was twice as wide across the shoulders. The servant cleared his throat before speaking. "The lady does not wish to be disturbed."

Onin cast him a withering look. It had the desired effect, and the man visibly shrank away. "That's too bad because I intend to disturb her."

With those words, Onin pushed the door open and stepped into the room unbidden. He had been in Yolan's private chambers a scant number of times, and as usual, he was struck by its opulence. Decorative furniture, tapestries, and works of art festooned the place. The finely crafted pieces crowded the eye with an explosion of rich colors. A pair of handmaidens bustled about, tending the fire, pouring wine, plumping pillows, and serving food from silver trays. Another handmaiden plucked a yearning tune on an elaborate harp in the corner. Smoke from the braziers filled the air with a haze as well as an earthy scent.

Yolan lay in the midst of luxurious cushions, attended by two servants; a large, well-muscled man who fanned her while an adolescent boy with refined features read poetry aloud to her.

Everything but the smoking braziers ground to a halt when Onin entered the room. Collectively, the attending servants looked at him with cold, blank stares then turned back to their mistress, awaiting instructions. Yolan, clearly irritated at the interruption, reacted as Onin expected.

"What do you want?" she asked with venom.

Onin shrugged. "Nothing in particular."

"Then what are you doing here?"

"Just wanted to see you."

"Now you've seen me. Go away." She started to motion for the servants to resume, but Onin interrupted her.

"No," said Onin.

The look of shock on her face was priceless. The servants exchanged nervous glances with one another.

"No?" she repeated. Her voice had risen noticeably. "Get out of my rooms!"

Onin rolled back and forth on his feet like a mischievous schoolboy. "No."

Yolan grew livid. She clambered from her pile of cushions to stand defiantly before him. "What is this?" she screamed. "Overcome by carnal need and here to claim the husband's right! Well, I'm not your breeding sow, to be used at your discretion!"

"No," he said firmly. "That's not it."

"Then what?" she raged at him. "What in all the Heights has moved you to disturb my privacy and invade my rooms?"

"Ever since we were married, I've been as civil to you as possible, and you show me nothing but contempt," Onin said. He thrust out his jaw. "Well, I'm sick of it. I'm not going to walk around here, scared of you anymore. Be a shrew if you like. I'm not going to let it get to me."

Her hand lashed out like a viper. The slap rang through the air, leaving an angry red welt on Onin's cheek. He stood solid as a stone, unflinching.

"Get out of my rooms!" she screamed again, red faced.

Onin looked her squarely in the eyes. "No."

Yolan snarled and snatched a crystal decanter from the hands of a nearby handmaiden. She swung it in a wide arc and smashed the delicate vessel over Onin's head. Onin held his ground stubbornly, shards of crystal scattered across his shoulders. A trickle of blood ran down his cheek from his scalp. Without moving, he fixed her with a cool stare, and they locked gazes for a few silent moments.

With a short leap, Yolan was upon him. He braced himself for another blow when he saw her quick movements and was unprepared when her arms wrapped about him passionately and she smothered his lips with her own. They kissed madly, with abandon, and it was several seconds before Onin could disengage himself enough to speak. "Get out!"

The servants ushered themselves from the room, closing the door as they left.

Chapter 13

Any fool can swing a sword, but it takes finesse to talk to a woman.
--Yolan Manespike

* * *

The Broken Wheel tavern hosted a noisy crowd on most evenings. The patrons consisted of tradesmen and laborers, by and large, which meant the ale was cheap but plentiful. Like many such establishments, the reek of stale beer clung to the very stones of the floor. The cheery red glow of lit pipes dotted the hall, and a smoky haze and rich aroma filled the air. The pair of serving girls and the proprietor were kept busy, ushering food and drink to wherever needed.

By the time Onin arrived, Hangric had already secured their usual table by the fire. They clasped hands, and Onin gestured to the nearest serving girl. In less time than he would have thought possible, a full tankard sat in front of him. He and Hangric lifted them in the customary toast.

"To the king."

They made a point to meet at least once a month, as their respective assignments allowed. They had tried several other establishments before settling on this one. Initially the friends would rendezvous at inns or taverns closer to their homes, but the circumstances never quite worked out. In those places too many patrons were social peers--members of other Great Families, other Guardsmen, officials of the chancellor, and so on. It made it impossible to speak on any subject comfortably for fear of eavesdroppers. Instead, they settled on the Broken Wheel. No socially conscious people of the Heights would ever be seen there. The place provided a haven where they could speak freely among themselves, a surprising rarity.

"What news from the outside?" said Onin.

Hangric had just returned from a short stint in the Midlands, and Onin was due to ship out himself the next day.

"Three feral attacks in the last two weeks," said Hangric grimly. "In one case, a single beast demolished a remote farmstead, but the two most recent were flocks attacking verdants. The most recent happened yesterday. We caught wind of it as we were shipping back to the Heights. From what we heard, the verdant dragon went down somewhere over Wheatmarch."

"Flocks of ferals? I didn't know that could happen."

"It's rare. Usually only happens over the black swamp."

"Did you see any ferals yourself?" asked Onin.

"No," said Hangric with a sour expression. "Never in the right place at the right time. If the attacks had some rhyme or reason or if we could guess what the targets might be, we could take better precautions. As it stands, by the time we even hear about a feral dragon, it's long gone."

Onin could only nod in agreement. "The great beasts are too cunning to attack our strongly defended outposts," he said. "But two attacks on verdants? I wonder if there's a pattern forming there."

"Hard to say," replied Hangric sagely. "The skies were clear when I flew, both there and back. The most dangerous thing I had to do was climb into the blasted tierre for the return trip." He took a long pull from his tankard. "I'll wager your unit is on its way to the downed verdant," said Hangric. "For all the good it will do. Once one of those beasts goes down, it stays down, my captain says." He looked up. "Here comes Fargin."

Fargin plopped himself down at the table, snatching a tankard from a passing tray over the serving girl's protests. He drank deeply then wiped his mouth with his sleeve.

"He seems full of vigor," Onin said to Hangric with a sly grin. "I think married life agrees with him."

A smile split Hangric's face. "Well, I'd be agreeable if I were married to the sweet little dish he calls wife," joked Hangric.

"Speaking of which, how is Horseface?" asked Fargin. No one dared call Hangric's wife by the name in her presence, but her equine features remained undeniable.

"Norietta is doing just fine," said Hangric. Then he frowned thoughtfully. "Her new passion is dancing. Courtly dancing." The big man shuddered. "I always step on her feet. But she insists I accompany her all the same."

The three friends drank, laughed, and ate while waiting for the last of their number to arrive.

"Where is Rabbash?" asked Hangric while waiting for more ale. "He's the one who called us together. Said he had something very interesting to talk to us about."

Hours later, Rabbash had still not shown, and a bad feeling grew in Onin's gut. If not for the need to get up early for his deployment to the Midlands, he would have accompanied Hangric and Fargin to Rabbash's home, but they assured him they would let him know if there were something he could do. No matter what they said, it was an ill omen.

* * *

The grounded verdant cried its anguish to the sky, answered by another circling overhead. Onin usually heard a verdant roar its displeasure with sass and attitude. This sounded different; the honking cry of the massive beast expressed heartache, and the replies from the airborne verdant echoed it. Onin pined for the creature as it stretched its neck to the sky and its fellows.

Claw wounds marked the back and flanks of the great beast. Only the barest remnants of the harness and rigging that held the tierre in place remained intact, flapping about like loose strands of hair. Of the tierre, there was no sign at all.

"Glory be, that's a sight," said Captain Bolg from beside him. Onin had been pleasantly surprised to find the ugly man had not only been promoted but also assigned to lead this mission. "Once one of those brutes goes down, it's all over."

The dragon shifted its bulk, taking a few halting steps before settling to the ground again. Once again, it released a mournful cry, echoed by the airborne dragon.

"Couldn't enough food be brought to her?" asked Onin, grasping at solutions.

"Possibly, but even then there's no way to get her back in the air," said Bolg. He rubbed at the red scar on his face. "She'd have to walk all the way to Dragonport and climb up the mountain to have enough altitude to take flight again."

Onin nodded grimly. The dragon could hardly take a dozen steps before needing to rest its legs. It seemed unlikely it would be able to scale a mountain, even if it could cover the distance overland. Verdants were built to fly, not walk. It made him think breeding the dragons purely for size had been a huge mistake. *How could people have been so foolish?* he asked himself, but he already knew the answer: greed. It was a problem that ran deep and would not be so easily remedied. "What do we do, then?" he asked.

"The only thing we can do," said Captain Bolg. "Find a humane way to put the poor beast down."

Onin didn't like that answer one bit. It seemed like such a waste. His association with the Manespike family business gave him a deep appreciation for the amount of work that went into breeding, hatching, and raising dragons. But he was also without any notion of an alternative.

"How does one go about such a thing?" Onin wondered aloud. Verdants were enormous and their scaly hides, unbelievably tough.

"I don't know," said Bolg. "The dragon riders have a concoction, I hear, but it is slow to act and unpleasant. They dislike using it in the extreme." Which made sense to Onin; the dragon riders were notoriously meticulous when it came to the care and feeding of their charges. "In cases like this, it's poison or let the creature starve to death."

Both men grew silent as they contemplated the situation. Their reverie broke, however, as sudden darkness engulfed them. Onin realized he stood under a shadow, one in the form of a dragon. A feral dragon.

The feral soared over them and pounced upon the unsuspecting verdant. The dark dragon sank its teeth into the base of the verdant's right wing. The black-scaled form clung to the larger dragon's back tenaciously, digging its claws into the great scaly flanks for better purchase. The verdant raised its snout to the sky and roared in pain while a second feral dragon swooped in, maw gaping to snatch the great throat.

The verdant wasn't completely defeated, however. At the last moment, the great snout turned to meet the second attacker, and the verdant's massive jaws closed over the head of the feral. The feral's wings flapped erratically a few times before the verdant bit down, ending the dark-scaled dragon with a single bite. The verdant swung its mighty head, flinging the dead feral through the air.

Bolg and Onin scrambled for cover as they realized the dead feral sailed directly at their location. Onin made it a half dozen steps before tripping, landing face-first in the dirt. Instead of trying to rise, he covered his head with his arms and hoped for the best.

The ground lurched. A cloud of dust and debris engulfed them. Onin coughed dirt from his lungs but was again plunged into persistent darkness. Something soft but heavy, like a leather tapestry, draped itself over him and pressed him to the ground. He fumbled about and pushed against it, scrambling toward slivers of daylight.

From the dead feral dragon's wing, Onin emerged. His fellow Guards were dashing about, calling out to one another. He could hear the cries of the wounded. Not all of them had made it a safe distance away.

Another tremendous roar tore through the air. Onin felt it in the pit of his stomach. A third feral dragon attacked the ailing verdant. This one had more success in its swooping ambush. As Onin watched, the newly arrived feral pinned the verdant's head to the ground and savaged the long, scaly neck with its claws.

Yet another verdant roar drew Onin's attention skyward. He looked up to see the airborne verdant dragon under attack by ferals as well. Easily a half dozen ferals darted in and out, attacking the bulky dragon from multiple directions, enough to overwhelm the great beast. The verdant, or its handlers, decided to exercise discretion and set its course for home with the ferals in hot pursuit.

The cacophony of dragons locked in mortal combat brought Onin's attention back to the ground. The grounded verdant still struggled but seemed unable to resist the two vicious feral dragons. With the pair of dark-scaled dragons on its back, the verdant lacked the strength to even stand, let alone fight effectively. Despite the noise, the fight was as good as over. Onin wasn't the only person to realize it.

"Retreat!" yelled Bolg to the Guardsmen. His voice cut through the snarls and bellows of the dragons. "Grab the wounded and get out of here! Now! While the ferals are distracted!"

The men, realizing the sense of his words, made haste. Onin stopped to lift a wounded man to his feet. The fellow's leg was broken, struck by the hard edge of the wing as it landed on them. Onin tossed the man over his shoulder, to his protests, and ran as fast as he could.

The sound of dragons fighting receded in the distance, and the Guardsmen made good their escape.

* * *

The rest of the two-week tour of duty proved blissfully uneventful. Onin was thankful for some time to digest the events he had witnessed. He hadn't quite acclimated to the sheer scale of full-grown dragons yet. To see them locked in mortal combat overwhelmed him. For days afterward, Onin suppressed shaking in his hands.

Feral dragons were unsettling on a primal level and haunted his nightmares. Onin experienced his recurring dream again but with differences. Battling dragons filled the sky. Ferals attacked and slaughtered another kind of dragon, one Onin didn't recognize. They weren't verdants. He could tell by the shape alone. These new dragons had only two legs and wings, with serpentine bodies, like the ferals, instead of four legs and a thick torso like the verdants. The new dragons were the same general size as the ferals too. They were in bright, sparkling colors, contrasting the blacks and grays of the ferals. In the dream, ferals battled these majestic dragons until none remained. The landscape was littered with fallen, crumpled bodies.

The eggs remained the same. The dream shifted focus until the mound of eggs predominated, and the foremost egg, with the many striations, came to be the center of his vision. The striations he now knew to be a mark of poor health in an egg, but the shieldlike shape formed by the gray patches glowed with a life of its own. This was new; the symbol had never glowed so distinctly in previous dreams.

The amber-colored glow became stronger, until Onin could no longer see for the brightness of it. Finally a different scene, a different place came into view as the light dimmed. It was a baby, floating down a river on a bed of reeds resembling the shape on the eggshell.

* * *

"I can't believe this," Onin said. He scanned the letter in his hands again. "Two weeks and no sign of him? A man doesn't just disappear into thin air."

Yolan popped a grape into her mouth. The night was pleasantly cool, and the gentle breeze, refreshing.

"I agree," she said. "He must be somewhere; you just can't find him."

He found her flippant, matter-of-fact tone irritating but bit back a rude response. He had just returned home and didn't want things to turn sour between them so soon.

"True," he said. "But we're running out of places to look. He hasn't been seen at home, hasn't reported for duty, and hasn't been to his usual taverns or haunts. He hasn't been seen by anyone in his neighborhood since the day he went missing. His wife is beside herself."

"Yes, poor thing," said his wife while eating another grape. "Rabbash is clever; you've said so yourself. Maybe you should just trust that he'll turn up."

"Not sure I have any alternative," muttered Onin, but Yolan perked up.

"Oh, come now," said Yolan in a musical tone. "You have just returned and shouldn't worry yourself over such bad tidings. Take some time to recuperate first."

Onin sighed. Perhaps she was right. "How is the clutch doing?" he asked, hoping to change subjects to a brighter note.

"Not well, I'm afraid," she replied, dashing his hopes. "The master incubator reports the clutch has gone bad."

"Bad?" Onin exclaimed. "All of them? The entire clutch?" His disappointment ran deep. Almost all of his free time was spent at the hatchery. He knew the striations of color were a warning sign, but they had progressed farther than he thought possible in his absence. He hung his head.

"There, my husband," she soothed him, stroking the back of his head, her touch soft and inviting. "We recouped our losses by selling the remains. There is also good news, so do not brood so."

He looked up into her face, wondering what could possibly assuage the dark feelings he was experiencing. His missing friend, the lost clutch of eggs, and the death of the grounded verdant left him in a bleak frame of mind. She took his face in her hands and smiled at him.

"A new clutch was dropped this morning." She smiled. "You can return to nursing eggs immediately. Who knows? You might even hatch a dragon."

Chapter 14

Women are the givers of children. Respect them and the sacrifices they make on behalf of us all. To dishonor a woman is to dishonor your own mother.
--Zorot Durantis, trade ambassador

* * *

Cloaked and masked bodies packed the underground amphitheater. Each wore a nondescript, deliberately simple mask, and the hooded cloaks were simple wool. Incense hung in the air, and people spoke in hushed whispers. The entire affair seemed solemn yet officious. Sensi attended four gatherings prior to this evening; each time the meeting place was slightly larger, to accommodate the increasing numbers. Attendance had doubled in as many months. With each meeting, the atmosphere sobered, and the gatherings gradually became ceremonial in practice. The attendees spoke excitedly among themselves in anticipation of the proceedings.

Sensi engaged in simple, even inane, chat with the woman to his left. He had no idea whom he talked to, which was the point. Short of recognizing voices, there were only two ways to know the true identity of a person here--to have invited or been invited by him or her. Sensi had brought no new recruits to the secret circle. As a consequence, he knew only the twins for certain.

"But when it comes to a hanging garden," concluded the mystery woman. "I find the best moss to be grown here in the Heights. Imported from the Midlands is cheaper but of lesser quality."

"Considering the cost of dragon shipments, I'm surprised anything from the Midlands is cheaper here," he replied.

"Well, the imported moss is inferior but abundant. To them it is essentially worthless, so to even get a bit of coin for it is something to the Midlanders."

"Makes sense to me," said Sensi. "I suppose if I could gather up something worthless and sell it for cash, I would do it too."

A delighted giggle escaped from behind the plain white mask. The woman covered the thin line of the mouth with her hand out of habit.

A man in the same gray robe and white mask stepped to the center of the stage that occupied the amphitheater. He tapped on the floor a simple wooden staff to gather everyone's attention. The various conversations died off, and the strangely clandestine meeting came to order.

"Fellow Unknowns," the robed figure said, "we have gathered here to reaffirm our goal to rid our society, the greatest on Godsland, of the superstitions and religious claptrap which holds us back from achieving true greatness. While we are assured people of the Heights have created the greatest of living societies, we also know for certain that the ancients, our direct ancestors, achieved far more in this world than we have ever dreamed."

The meetings had been growing steadily for months and were getting better organized all the time. For an organization that ostensibly didn't have a leader, things were coming together nicely. The speaker continued.

"Despite our lofty ambitions, there are those who would oppose us. Those who cling to outmoded ways and obsolete traditions. Those who would keep us in a state of perpetual darkness and ignorance. Those with minds so closed, they cannot understand when the world has moved on and left them behind."

The man paused for dramatic effect. An angry muttering moved throughout the crowd; Sensi could tell the sermon reached them. Sensi almost felt something himself. The words were passionate, but his cynicism ran too deep to allow him to respond.

"So we remain Unknown, so we may stay hidden and continue our work. That we may bring a brighter, more glorious future to our descendants. That we may challenge the accomplishments of the ancients-- nay! Eclipse them!"

His words brought cries of agreement from the crowd, whose fervor infected the air.

"The unenlightened will hold us down until our doom is upon us," said the orator. "The priests and elites would keep us ignorant, forbidding us from the dangerous magic of the ancients. They say it is evil, unnatural, and was the destruction of our ancestors.

"But we know it to be untrue! The ancients were powerful, yes, and perhaps even magical, but they were not evil and destructive. By studying what they have left to us, we may advance ourselves and our people and leave a great legacy for our descendants."

The speaker shook the staff in his hand as if challenging the gods.

"The priests will tell you the ancients were destroyed because they dared challenge the power of the gods. But we know there are no gods! There never were! Why do we restrain ourselves based upon old superstitions? Why do we refute our greatest birthright, bequeathed to us over thousands of years? Why forsake power for imaginary beings?"

Sensi began to enjoy the rhetoric. This kind of talk circulated throughout much of the Heights these days. Certainly many were still devout servants of the gods and the religious orders that espoused them, but many were also tiring of the priesthood's influence and that of the Great Families over the affairs of the city.

"We will not give up. That is our answer," intoned the robed orator. He tapped his staff on the stage for emphasis. "We are Unknown. We will persevere. We will overcome. We will inherit."

The man bowed with grace and dignity and backed off the stage.

The audience didn't react at first. Then a few began clapping hesitantly. Some more joined and before long, the entire room enthusiastically applauded the speech.

"Quite rousing, don't you think?" said the mystery lady. She yelled slightly to be heard.

"I agree! Can't wait to see what the next gathering will be like," Sensi responded.

* * *

When Sensi met with the twins later, the euphoria still gripped him. The sheer energy and excitement fostered by the speaker had rubbed off on him, despite himself. Lornavus and Altavus, however, were their usual reserved selves.

"Well, tonight's gathering was certainly something to see," said Sensi. "I might have been skeptical at first, but the speaker really changed the tone of the meeting." A tray laden with goblets and a decanter sat nearby. Sensi poured himself some wine.

"Agreed. His powers of speech are compelling," said Lornavus. The twins had another tray, this one full of food, between them and were busy picking at a pair of roasted fowl.

"It was also interesting to see all of the Unknown in one place," said Sensi. "There's getting to be quite a few of us."

Altavus raised an eyebrow at him. "What makes you think those were all of the Unknown? That was but one small gathering. Others just like it are happening all over the city. Our message is being repeated, and the people are receptive."

Lornavus added, "It also wouldn't be smart to gather every single member in the same place at the same time. Far too easy for the movement to be wiped out in one fell swoop by a single informant. No, we continue to gather in small groups, like you saw tonight."

"Small?" replied Sensi.

"That is but a fraction of our total number," said Lornavus. "Before much longer, it will be impossible for us to remain hidden."

"When that occurs, the true purpose of the meetings will become clear," chimed in Altavus. The twins exchanged a cold smile, the nature of which sent a shiver down Sensi's back. The fat man shook himself deliberately and continued to speak.

"There is another complication," he said, chasing the smiles from the faces of the twins. "Some matter about a missing Guard."

* * *

"Are you sure this is correct?" asked Onin, his skepticism obvious.

Fargin shrugged. "It's the only lead we've found," he said. "It's the last place anyone saw him."

"What would Rabbash be doing in the underbelly?" asked Hangric. Officially the king didn't acknowledge the existence of the underbelly, so officially the Guard had no business there. To be caught there might force the king to acknowledge the existence of the place, and thus the Guards avoided it.

"Whatever it might be, it must have been important," concluded Onin. He looked at the other two friends imploringly. "He wouldn't do such a thing on a whim."

"Could he have been blackmailed?" said Hangric. "Extortion would explain why he had to go there. He could have been ordered against his will."

"I've never known him to do anything worth the trouble of blackmailing," said Fargin. All three recognized the truth of the statement. Rabbash had been inconveniently scrupulous during their academy days, even refusing to cheat during academic exams.

"We might get away with it, but there would be a price to pay," Rabbash would say. "Mark my words."

Each friend seemed to have those remarks echoing in their memories. Onin decided to break the silence and utter what each had been thinking.

"If we're going to go into the underbelly," he said, "we're going to need some nondescript clothes. And some gear. Nothing that will mark us as Guards."

"No armor," said Fargin. "Armor will make us stand out there as much as wearing our uniforms."

"I have a blacksmith cousin who has a few simple swords he can be convinced to part with," said Hangric. "Some daggers, too, I imagine."

"What about a guide?" said Onin. "We're sure to get lost down there without one. Stories say it goes on for miles."

"Rabbash certainly wouldn't have gone without a guide," said Fargin. "Although he was seen entering the underbelly by himself."

"Then he must have met a guide on the inside," said Hangric. "How do we know who to talk to?"

"The watch," said Onin, scratching his beard. "The watchmen come and go from the underbelly. They must know someone. Come to think of it, I wonder if a watchman could be persuaded into leading us there."

"Who knows someone in the watch?" asked Hangric.

The three of them exchanged glances, and they surmised none of them did.

JACK MCCARTHY AND BRIAN RATHBONE

"Well, then," said Fargin. "It can't be so hard to make friends with the watch, can it?"

"I suppose we're going to find out," said Onin. He drained his ale. "But not tonight. I have to be home. Can we meet here tomorrow night, and we'll plan further?"

His friends gave their assent. Then Onin was off to his home.

* * *

Howle, the Manespike steward, met Onin at the door, as usual. He had a knack for anticipating Onin's arrivals, always on hand to take his cloak, apprise him of the situation in the manor, and otherwise see to his needs. He also seemed to know when Onin would be hungry or thirsty, and always had food or drink on hand at the right time.

It being a warm night, Onin had no cloak, and comestibles were far from his mind. To his unspoken question, the steward said, "Her ladyship is on the terrace."

Onin headed straight there; though, in honesty, he still felt uneasy in her presence. Things had improved dramatically with the happy news of the new dragon clutch, and they could be in the same room without squabbling incessantly, but Onin still had the nagging feeling Yolan didn't like him much.

The terrace provided a spectacular view of the mountainside below them. The Cloud Forest formed a base around the city, like a protective ring of the brightest colors, from emerald green to sapphire blue to the richest purple of amethyst. The only sounds to reach them were the distant cries of birds and forest creatures from below and the whispering breeze ever-present in the Heights.

Yolan reclined on a divan, looking like a lazy cat. She was absolutely alluring, and her shapely legs were revealed from beneath the folds of her robes. Yolan's usual gaggle of servants attended her--a pair of serving girls and the well-muscled fan-bearer, despite the cool breeze. She dazzled him with her smile when he approached. Despite all she put him through, Onin still got weak in the knees when she looked at him in such a way.

"Ah, my husband," she said. "Come and grace your wife with a kiss."

Onin leaned forward willingly, bringing his lips closer to hers, but at the last moment, she wrapped her arms around his neck and pulled him onto the divan with her. Their lips met and the moment seemed to go on for a long time. Onin struggled not to crush the slight woman under his full weight. He certainly liked the way her lips felt on his own. But just as he was beginning to enjoy the intimacy, she pushed him away.

"All right, get off of me, you great oaf," she said. Her tone sounded playful, but Onin sensed the sincerity in her words. As usual, she could shift from one extreme to another in seconds. Onin had no sense of boundaries with her. Acceptable behavior one day would be considered a great offense on the next.

Onin sat up on the edge of the divan while she beckoned to a servant girl.

"Bring me the new dresses," she commanded, and the girl scurried to a pile of objects to the side of the terrace. No doubt the pile represented the day's "spoils," as his wife often described her purchases. "I visited the most amazing dressmaker this morning. He's only been operating his own shop for a year, but his designs are fabulous. Every lady of courtly bearing is waiting for one of his newest dresses, and I got six of them today!"

She clearly took great joy in her victory over her peers, and her voice dripped with pride. Onin watched with feigned interest as she displayed each of the gowns to him, pointing out the intricacies of the patterns or the accessories she had picked to accompany them or the nuances of the stitching. They did seem fine to him, even beautiful, but the true genius of the dressmaker remained lost on him. He smiled in thanks when one of the serving girls placed a goblet of wine in his hand, unasked. The girl responded to his grateful look with a shy smile and curtsy.

"I'm hungry," announced Yolan. She began to look around, and the other serving girl presented a tray of fruits and cheeses. Yolan surveyed the tray and wrinkled her nose. Her voice took on a petulant tone.

"I want eggs," she said. Her bottom lip turned down in the slightest pout, and Onin smiled despite himself.

"Eggs?" he repeated.

"And yogurt," she added. Her face brightened. "Made from goat's milk."

"Eggs and yogurt made from goat's milk," Onin said. "Do you want them cooked together?"

"No," she wrinkled her nose at him. It only made her more adorable. "I want the eggs poached and the yogurt served separately. And a steak. A rare steak."

Onin wondered if she just enjoyed testing him. Still, he grasped at anything to improve their relations. "Howle!" he yelled.

The steward was present within moments. He stepped onto the terrace, not moving more than a foot beyond the threshold.

"Yes, m'lord?"

"Some poached eggs, a rare steak, and some goat's yogurt for m'lady," said Onin. "We have all of those things on hand, yes?"

"Indeed, we do, sir," Howle said and departed the terrace promptly.

Good old Howle, thought Onin.

* * *

Onin arrived late at the chosen tavern, the Dancing Dove. Fargin waved him over to a corner table as he entered the place. After some discreet inquiries, this location had turned up as a tavern favored by the watchmen. Perhaps it was a bit more rowdy than most places, specifically because it catered to men of the watch. After all, who was going to show up and break up any scuffles? Onin took his seat and ordered ale from the passing barmaid, who gave him a bored look in response.

"How goes it so far?" asked Onin.

"Seems to be moving along," said Fargin. "No one has taken serious notice of our presence here. Apparently we are unrecognized."

As a member of the Guard, moving around without drawing attention was often difficult. Many members of the elite order were prominent public figures and recognized almost everywhere in the city. While none of the circle of friends had such distinction, they could be known by sight to total strangers.

A boisterous outburst came from the back of the tavern's main room. Onin looked quizzically in that direction then at Fargin.

"Hangric," they both said together.

"He's making friends," Onin added.

Onin took his ale and went to observe. There were about a dozen people huddled around a table, with two figures seated across from one another. Their arms were locked together in a contest of strength, muscles bulging and faces turned red with exertion. Onin recognized Hangric just as the big man slammed his adversary's hand to the table with a crash. Hangric threw his arms in the air and bellowed his triumph. When he spied Onin, his eyes lit up.

"Onin, old friend!" Hangric shouted and in an instant jumped out of his seat and had Onin wrapped in a bear hug. Hangric belched in Onin's face while embracing him, and Onin swooned slightly from the reek of ale. Hangric just as abruptly released him and spun around to the man he'd just been arm wrestling.

"Caris! This is the friend I was talking about," said Hangric. His voice was slurred and his balance unsteady. "We must have another drink together and get you two acquainted."

The man peered at Onin owlishly. He was stocky, with thick arms, and his beard was shot with gray. He wasn't one to bet against Hangric, but he would have given this man good odds in a test of strength.

Apparently deciding he liked the look of Onin, Caris extended his hand in greeting. "Caris." He slurred so badly that Onin couldn't make it out completely. He was glad Hangric had spoken the name first.

"Onin," he said and clasped the man's hand.

With one giant stride, Hangric was between them, an arm around each of their necks. "Now, Caris," said Hangric. "A bet is a bet."

"Aye, lad," said Caris. "You won but don't rub it in."

Hangric detached himself and held his hands up in front of him. "Surely not, surely not. I am just excited about my winnings."

"Winnings?" said Caris. The grizzled watchman looked incredulous through the drunken stupor. "I thought you were joking. Who in their right mind wants to go *there*?"

Hangric grinned at Onin, obviously gloating over his success.

"Oh, we are not in our right minds," said Hangric with slurred conviction.

Chapter 15

If dreams were coin, coin would cease to have worth.
--merchant's proverb

* * *

"This way," said Caris. "Watch your step. Some of the spots around here will be slick with refuse."

The friends didn't doubt his words to be true, based on the odors of the underbelly. The seemingly endless corridors wound in every direction, with staircases cut from the stone leading up or down to other levels, and the passageways sometimes doubling back on themselves, or emptying into cavernous chambers. The chambers were filled with makeshift tent communities, like so many refugees fleeing war-torn lands. Cooking fires dotted the large chambers and contributed to the haze of the air around them. The inhabitants were filthy, disheveled, and sickly. Many of them exhibited symptoms of disease, from racking coughs to boils. Onin would not have believed people could live this way had he not seen it with his own eyes.

"By the gods," said Fargin, his voice heavy with emotion. "These people." He was obviously having the same thoughts as Onin.

Caris the watchman turned the light of his hooded lantern on them. While the three friends could not see his face, his tone betrayed his lack of compassion for the unfortunates around them. "Beware the pity you feel," said the watchman. "Despicable wretches they may be, but they would cut your throat for the boots you're wearing now." He turned back and continued to lead them further into the recesses of the great mountain.

Onin rankled at his words; they went against all he had been taught to believe. Yet looking at the faces hovering over the meager cooking fires in the underbelly, Onin sensed the danger for himself. He could see the inhabitants were watching the small band travel by as a predator would watch potential prey. No hint of goodwill lay in those faces. Onin was thankful for the simple sword and dagger belted to his waist.

"What in the world would bring Rabbash here?" asked Hangric. Each of them had asked the question more than once, and none of them had a plausible notion.

One blessing was that running water was common. Many of the chambers and rooms had a series of fountains and channels allowing clean, cold mountain water to flow throughout the underbelly. Many inhabitants could be seen filling pots, pans, or even old boots, anything that could hold water to carry back to whatever hovel they camped in. Hangric stopped to drink from one of the fountains they passed, but Caris stopped him.

"The water is fouled," said the watchman. "It contains the waste of the people from the upper city. Every watchman who has ever drunk the water here has gotten sick, and many have died."

Hangric backed away from the fountain slowly.

"Best to keep moving," said Caris. "We're close now, but Demitus is shifty. He doesn't like to stay in one place for long. He might disappear before we get there."

"Are you sure this man is reliable?" asked Onin.

"As reliable as anyone down here," replied Caris. "He knows something about everything that happens in the underbelly, it seems. If your friend came this way, Demitus is bound to know about it. Ah, here's the place." They stopped outside a nondescript door. Onin couldn't tell what was different about this one from the last dozen or so they had passed.

Caris opened the door and stepped into the room on the other side, and the friends filed in after him. The room had two other doors on the opposite wall, and the place was lit by a few flickering candles set in crude wooden sconces. They found a grimy, fat man waiting for them. He wore a sleeveless tunic, his exposed arms and face covered with boils. Onin was repulsed at the sight of him.

"Demitus," said Caris by way of greeting. Judging by his tone, the watchman felt much the same way about Demitus as Onin did.

"Caris," wheezed Demitus. Onin could see he lacked most of his teeth; this didn't surprise him. "I was about to leave. You know it isn't healthy for me to be seen talking with a watchman. People will get suspicious."

"What a shame, you being a soul of integrity and all," said Caris drolly. The big watchman jabbed a finger at the informant's chest. "You go wherever the coin is, and my friends have coin to spend if you've got information they want to hear."

For the first time, Demitus seemed to look over the three friends. His eyes were shrewd and greedy, and Onin felt dirty from his gaze alone.

"What are you looking to know?" said the greasy man.

"Our friend came down here some weeks ago," said Onin. "He hasn't been seen since. We want to find him."

"He must owe you a lot of money," said Demitus.

"What do you mean?" he said, his tone indignant.

"Well, he's lost himself in the underbelly," said Demitus. "And you're here looking for him. The only thing that makes sense is money--lots of it."

"Here it comes," groaned Caris.

"What?" said Demitus. It seemed like his turn to act indignant. "You expect me to believe they're down here because they're such good friends? Don't take me for a fool."

"It makes no difference why we're here," said Fargin. "Do you have the information we need?"

"Perhaps," said the dirty man evasively.

"Then *perhaps* we have coin for you," said Fargin. Onin was a little surprised at the exchange. Fargin rarely took the initiative in such a way.

"I'll need some time to ask around," said Demitus. "What does your friend look like? Would he have any sort of clothing or jewelry which would make him recognizable?"

The friends did their best to describe Rabbash. They often spoke over one another to add details or correct a statement. After a few minutes, Demitus seemed to have an idea of whom he would be looking for.

"Meet me back at this place in a week," said the scruffy man. "I'll have something for you then." Demitus held his hand out, palm up. "I'll need my retainer before I begin working."

Fargin dropped a pouch of coins in the outstretched hand. Demitus hefted it and shot a glance at Fargin which implied he thought it light.

"You'll get more if your information is good," said Fargin. "One week."

Demitus locked eyes with him for a long moment.

"One week," said Demitus. Then he left through one of the other doors in the room.

Caris led them away from the meeting place, presumably in the same direction they had come. Onin found it impossible to know for certain. The twisting corridors and scattered chambers of the underbelly made an inscrutable maze. They seemed to climb stairs more than descend them, so Onin could only conclude they were heading for the surface. It made sense to him; wherever you might be down here, if you kept heading up, you would find yourself under open sky eventually.

The band hadn't reached the more populated sections of the underbelly when they found the way ahead obstructed by a group of unsavory-looking men. Onin guessed there were at least ten of them, probably more. They were filthy and covered in tattered rags, but each also held a naked blade in hand, whether a crude short-bladed sword or a rusty knife.

Onin brought up the rear and glanced behind them to plan an escape route. To his chagrin, he could see a similar-sized group of men crowding the corridor behind them. A nearby door offered the only possible escape. The three Guardsmen waited for a cue from the watchman, but Caris had already yanked his own sword from its scabbard and bolted for the door.

"This way!" the watchman yelled as he threw the door open and disappeared into the darkness beyond. Quick to respond, the three friends were close on his heels. Unfortunately the mob of attackers streamed after, screaming for blood.

They turned left and right frantically, ducking through doors, sprinting through rooms, hurdling ragged tents, in their attempt to lose the attackers. They found themselves in a vaulted chamber that was surprisingly empty but for a wide staircase that curved up and away into darkness. Caris raced up the staircase with the friends close behind.

Hope seemed lost when they reached the landing at the top as there were no exits. The entire landing was nothing more than an oversized balcony, and all sides were bounded by flat, gray stone. There was no way down except the stairs or to jump over the railing. Caris released a string of profanities as he cast about for an escape route that refused to present itself.

Realizing the predicament, the three friends turned about and formed up shoulder to shoulder with swords in hands. They had no shields to overlap for defensive purposes but descended the staircase a few steps to command the high ground. Whatever advantage they could snatch from their circumstances would be needed, Onin was sure.

The attackers met them on the steps, their forward momentum broken by the sudden ascent. They were a rabble, attacking as a mob with no coordination or planning. Two fell in the initial attack, taking a third and fourth with them as they tumbled down the staircase, only to be trod upon by their fellows. Regardless, the enemy's superior numbers forced the companions backward, one step at a time. Fargin cried out as a knife bit into his forearm. It was not his sword arm, however, and he fought on, undaunted.

Hangric, meanwhile, locked blades with an assailant. With a defiant roar, he reached forward with his other hand and grasped the front of the attacker's grimy tunic and, to the man's surprise, casually tossed him over the railing of the staircase with one hand. The attacker plummeted fifteen feet or so to land on the hard stone floor below.

Seeing an opportunity, Onin vaulted over the railing after him. He let out a hoarse yell as he landed feetfirst on the attacker who had just been thrown below by Hangric. The man convulsed with the impact and lay still. Onin pressed his sudden advantage and attacked the body of surprised men clustered at the bottom of the stairs. Caris the watchman had taken his place next to Hangric and Fargin; a fleeting part of Onin's mind was impressed by the man's mettle under duress.

He had no room for extraneous thought as he cut a path into the enemy. Two men fell before they even realized what had happened, and a third narrowly avoided the same fate with a clumsy parry. Onin flicked his wrist and sent his opponent's weapon flying from his grasp then dispatched him with a backhanded swing.

Onin's rampage continued, driving his adversaries before him with each stroke of his sword arm. His momentum carried him through their center, and he found himself climbing back up the first few steps of the staircase. Following Hangric's example, he reached out with his free hand in the chaos of the melee and was rewarded with a handful of beard. Onin yanked as hard as he could, and the man on the other end of the beard sailed over his shoulder to be dashed on the stone floor below.

The twanging sound of bowstrings split the air. Sudden pain erupted through Onin as two powerful blows struck him from behind. He fell to his knees on the staircase, his sword tumbling from his grasp. One of the attackers seized the opportunity to kick him in the face. Onin tumbled backward to land in a heap and descended into unconsciousness. As the darkness claimed him, he could hear his friends screaming his name.

* * *

The dream had him again; the details were the same, but the focus, different. Dragons in the sky, at war through tooth and claw, and none of them verdants. Scaled carcasses littered the landscape. The eggs, in a nest carved into the mountain. A single egg showed dark striations throughout the shell, the pattern in the form of a shield. The eyes, one yellow like a cat, the other a glittering gemstone, superimposed over the egg. Then, behind the eyes, the shield-shaped reed boat floated on a river with an infant nestled inside of it. Unlike previous dreams, this was not fleeting; he relived it over and over again, each detail burning itself into his memory. It remained the same dream but new and different, vividly real in a way like never before.

The egg. The eyes. The shield. They all meant something. If only he knew what.

* * *

Onin realized he had been hearing a solitary voice for some time, but it was the awful smell that finally lifted him back to wakefulness. The air reeked of rotten eggs and sweat. Onin struggled to open his eyes and, with a concentrated act of will, succeeded. He blinked his way through the dried crust threatening to keep his eyes sealed shut. The room felt small and cramped, the air very close but warm and comfortable. He took a deep breath, and jolts of pain shot from his back. He groaned and coughed, which only made the pain worse. Onin spent several moments suppressing his urge to cough; it sent only tiny daggers of pain through him. His head pounded and he feebly lifted a hand to his brow. He felt a bandage there, the flesh beneath felt sore and bruised.

He became dimly aware of another figure moving about in the smoky gloom of the cramped space. The voice he had been hearing issued from the shrouded form, the voice of an old woman, apparently talking to herself.

"He's coming awake already," came her scratchy but high-pitched voice. "Aye, he is, and much sooner than I would have reckoned possible." For some strange reason, Onin thought she wasn't speaking to him.

"I can't cook without the proper ingredients," she continued. "The proper ingredients are nearly impossible to obtain. It's why I send the others to get them. I'm an old woman. I can't be expected to go all over the place to find these things. Yes, if they want me to cook for them, they must simply bring their own ingredients."

Onin's vision cleared, and he could see the old crone stirring an iron cauldron hanging over a fireplace. She lifted the large wooden spoon to her nose and sniffed several times. She returned to stirring the mixture while fishing in her old, ragged clothes for a handful of something. Onin couldn't see it, but she dropped the mysterious handful into the boiling pot. Within seconds the scent in the room changed, not really any better, just different. It now emitted an earthy, even moldy, smell.

"The dreams disturb him, that's obvious enough," the old crone went on. "Of course they do. He has nothing to compare them with, not even other dreams." She threw back her head and let out a harsh laugh. "Imagine it! Spending your entire life with only one dream. I never thought about it that way. It sounds terribly limiting. It would be like cooking with only one recipe! One recipe for an entire lifetime! How could one recipe satisfy all of life? It simply can't; that's obvious enough. Sometimes the right ingredients come to you; sometimes they don't. Sometimes they just land in your lap and are waiting for the person to come along who needs the recipe."

The old woman put a lid on her cauldron and hobbled over to where Onin lay swaddled in smelly furs. The lighting was poor, the only illumination coming from the bed of coals in the fireplace and a single candle on a wooden table. Onin could make out only the vaguest sense of her features. He could sense, more than see, a toothless grin on her face.

"Where--?" he croaked, but his dry throat choked off the rest of his question. The resulting coughing fit caused waves of pain from the wounds in his back. His head still hurt too much, and nausea assaulted him as his cranium pounded.

"He doesn't even realize he's still dying," said the old crone as she pushed him firmly down into the furs. "He probably thinks I like the way all of this smells. A dullard and a brute he is. Hardly what I hoped fate would provide. Sometimes the right ingredients are there; sometimes they're not. Sometimes you need to adjust the recipe. I hate making due. I really wish I had the right ingredients."

Her gnarled hands had fished another mysterious handful from her ragged clothes. She forcibly crammed the handful of whatever into Onin's mouth. It was dry and bitter and clogged his throat as it crumbled into particles on his tongue. Unable to resist, Onin could only chew the ghastly substance, which felt like dried moss on his palate. He would have gagged, but she held a waterskin to his lips and squeezed a mouthful for him.

"Sometimes you need an entirely new recipe. Well, of course, don't think I would forget that, do you?"

A sudden light flared in front of Onin's eyes, and her face came into clear view for the first time. It simultaneously reassured and frightened him; she was equal parts nightmarish hag and doting grandmother. Deep lines and sagging skin defined her features, and sparse white strands hung from her scalp. A rare breeze sent smoke from a nearby brazier into Onin's face, filling his nostrils with a sickly sweet aroma.

"It will put him in a frame of mind better for healing," said the old woman. "His mind is as rigid as his spine. His kind snaps in the wind instead of bending. Do not judge so quickly. Perhaps his rigidity is what is needed. It doesn't fit the recipe. Is this a new recipe or an old one?

"Whatever the case, the dish always turns out. Sometimes it turns out terrible, but it always turns out. And there's always the next time I cook. Maybe the recipe will be better next time, or I will have better ingredients."

A light-headed sensation had begun to descend over Onin. He had a hard time focusing on the old woman before him, even as she took repeated tokes on the pipe in her hands and blew the smoke into Onin's face. It was really quite pleasant, once you got over the sickly sweet smell of it, thought Onin.

Soon enough, the big man found blessed, peaceful sleep again.

Chapter 16

Mountains will shake, belching their guts to the sky and sending shards of earth and fire to the corners of the land. The skies will swim with ships and beasts, and men shall claim the heavens as their domain.
--excerpt from *Testament of the Augur*

* * *

Onin lost track of the days as he slipped in and out of consciousness. The lack of sunlight in the underbelly would have made tracking the passage of time impossible, even if he remained awake. Whenever he awoke, the old woman cared for his hunger and thirst. She tended his wounds, changed his dressings, fed him broth or held a waterskin to his lips, all while talking to herself. In the time he spent with her, she never seemed to notice his presence or talk to him directly; her conversation was reserved for herself, and she talked about him in a most unusual fashion. Despite her seemingly unhinged mind, she proved an attentive nurse and competent healer, and Onin grew stronger day by day.

"How did I get here?" he asked one day after being fed a salty stew.

"He acts like he doesn't know where he came from," said the old woman. "Doesn't he know he had a mother, just like the rest of us?" The old woman giggled. Onin began to respond, but she continued to speak over him.

"That's not what he means. Of course it isn't, but the answer to his question would make no sense to him. Ignorance is better than confidence built on incomplete knowledge."

Onin wondered about that last statement. It reminded him of lessons from Teacher Doren at Scaleback Academy. However, his fatigue and lack of success with questioning the strange old woman kept him from pressing for more.

Unable to move due to his wounds and fever, Onin was unable to see to his most basic needs. He was helpless as an infant, but the old woman never fussed. Each day she removed his soiled bedding, and hand-bathed him with wet rags. He vaguely wondered where and how she cleaned the furs he slept upon.

Onin had the dream frequently while under the hag's care. The details were more vivid than ever before, and they haunted his waking hours as well as his sleep. With each iteration, the same images were reinforced--the egg, the eyes, and the shield--but the meaning remained obscured from him. It always ended the same, with an infant floating downstream in a bed of reeds shaped like a shield, the same shield symbol that grew on the shell of the egg.

"The shield is the tool and the conveyance," said the crone. Onin started at the sound of her voice. She seemed to hear his thoughts and offered her own commentary on them. "It is the purpose of the shield to protect that which hides behind it, but that is not the only use it can be put to. The river guides but the shield floats."

"Where does the river guide me?" asked Onin. Her words were starting to make sense, which terrified him. He wondered if he would eventually forget his life under the open sky, his friends and family, and would live out the rest of his days here, trading nonsense with a babbling hag. He could not push aside the power the dreams had over him, however, and listened raptly to her for any snippet to help him make sense of it all.

"He knows it is him floating on the river. It is some progress," said the crone. "I don't know about that. The gods do not require us to understand our purpose in order to fulfill it. To seek meaning can interfere with doing what comes naturally. To act in ignorance can lead us astray." Onin never knew what to make of her apparent contradictions. They seemed to make perfect sense to her.

"Where does the river guide me?"

"Wherever the river goes, of course! How else does a river work?" she replied. It was rare when she would respond to him at all, let alone directly answer a question. Still, he was aggravated that even her direct answers were of terribly little help.

The day finally came when Onin felt strong enough to stand on his own two feet. Unsteady at first, he held the walls for balance, but it felt good to have some control over his own movements. His wounds were sore and painful but restricted him less than he'd feared.

The old crone appeared in the doorway to the room. She held a bundle in her arms and thrust it into his hands without a word. He opened the dirty old satchel to find a round of cheese and some stale bread inside.

"What is this for?" he asked her.

She looked at him directly, meeting his gaze for the first time. "You leave today, protector," said the old woman. "Your time with us is over."

She squatted down with a groan of effort and rummaged through a pile of furs and clothing. She arose a moment later with Onin's sheathed sword in her hand. The old woman looked at him with mischief in her eyes.

"If you remember nothing else from your stay here, heed this advice," she said solemnly. "Don't get shot with arrows."

* * *

Sensi rushed along the corridors, his mind juggling a long list of tasks to be accomplished. The short, pale, fat man sweated, waddling as fast as his feet would carry him. He dreadfully feared forgetting a task. He'd have made a list had all of them been legal.

These other activities had begun to leave Sensi feeling uneasy. He wanted to see the twins, Lornavus and Altavus. He hesitated, however, because he knew they didn't like to be bothered too often; they considered it a sign of incompetence. Recent news provided sufficient reason to break the ban. A Guardsman missing in the underbelly for some weeks returned alive, against all odds.

Sensi entered the new office they occupied after being admitted by the Guardsman at the door. The twins must have risen quickly and substantially in the king's service to warrant a personal Guardsman. Despite his current unease, Sensi took it as a sign that his instincts were accurate and attaching himself to the twins had been a good move on his part. With no family of prominence, at least not any who would recognize him, Sensi made what friends he could in the world. The twins ended up being worth the investment.

When he entered the room, Sensi saw only one of the twins sat at the desk, scribbling notes while going through a stack of papers. The twin, as ever, appeared thin, almost underfed. Sensi looked carefully into the man's eyes and, for the first time since he had known them, wasn't sure which one he talked to.

"Lornavus?" asked Sensi, his tone tentative.

"Yes," said the twin. Sensi detected a slight pause before the response. Was it a lie?

"I've news you want to hear," said Sensi. His tone was even, though he was still slightly out of breath. "The Guardsman who disappeared into the underbelly has returned."

The twin's eyes narrowed dangerously. "The small one? Rabbash?"

"No," said Sensi, shaking his head. "One named Onin. He was part of the search party from three weeks ago. They went into the underbelly seeking Rabbash. He was presumed dead, along with the watchman. Now he's been found near the surface by the watch and sent to his home after thorough questioning."

"How did he survive? According to the accounts of the other two, the oaf was wounded in battle and they were forced to leave him behind." The twin obviously remembered the search party. Sensi was fairly certain he had talked to Lornavus at the time as well, but it meant nothing. One twin could have informed the other by now.

"By his own account, some old crazy woman nursed him back to health and then turned him loose to make his escape," said Sensi. "Some of the townsfolk are saying she must have been the Hag." Sensi openly scoffed at the notion, but Lornavus did not. "What, that old folktale? Parents scare their children into behaving with stories of the Hag."

"There is more to our myths than you would believe," said the twin. "And more yet to come." Sensi didn't know how to respond to the notion.

The twins were often enigmatic. Sensi decided it was an opportune time to broach the other topic on his mind.

"There was something I wanted to discuss--" he began but Lornavus interrupted.

"What did he tell the watch?" said Lornavus. "Does he have any knowledge as to why his group was attacked?"

"He seems to know nothing," said Sensi. He was a little testy at the rude treatment but tried to keep it from his tone. "He doesn't even remember how he came to be at the old woman's dwelling. My information comes from the watchmen who questioned him."

"Interesting. Keep me informed of further developments," said Lornavus. "What is it you want to discuss?"

Sensi hesitated to bring it up, but he swallowed hard and began, "It is the Order of Unknowns. I am becoming a little unsettled by recent changes to the organization."

Lornavus arched an eyebrow, but his expression remained otherwise unchanged. "Tell me more," he replied smoothly. Sensi could always tell when he was being worked, whichever twin it was; the voice always became as smooth as the finest cream.

"It was rather loose and, frankly, a bit silly in the beginning," said Sensi. He smiled nervously. "Responsible adults sneaking around with masks and robes, gathering in secret to discuss radical social ideas. Usually good fun and harmless enough. Recently, though, it's been much more serious. Perhaps even a touch militant."

"This causes you concern?" said the twin. "I did not take you for a timid one at heart."

"I'm not, really," said Sensi. He spread his hands in supplication. "But I don't know what's going on, and that makes me nervous. The order was almost like a game when we joined. Now it is organizing into something with a serious message. A violent, revolutionary message. To what purpose?"

"The same purpose the order has always been dedicated to," said the twin with surprising conviction. "Saving our civilization from the rule of superstitious nonsense. The priests and the temples have lied to us for countless generations."

"So the order intends to bring down the temples of the gods?" said Sensi. "That's a lofty ambition indeed. Might as well rearrange the heavens than oppose the gods."

"You are wrong, Sensi," said Lornavus. The twins almost never called him by name, and it made him snap to attention. "The ancient founders were not the gods the temples and Great Families claim them to be. They were simply men and women, flesh and blood, same as anyone else. There was nothing divine about them, nor is there anything divine about their descendants." Such openly defiant talk would earn serious responses from the Great Families. The many temples of the Heights and the lineage of kings and successors were founded on the one principle: the Great Families comprised the descendants of the gods who created the city thousands of years ago. To challenge that notion was to challenge the basis of the king's dominion.

"So this is the truth behind the order, a revolution against the temples?" said Sensi. "That's madness and would end with blood in the streets. It's the only way it can all end."

"Of course," said Lornavus. "But we do not mean now. The time for action is coming, but there is much to be done before the time is ripe. You want to be on the right side of things when it happens, I promise you." The twin's gaze turned cold.

"Yes," said Sensi. He swallowed, nervous. "I do."

* * *

Onin crossed the threshold of Manespike Manor, greeted by Howle. He had never been so glad to see the steward and gratefully accepted the goblet of wine offered. The entire household buzzed with news of his return; apparently word had reached here before he could.

"Welcome home, m'lord," intoned Howle. His attitude was casual, as though Onin had been gone an afternoon, not several weeks. The man seemed capable of maintaining his composure no matter what the circumstances might be.

"Thank you, Howle," said Onin with genuine warmth in his voice. One of the serving girls approached and offered a washing bowl. Onin washed his hands and splashed his face. The water became murky as the grime washed away.

"Her ladyship has been informed of your return," said the steward. "Will you be going to her straight away?"

Onin looked down at his dirty, ragged clothes. "No, not like this," said Onin. "I will bathe first. Have some fresh clothes brought to me, and burn these rags afterward. Also, send a messenger to my fellow Guardsmen Hangric and Fargin."

Howle bowed slightly and departed. Onin, in turn, went straight to the bathing chamber. One of the extravagances of life in the Heights that Onin appreciated was the hot baths. Whether from a naturally heated spring or some clever arrangement of furnaces and pipes, most manors of the Great Families boasted a bath that was always heated. The wealthiest families even had separate bathing chambers for the servants.

Onin welcomed the cloud of steam. Warmth seeped deep inside his bones, and he settled down into the hot water with a contented sigh. He scrubbed vigorously, trying to rid himself of the clinging filth and rude stench of the underbelly. Onin sincerely hoped he would never have to return to the horrid depths.

Drowsiness must have claimed Onin, for he awoke with a mild start a short time later. In a dreamlike state, his mind had wandered to his wife, and he wondered why she hadn't come to him yet. Had she even missed him, to be so casual about his return? He felt taken for granted and considered retiring to his own chambers straight away but then thought better of it. With reluctance, he rose from the scented waters and toweled himself dry before seeking her out.

Onin found her in her own chambers, attended by her usual gaggle of servants, including the muscular fan-bearer who invariably fanned Yolan while she lounged. Onin felt a stab of jealousy; this servant seemed to spend far more time in his wife's company than he did. He pushed the thought away as unreasonable; after all, Onin was not always home, and the servant had no choice in the matter. At times, Onin wondered if he would even want to spend that much time in the same place as Yolan. She was difficult on the best of days and a terror on the worst.

"Husband!" exclaimed Yolan. She sounded sincerely happy to see him but made no effort to rise from her divan. "I was afraid you had run back to the Midlands." Her serving girls giggled at her comment. Onin thought he even detected a smirk on the face of the normally stoic fan-bearer.

"Your humor in the face of my absence is a testament to your concern," said Onin. He mustered all the sarcasm at his command. "You do realize I've been missing for some weeks?"

Yolan looked cross with him. "No doubt in the bed of some whore!" she spit in reply. "I'm sure you were off doing whatever it is you Guardsmen do with your time. Drinking, womanizing, and whatnot. It's a surprise you made it home at all."

Onin felt his face flush with anger. She could be nonchalant about his return, but to accuse him of disappearing to indulge his basest instincts crossed the line.

"I was wounded while looking for Rabbash," he said hotly. "You know it to be true!"

"But I don't!" she screamed. "I know what you tell me, but how do I know it's true? For all I know, when you leave here, it is to leap into the arms of another woman. I notice you don't visit my chambers very often."

"Because I'm unwelcome!" screamed Onin. The situation quickly escalated into something quite different from the happy reunion he envisioned. "I don't like to come to you. I feel like a beggar asking for scraps, and you act so generous for gifting me with your favors. Well, you can keep your attitude and your favors!"

Onin stormed from her bedchamber, slamming the door behind himself. Yolan's shrill voice chased after him, but he ignored her words.

Chapter 17

Destiny, fate, luck ... what difference does it make? What happens happens, and one must simply deal with the circumstances as they are presented.
--Doren, teacher at Scaleback Academy

* * *

Onin stomped his way through the manor with no real destination in mind. He truly wished things would go smoothly between himself and his wife, but she never made it easy. It seemed every word he uttered could be twisted into a vile insult, and it wore his patience thin. Every time they had a disagreement, Yolan would say the most hateful things he could imagine. His anger would become so great, he often fled rather than risk losing control of himself, as he had just done.

He meandered his way through the many hallways until he found himself on the terrace that offered such a fine view of the city below. It was late afternoon, the warmest part of the day, and the sun bathed the white stone and cobbled streets of the Heights with its light. He stopped and looked out over the city, down the mountain, into the Jaga. He imagined his gaze could reach all the way to his hometown of Sparrowport, and his mind mused over the direction his life had taken since his childhood. He had envisioned himself serving out his years in the local militia with its modest salary and social status. But life was not what he had expected it to be, and he found himself a Guard in the Heights, where everything felt strange to him. His childhood home a world away, he suddenly felt very homesick.

Onin heard a soft cough to one side, and he glanced in that direction to see Howle standing with a goblet on a silver tray. Onin gratefully accepted the refreshment from his steward and once again noted how the man seemed to have a preternatural sense of where he would be and what he would want. Howle gave no reaction at all and merely stepped back to resume his place quietly, leaving Onin to return to his ruminations. His thoughts were morbid and hopeless where his wife was concerned, so Onin was happy to be interrupted by Howle a short time later.

"Lord Hangric is here to see you, sir," Howle said and stepped aside to let the big man through the door. Hangric rushed across the terrace to embrace Onin, who returned the hug with feeling.

"Thank the gods," said Hangric. "We thought you lost forever in that stinking pit. What happened to you? Where have you been? It's been a full three weeks since you disappeared."

Onin related the story of his recuperation under the strange old woman. Hangric interrupted many times with questions or comments, but it didn't take long for the story to be completed. Onin described the crone's erratic behaviors but omitted any mention of his dreams. It was too personal yet, and he was not comfortable enough with it to share, even with his friends. He needed to understand it himself before he could talk about it to anyone.

"Well, crazy or not, I am thankful she kept you alive and well," said Hangric. "It is a blessing in what has otherwise been a difficult time."

"You know my story now," said Onin. "What happened to all of you? I remember being struck down and no more until I woke up in the old woman's dwelling."

Hangric's expression turned grim.

"After you took those arrows to the back, we knew the staircase was an exposed position, so we charged them. We covered the distance to them quickly, but not before they could fire another volley at us; there were about four of them in all. Caris, the watchman, fell in the second volley. I don't suppose there's a chance the old woman found him too?" Hangric looked hopeful for a second, but Onin grimly shook his head. "Then he is probably dead. We presumed you were dead too." Hangric looked guiltily at Onin then turned away in shame.

Onin put a reassuring hand on his friend's shoulder. "I'm as surprised as anyone else to be alive," said Onin.

Hangric glanced at him again, guilt written on his features.

"What happened after that?"

Hangric shrugged his wide shoulders. "We fought," said the big man. "The archers we killed were different than the other rabble. They were better dressed and equipped, for one thing. They also looked healthier, not at all like people who lived in the underbelly.

"But we had no time to think as more of the mercenary rabble was upon us. We retreated back into the maze of passageways, and it took us quite some time to lose our pursuers. Of course, by the time we did so, Fargin and I were completely lost and without a guide to lead us to the surface. It took us days to find our way out. It was sheer luck that we stumbled across a unit of watchmen combing the underbelly for a pickpocket. By then, Fargin was in a poor state."

"What about Fargin? What happened?" Onin was concerned by the desolate expression on his friend's face. "Is he alive?"

Hangric's shoulders slumped. "He is alive," said Hangric. "But not well. If you are fit enough, we should go see him."

Onin nodded silently, and the two friends set out for Fargin's home.

* * *

Sensi had been watching the stack of papers grow in fits and starts throughout the day. It represented his life, this stack of papers, because it was the list of items comprising his official duties of the day. How and why he was assigned these tasks was a bit of a mystery, and he had yet to successfully clear the stack in a single day. He simply strove to get as much as possible done and keep the stack's growth to a minimum. Sensi wasn't even certain what his station was or what he should be called. He did whatever was requested of him, and he reported directly to Lornavus. Altavus wasn't anywhere to be seen these days, and his brother insisted that he had sequestered himself away for scholastic pursuits. Sensi could only wonder what sort of knowledge would occupy the attention of either of the twins. They were the most inscrutable men Sensi had ever known, but their ambition seemed to know no bounds. Whatever occupied Altavus's time, Sensi was certain it wasn't strictly academic.

Another paper was added to the stack by another functionary whose exact position and status within the king's service was likewise ambiguous. Sensi snatched the paper up with irritation, even though he tried not to begrudge the other man for doing his job. Sensi groaned as he surveyed the contents of the missive; it required a complete inventory of the king's dry goods held in reserve. The storage houses of the king were immense, housing an unbelievable amount of goods within them, from textiles to salted meats to stacks of iron bars. It would be a monumental task to inventory them.

The task was further complicated by the term "dry goods." Sensi had a recent clash with another administrative clerk in the service, and it was caused by an argument over exactly what constituted dry goods. The clerk in question took the term quite literally and assumed authority over everything not wet or itself a liquid. Sensi tried to explain that he thought his interpretation to be broader than intended, but the man proved intractable. Sensi had decided to obtain a clarification of the term from a higher authority (Lornavus, naturally), and the resulting decision limited the man's power to textiles and cloth, which the clerk took as a mortal insult. This new task would have him rubbing elbows with the same man for days on end.

Sensi spent a few moments wondering if he had done something to offend the gods before he remembered he wasn't supposed to believe in them anymore. Old habits die hard, he thought.

"Sensi," came a voice from his door. Sensi started a little, even though the voice was soft and calm in tone; he was normally aware of people entering his office. He looked up to see Lornavus hovering on his threshold. He was more than slightly shocked as the man had never come to his office before.

"Come with me," said Lornavus. Sensi rose from his desk without question, despite his burning curiosity. He wondered if something were wrong but could think of nothing that would prompt a visit from either of the twins.

Sensi stepped into the hallway to find himself amid a retinue of civil servants. He recognized most of them; there were about ten in all. No one spoke, but the people he knew exchanged quick nods of recognition as Lornavus led them away at a brisk pace.

Sensi fell into step, and they were led up to the next level of the palace. The location of an individual's workspace and living quarters were formally tied to one's place in the king's service. The lowest servants, such as scullery maids and laborers, lived on the lowest levels, with each level of the palace housing staff of successively higher social station. The highest level, the ninth, was where the king lived. The lord chancellor was the only civil servant to reside on the same level as the king and his family. Sensi currently worked on the seventh level of the palace, a place of important but generally mundane responsibilities. Lornavus led his small retinue up to the eighth level.

There he entered what appeared to be a recently vacated office. The furnishings included an ornately carved desk made of polished hardwood and several chairs with plush velvet cushions. A few tapestries devoted to the line of kings adorned the walls. The desk still sported the remains of a meal, still steaming, sitting on a silver tray.

"This is your office now, Sensi," said Lornavus. "You are now the direct assistant to the royal treasurer. He is of relatively sound mind but is advancing in years so will likely need you to shoulder many tasks on his behalf."

Though surprised by the sudden promotion, Sensi was keen enough to catch on to the implied assignment: Take control of as many functions of the treasury as possible. He inwardly gathered himself then pointedly walked around to the other side of the desk to take his seat. Lornavus seemed pleased at his decisiveness, and his lips curled upward slightly in a smile.

"These are your assistants," said Lornavus. "They report directly to you from this moment on." As a group, the members of the retinue bowed slightly to Sensi. "You have proven yourself to be diligent and prudent. This station will be better suited to your strengths. There is no need to waste your talents on trivial matters any longer."

Sensi's mind immediately flew to the copious stack of incoming papers on his old desk. Giving up his previous duties filled him with relief. *So much for the dry goods inventory,* he thought.

"I will leave you to it now," continued Lornavus. "Please, stop by in a week or two and let me know how you are settling in." Lornavus departed without waiting for a response.

Sensi leaned back in his chair, the cushion under him soft and plush, and he breathed a sigh of relief. One of his underlings stepped forward a deposited a stack of parchments on the table.

"Today's requisition forms, sir," he said and stepped back once again.

He was replaced by another, also bearing a stack of papers. The new bureaucrat placed the stack next to the first. "Expense reports from the dragon docks."

The man stepped back, and another took his place, again putting a stack of papers next to the others already present. "Budget recommendations on agricultural development."

One by one the assembled functionaries placed papers on his desk. Sensi watched his tasks grow, mentally taking note of the various areas he would have at least indirect influence over. By the time each had stepped back from his desk, the amount of papers before him was greater than the one he had left behind at his previous desk.

"Very well," said Sensi. "Leave me now and I will get started." They each bowed and exited without another word. With a deep sigh of resignation, Sensi picked up the first sheet and began to read.

* * *

Hangric and Onin arrived at Fargin's house as the sun set. The red rays cast a bloody hue over everything in its path, and it filled Onin with a sense of foreboding. Hangric said almost nothing on the way over, and Onin couldn't muster idle chatter, in any case. The household exuded somber quiet when they crossed the threshold. The servants greeted them with courtesy but no enthusiasm. The first member of the house to meet them was Carnella, Fargin's wife. Normally sweet tempered and effusive in her speech, today they found her subdued and withdrawn. Legitimately happy to see Onin alive, she embraced him warmly by way of welcome.

"We thought you lost," said Carnella. She looked up at Onin, and her eyes were rimmed with tears. Her face was blotchy and red, and Onin thought she had been crying a lot recently.

"There, there, little one," said Onin. He patted her tiny shoulder uncomfortably. Giving solace had never been a strong suit for him, but he had always liked Carnella and hated to see her in such pain. "Take me to him."

Carnella nodded and blinked away her tears. She led them to the dining hall. Despite being warm outside, a fire burned in the hearth. A crumpled figure wrapped in a blanket slouched in a chair in front of the fire. His shoulders were stooped and his posture that of an old, tired man. It took a few seconds for Onin to realize he was actually looking at Fargin.

Onin was shocked at the change in his friend. Fargin had always been reserved in speech, but strong of body. Onin could not reconcile his memory of his friend with the pale ghost of a man who sat before him. He was drawn and thin, his complexion like wax. His beard was scraggy and unkempt, as was his hair.

"Gods damn it," said Fargin. "Will the blasted itching never stop?" His voice was dry and cracked. He never looked up, so Onin wasn't sure if he was talking to them or himself. "It's gone but it itches nonetheless. I need more wine. Steward!"

Fargin lifted his gaze as he called out. His eyes fell on Hangric first, due to the sheer size of the man, then went to his diminutive wife. He seemed to have nothing to say to either of them. Then his gaze fell on Onin.

A range of emotions crossed Fargin's expression. Amazement gave way to glee, then to confusion, then to suspicion.

"So you're back from the dead," Fargin said with a smile, although his voice held no humor. "Two arrows, right in the back. I saw it with my own eyes." Fargin's left hand emerged from under the blanket covering him. He gestured vaguely at Onin. "Yet here you are, looking quite fit."

The steward arrived with the requested wine. There were enough goblets on the tray for all of them to partake, but Onin had no taste for wine at the moment. Fargin grabbed up his own goblet without hesitation and thrust the empty vessel at his servant with apparent irritation.

"Well, fill it already, man," said the master of the house. "I can't pour it myself, in case you hadn't noticed." The steward poured nervously, and Fargin seemed impatient at how long it took the wine to make its way into his goblet. Wine splashed over the goblet's rim as Fargin lifted it to his lips and drained it in one gulp.

Onin struggled for something to say. Of them all, Fargin had been the optimist, the one to look at the bright side of any situation. To see him so despondent was devastating. He opened his mouth to speak, to say something, anything, but Fargin cut him off.

"Two arrows! You should be dead!" Fargin screamed. Tears streamed from his bleary eyes. "But no, the gods have seen fit to return you home, safe and sound, looking hale and hearty. Old Fargin, though, he takes a scratch, and loses his arm for it." Fargin coughed with the exertion of his yelling. Despite his venom, his voice came across as wheezy and weak. He raised his goblet to his lips before continuing.

"More than my arm, you've cost me my health," he said, jabbing the goblet in his hand at Onin accusingly. Wine spilled over the edge and onto the floor with his movements. Shocked by the accusation, Onin took a step back.

"Husband, don't accuse your friend like that," said Carnella. Tears were flowing freely from her as well, and her voice shook with emotion.

Fargin turned a baleful gaze upon her. "Stupid cow!" he screamed. "Get out of my sight! You don't have a husband anymore; he died in the filth below!"

The petite woman turned pale and fled from the room, sobbing.

"Fargin, I am so sorry this happened to you," said Onin. "If I could change it, if I could give you my own arm, I would--"

Fargin laughed bitterly. "Oh, yes," he said. "But you can't, can you? It's done and that can't be changed. And now you're here to mock me with your wholeness." Fargin raised the goblet to his lips again; finding it empty, he flung it away angrily. The clattering echoed through the dining hall. "Before you came back, I could take some solace that I survived. Now I don't even have that."

Hangric finally spoke up. "You still have that solace," said the big man in a soft tone. "You have your life, at least."

"Oh, yes, I have a life," said Fargin. Sarcasm and bitterness dripped from his words. "A life of infirmity. A life as a broken man, not a Guard. A life of constant reliance on servants. No, better to think of me as dead because the man you knew is no more. Leave me."

Both Hangric and Onin hesitated. They exchanged glances. Fargin had hardly ever raised his voice to them, let alone banished them from his presence. When they didn't immediately move, however, Fargin's ire grew.

"Get out of my sight!" he screamed and descended into a fit of wracking coughs. His steward attended him loyally, but Fargin brushed him away. He turned back toward the fire and wrapped the blanket tighter around himself.

When it became apparent Fargin had no intention of acknowledging his friends again, they withdrew, feeling defeated. Onin left the manor looking through tears of his own.

Chapter 18

Honor? Honor is just a word men use to justify their actions.
--Yolan Manespike

* * *

After leaving Fargin's house, Hangric seemed uncomfortable looking Onin in the face. Did the big man also harbor resentments, Onin wondered as his friend walked away.

Fargin's accusations had rattled Onin. His feelings were raw, and he wanted to drink himself into a stupor to forget the pain as well as the pain of his friends. However, experience taught him the value of temperance. A night of revelry may seem cathartic, but the next day brought the inevitable hangover with the problems precipitating the binge unresolved. Still, much as he thought the situation over during the walk home, he came to the opinion perhaps a drink or two would not be out of order.

With the thought of ale firmly in mind, he accepted the goblet proffered by Howle as he crossed the threshold of his home. Onin immediately retired to the terrace. He wanted to feel the cool breeze and hoped it might cleanse his mind of its dark thoughts somehow. Onin finished his wine in just a few gulps but refused when offered a refill.

His mind preoccupied with thoughts of his friends, Onin struggled with the disappearance of Rabbash and the fact that the Fargin he knew and loved seemed to be no more. He also felt self-conscious, wondering if there might be truth to his wounded friend's accusations. Was he somehow responsible for Fargin's loss? It had been his idea to go into the underbelly to search for Rabbash. Onin's memories also conjured another old friend, a smiling one with sharp wit and sharper tongue. Onin hadn't thought of Flea in years, but his recent grief made his friend's absence ache within him.

Onin looked out over the city below him. As the manor of a Great Family, his home sat well above the lower sections of the city, where the common people lived. In the evening, many lights could be seen, and the bustle of the city's inhabitants continued undeterred. Onin considered the many people living in those lower levels and knew yet another level, another city, existed deep below, where the light of the sun never reached at all. The immensity of the Heights staggered him in the moments he thought of it, and it did something to turn him away from darker thoughts.

"You look well for someone who's supposed to be dead."

Onin turned to see his father-in-law, Torreg, stepping onto the terrace. He embraced Onin warmly and held him at arm's length, appraising him. After satisfying himself the younger man was whole, Torreg looked deeply into his eyes.

"I take my compliment back. You don't look well at all."

Onin had no response to the comment but didn't doubt its truth. Instead of speaking, he gestured for Howle to bring wine for Torreg and accepted a refill of his own goblet. Within moments, the two were seated comfortably, enjoying the breeze while sipping wine. Neither spoke for some time, but eventually Onin broke the silence.

"It's not even the same man," he said. Onin rubbed the back of his neck wearily. "Fargin was always so . . . full of hope."

Torreg nodded solemnly. "The injuries of battle are not confined to the body," said the older man. "I've seen men under my own command survive a battle without a scratch but later be unable to lift a sword for the trembling of their hands. His wounds were grievous, and he must now face the prospect his days as a Guardsman are over."

It hurt to hear the truth out loud, but Onin couldn't refute it. The circle of friends worked so hard together over the years, he couldn't accept that one would not be able to continue on the same path. Fargin lived but had lost the primary thing he lived for.

"I'm sorry for your friend's pain," continued Torreg. "But I confess it is overshadowed by the happiness of your return. You know I love my daughter, but if she were the only person to talk with around the manor, I might get myself reassigned to the Midlands again."

"Whatever are you talking about? You're hardly ever here, even now that you're home."

"Well, that's true. It seems every detail of the order is mired in bureaucracy these days. Every little suggestion has to pass a dozen reviews from as many officials. More time is spent in formalities than productive work."

"Watch yourself. Isn't that the kind of talk that had you assigned to the Midlands?"

Torreg gave him a disgusted look. "At moments, that fate doesn't seem so bad. The Midlands is far away from all this pointless bureaucracy. But what else am I supposed to do? I must persist or these problems only become worse."

"What news from the order, then?" said Onin, changing the subject. "I've been away for some weeks now. Have we received confirmation yet?"

Torreg broke into a wide grin. "Indeed, we have," said his father-in-law. "My promotion to commander is official. The ceremony is next week. I'm being assigned the palace detail, which is something I wanted to speak with you about. I'm hoping you'll accept reassignment to palace duty."

"Palace duty?" said Onin. "Isn't there a long list of applicants? It's our most prestigious assignment."

"Yes, but these applicants you speak of want the assignment for the wrong reasons," said Torreg. His lips curled in a sneer. "Palace detail has become the easy, no-risk assignment of any Guard. Those guarding the king and successor never face danger, and they have almost constant access to the wealthy and powerful of the Heights. It's a fawning conniver's dream." Torreg paused to drain his goblet and have it refilled by the dutiful Howle. "The men currently on palace detail see it as an opportunity for social advancement, not a sacred duty. Despite the large numbers of men to be found there, security around the king is astonishingly lax. My goal is to change that, to restore discipline and vigilance, and I need men who recognize the need for proper measures around the king."

"I can see your point," said Onin. "But you have said yourself in the past, why would anyone target the king? It would make no sense and ultimately have no effect. The successor would ascend to the throne, and everything would be back to normal."

"Who knows?" said Torreg with a shrug. "But just because we can't think of a reason doesn't mean one can't exist. As Guards, we have no idea what may happen or why, but we must prepare for all the possibilities we can foresee. By my reckoning, the king is vulnerable. Did you know he's never even trained with a sword?"

With that, Torreg slammed his goblet on the table between them and clapped Onin on the shoulder.

"So say 'yes,' my son," said Torreg. "Help me to restore the sacred duty that is the reason for our order's existence."

* * *

The chicken was cooked to perfection, each bite juicy and succulent. Sensi could tell it had been braised with butter while roasting. To one side sat cooked vegetables and a selection of dried fruits and nuts, as yet untouched. The wonderfully prepared fowl occupied his attention, almost to the point he couldn't listen to the words being said.

"The current cost of raw iron is at an all-time high," said Tamzor, his assistant in charge of requisitions. Tamzor might be a terrible bore, but Sensi appreciated his keen attention to detail. "The Guard have requisitioned one thousand new blades of the strongest steel. To purchase the iron and pay blacksmiths is beyond the budget. In order to fulfill it, we would need to siphon funds from elsewhere."

Sensi knew ripples would emanate throughout the king's service at the suggestion. To divert funds from other budgets to support the Guard would be an unpopular move. However, they were beholden by law to provide the Guard with the materials and funds requested.

"What about the iron in the king's storehouses?" Sensi asked around a mouthful of chicken.

"We have sufficient iron in storage to fill the order," said Tamzor. "But just barely. I have already mentioned this fact to the captain in charge of the order, but he insists we must not use the iron in storage. We have a royal decree stating that we must keep a certain amount in the king's storehouses. We would go far below that amount using the iron for this project."

Sensi sipped wine from a simple silver goblet. It complemented the seasoning of the chicken.

"And you have calculated how much iron we can take from storage without dropping below the threshold," concluded Sensi. "How much of a deficit are we looking at?"

Tamzor seemed pleased with himself. "We can cover roughly one third of the order."

Sensi leaned back and thought things over. "Then place one third of the order. Purchase no iron, and use whatever we can from storage."

"Won't the Guard insist on the entire allotment?" asked Tamzor.

"They will get it . . . eventually," said Sensi. Satisfied with the chicken, he began to pick at the dried fruits before him. Sensi could never pass up a taste of something sweet, and he settled on some sugared raisins. "We must provide them what they ask for, but we will not impact other operations of the king's service to do it. We'll give them what we can now and fulfill the rest of the order when we can acquire iron at a reasonable price."

Tamzor nodded but did not seem pleased. "I see the reason behind your decision. But I feel the captain in charge of the order will not. I fear he will be intractable on this issue."

"A difficult captain? Forbid the thought," said Sensi wryly. "What is this captain's name?"

"Torreg," said Tamzor. "A most disagreeable sort, I can assure you. He spent many years serving below, mingling with Mudlanders. The crudeness seems to have rubbed off on him."

"Deliver my decision," said Sensi. "If Captain Torreg persists, I'll contend with him. Now if there is nothing else, I have someplace else I would like to be."

Tamzor inclined his head politely before withdrawing. Sensi left the remaining food where it was; his servants would see to its removal. Sensi had more responsibility than ever before but also enjoyed greater benefits than ever before. While substantial, most of his workload could be delegated to members of his staff.

Sensi wrapped a light cloak around his shoulders and left his office after a short discussion with his staff. His assistants were competent and well trained, and he felt confident leaving daily affairs in their hands.

Though he considered hiring a sedan chair for the trip, Sensi decided he would rather walk. It seemed more fitting for the occasion. The weather was sunny and bright, but the steady breeze kept the heat from being oppressive. Even still, Sensi was unused to physical exertion and was sweating profusely long before he reached his destination.

As he entered the chapel, Sensi dropped a handful of coins in the offering box. The attending priest made a gesture of blessing over him as he entered the mausoleum. Square stone panels covered the walls from floor to ceiling. Most had a tiny plaque with a name on it.

Sensi stood before one, his head slightly bowed. He remained silent for a long time but eventually spoke.

"Mother," he said. "It's been some time since my last visit, I know. Now, though, I don't have to be so concerned about your safety." She would have appreciated the dark humor in her younger days. "I never thought you were happy to see me. As a matter of fact, I don't know why I continue to come here at all. You refused my help at every turn." Sensi felt tears in his eyes and wiped them away angrily.

"I could've pulled you out of there," he said. "You could have lived somewhere better. But you refused to leave that place. Why? Did you really believe he would come and find you? What a fool."

Sensi heard the priest greet some other parishioners for evening prayers. He composed himself and cleared his eyes before speaking again, this time in a conspiratorial whisper. Sensi leaned closer to the plaque with his mother's name.

"My father has had every chance to recognize me. He never has, not even the slightest. I've no love for the man, and he has earned my contempt for letting his own flesh and blood rot away in the underbelly. One day, he will come to regret his decision."

Sensi touched his fingers to his lips then to the cold stone plaque. Feeling the fatigue from his walk, he went outside and hired a sedan chair to convey him to his home.

* * *

Onin fidgeted in full ceremonial dress, but palace detail required it. Onin had spent quite some time combing his hair and trimming his beard to prepare for his first day but still felt unkempt and crude. Howle, who had served Torreg for years before Onin came along, had polished his armor to a bright shine and had proven instrumental in arranging the long cloak in the appropriate bundles and layers. The intricacies of formal dress were beyond Onin, and he was glad for the help.

Like all Guards before him, Onin had memorized the layout of the palace soon after being inducted, so he did not have to contend with finding his way about, thank the gods. Many Guardsmen were about at any given time, but they hardly took the duty seriously. Most slouched against a wall or talked incessantly with one another or the servants. A few seemed to drop the pretense of being on duty at all and lounged about on the furniture when they thought no one of authority watched.

He made his way to the location of Torreg's office, as he had been directed. When he arrived, he saw Captain Bolg already seated in the office but no sign of Torreg. Bolg's ugly face broke into a grin when he caught sight of Onin, and the two clasped hands warmly.

"Aye, it's good to see you, lad," said Bolg. "I heard you had some trouble recently."

"Nothing to get excited over, I assure you," said Onin.

"A fortnight-long drunken bender, if your wife is to be believed," said Bolg with a harsh laugh. He furrowed his brow in apology, but Onin just waved it away.

"Yolan and I fight; everyone in the Heights knows that by now. But I'd rather hear what is going on in the Midlands. You can't have been back long."

"Two days now," said Bolg. "Things are far from peaceful, I'm sad to say. We've had five attacks by feral dragons in the last two weeks. During one attack, they succeeded in bringing down a verdant dragon. It's the second one this year."

Onin whistled. "Two in a year. I wonder what is making the ferals so bold."

"Old stories say this happens from time to time. Old timers will speak of such things, but I've not seen it in my days as a Guard."

Torreg entered the room. Both men rose to greet him, and they took turns clasping hands.

"Commander Torreg," said Bolg, placing emphasis on the title.

"I'm glad the two of you are here at the same time. We've something to discuss." Torreg took a moment to make sure his door latched. He motioned for the two men to follow him to the seats nearest the hearth. "I hope the sound of the fire will obscure our conversation," he whispered. "Keep your voices low, we may have eavesdroppers."

Onin was shocked at the implication. He had never considered such clandestine activities going on within the palace itself. He didn't like the thought of looking over his shoulder everywhere he went. He did as instructed, however, and the three men bent their heads together to talk in hushed whispers.

Chapter 19

Power comes in a variety of forms and manifests in more ways than you can imagine. No one contests the authority of a captain on his own ship, but no one questions the power of the cook either.
--Doren, teacher at Scaleback Academy

* * *

"We met while I was serving in the Midlands, Onin," said Torreg. "But we've never really discussed the reasons I was there so long. No doubt you've noticed most Guardsman are stationed in the Midlands but only for a few months at a time."

"Yes," said Onin. "I recall you spent most of my life there."

"I was vocal in my youth," said Torreg. "Still am, if truth be told. Hopefully a little wiser now, but it remains to be seen. Don't you say a word." The last bit he aimed at Bolg, who innocently stared at the ceiling with a wistful, knowing smile.

"Do you know why the Guard exists, Onin?" asked Torreg.

"The Guard was formed to protect the king and the successor and serve the king's will," intoned Onin.

"True," said Torreg. "Exactly what is taught in the academies, word for word. But tell me: What makes the king and the successor so important?"

Onin was speechless. He had never stopped to consider it in such a fashion. "Well, the king leads us . . . and protects the kingdom . . . and keeps the peace. Each king is chosen as successor by the previous king and represents the best of the Great Families. This ensures a blood descendant of the gods occupies the throne. It has always been the way of the Heights."

"Exactly what is taught in the temples and chapels of the city. Tell me, what is the king's name?"

Onin was surprised by the sudden change in direction. "What?" he stammered.

"His name. What is it?" asked Torreg, unperturbed.

Bolg appeared to be enjoying Onin's discomfort.

"I don't know. He doesn't need a name; he's the king," concluded Onin.

"Have you ever met him or spoken to him? Have you ever seen him?"

Onin fidgeted in his seat before admitting, "No."

"How can a man who is never seen be a leader?" asked Torreg.

Onin had no answer to that, and it made him uneasy. Torreg wasn't finished, however, and persisted with his questions.

"How does the king protect the kingdom and keep the peace?"

"He does that through the Guard," Onin breathed. He was relieved to have an answer to that one. "We go to the Midlands to advance the king's interests there, like when we met."

"Again, that is true," said Torreg. "But earlier, didn't we establish that the true purpose of the Guard is to protect the king and the successor? I've already spoken to you about the state of discipline here in the palace. No one has taken a threat to the king as a serious matter in a long time."

"No one has threatened the king in recent memory," countered Onin. "Which is not a bad thing."

"So if a region hasn't suffered through drought in many years, would you consider it wise for them to forgo stockpiling the surplus?"

"No, that would be foolish," said Onin.

"That's my thinking in this case as well," replied Torreg. "Just because it hasn't happened in a long time doesn't mean it can't happen. Go back and check the old histories. The early days of the Heights were filled with strife and conflict between the Great Families. Kings have been assassinated in the past, as unthinkable as it is today. The mortality of the king is what makes the choosing of a successor so important. What lengths would the Great Families go to if the throne were up for the taking?

"The king keeps the peace in the Heights by simply existing. Otherwise, the rivalries between the Great Families would have the streets running red with blood, I am sure of it. It's also why my deployment to the Midlands lasted so long."

"What?" Onin was confused again. "How did that lead to you getting reassigned?"

"Some of us in the Guard believe our original duty trumps all others," said Torreg. "We exist to protect the king and successor. Over time, we have become the king's private army, to advance his ambitions in the Midlands. At any given point, the vast majority of our numbers are out of the city, stationed in the Midlands, whereas the Great Families keep the bulk of their fighting men in the Heights. Any house could challenge the Guards protecting the king."

"Unthinkable," said Onin. "Who would do that?"

"Exactly what most say, both within and outside of the Guard," said Torreg. "Why waste valuable manpower and resources protecting against an event which can never happen? Better that we be deployed to the Midlands, where we will serve the good of the kingdom, instead of lounging around the palace. In my early days as captain, I pushed the limits on the issue, and as a 'lesson,' the grand marshal sent me on extended duty to the Midlands so that I might 'learn the value of our activities there.' The man is insufferably superior. But I digress. The point is, all these years later, I am still of the same mind. We must not neglect our original purpose, and that is the exact state of things currently."

Onin tried to absorb all of this. He had never been politically minded and found it difficult to grasp some of the principles at work. "So the order is under pressure from the Great Families to place more and more emphasis on duty in the Midlands?"

"That or eliminate the order altogether," said Torreg. "Yes, I know it also sounds unthinkable, but trust me, there are those that do more than think it; they voice the opinion. But I am not willing to let us be shifted to active duty in the lands below, the lot of us."

Bolg interjected, "It would turn us from an order of guards to a standing army."

"Exactly," said Torreg. "We live to serve the king, but we serve him best by protecting him." He seemed to hear a sound and looked at the door anxiously. "This is why I fought so hard to get the palace detail. I want to restore discipline and purpose to the Guards here. I want the both of you to join me here."

"You can count on me," said Onin. "But why all the secrecy?"

"There are Guards stationed here already who have no eye for the king's safety but a great interest in their own political future. The Guard is not their vocation but a stepping-stone to greater things. They are exactly the kind of men I want removed, but also those who can exact the greatest retribution on me. They have power and connections. I might not find myself commander of the palace guard for long. For that reason, we must proceed cautiously."

Bolg spoke up again. "How are you going to remove them? It's difficult to act against men with power and connections."

"I have a plan," said Torreg. "With a little effort, I won't need to remove them. The king will do it for me. Here's how."

Bolg and Onin listened closely as Torreg revealed his plan. It was risky, bold, and impetuous, despite Torreg's own call for caution. Onin was quite happy with it.

* * *

Resplendent colors graced the palace garden in the morning light. Indeed, it had been designed to present three distinct views, for the morning, afternoon, and twilight hours. The selection of exotic and colorful blooms were carefully arranged to offer breathtaking colors at any hour of the day, complemented by natural lighting, along with decorative walls, stone benches, and marble walkways winding throughout the grounds. The walkways meandered and interwove but came together to provide a main thoroughfare through the center of the garden. The outer walls were high and covered with a celebration of flowering vines and more than a few grape-bearing varieties. However, like any other thing of great beauty, daily exposure caused its grandeur to wear away on those so exposed, and with great boredom, the Guards Mekon and Henin surveyed the splendor before them.

The two men were passing the time with inane talk. They did not often agree with one another, so they would descend into argument on most occasions, but today they lacked the energy and will to do so. However, the previous night had proven a windfall for Mekon when his favored hound had won the primary race that day, and he had offered to share drinks with Henin. The pair had gotten carried away with themselves early in the night, and it had turned out to be a long, long boisterous night before Mekon's coin ran out.

Mekon didn't actually like Henin. He was a two-faced womanizer with a loose tongue, but Mekon wanted to be in his good graces. Henin, whatever his faults, would inherit a wealthy estate, replete with a splendid manor and significant holdings in the Midlands. He would also inherit responsibility for his unmarried sister, a plain-looking and simple-minded girl who served as nursemaid to their sick mother during her waning years. She would no doubt command a significant dowry and link the two families by marriage. Until then, Henin would habitually burn through his allowance from the estate and his wages from the Guard. Mekon knew his offer would be well received, and he considered his winnings well spent.

The night's revelry had taken its toll on the two of them. When they reported for duty with the sunrise, the two had been informed the king would be in their part of the palace today. The king often visited the gardens in the morning, so the two struggled to look fit, should he arrive without warning. Otherwise, the two men would have taken this opportunity to stretch themselves out on the lush, green grass and sleep away the rebuke of their debauchery. As such, they remained on their feet and at their posts. Even still, the two struggled to keep their eyes open.

As the sun rose fully above the high walls of the garden to pierce the eyes of the two beleaguered men, Mekon was surprised to see a dark shape scramble over the top of the high wall, and begin to climb down the other side, using the vines as handholds. As Mekon blinked and squinted to see more clearly, he could tell it was a man dressed in black leather armor and covered in ragged black furs. He also swore the figure was wearing some sort of white mask. Before he could decide if his eyes were playing tricks on him, the figure had reached the bottom and turned to face them. Even at this distance, Mekon recognized the mask as a crude skull shape, like the ones merchants would sell, claiming them to be real Jaga shaman masks. The figure drew two wooden practice swords and hoisted them in challenge.

"Mekon," said Henin. He continued hesitantly, even doubtfully. "I think we're under attack."

"Impossible," said Mekon.

In defiance of Mekon's assertion, the black-clad figure threw its head back and released a hideous cry, like a madman screaming for blood. The figure charged them with wooden swords at the ready. Both men stood motionless as the strange apparition loomed in their vision. Mekon realized the man rushing toward them was built like an ox. He suddenly remembered the sword at his side.

Mekon's hand shot to the hilt of his sword, and he drew with all the speed he could muster, but he felt as slow as dripping molasses. Henin was completely stunned, and remained stationary even as the bearlike assailant collided with him shoulder-first. Henin went sailing through the air until his legs collided with a stone bench, causing him to tumble over it backward. The palace Guard collapsed in a heap and lay still.

Mekon had his sword in hand and turned his gaze away from his fallen comrade just in time to parry a powerful blow from the fur-clad warrior. Mekon raised his light, polished shield to parry the follow-up strike from the other wooden blade. Little more than a decorative piece, the shield crumpled under the first blow, and Mekon cried out in pain as he stumbled back.

Other Guards, four in number, arrived at the garden's entrance, having been alerted by the cries and crashing sounds. They rushed to confront the savage attacker, who met them head-on with a charge of his own. The man was deft of hand and quick for his size and easily parried the clumsy attacks of the Guards. With each parry, the black-clad man would lash out with the other hand and strike a resounding blow. One by one, the Guards fell away to land in a heap on the ground. One lay completely still with a dented helmet. Others clutched some extremity or curled into balls to nurse ribs under dented breastplates. The decorative armor of the palace Guards, though impressive looking, proved ineffective against even hardwood practice swords.

More guards arrived, this time at least eight; Mekon couldn't exactly tell. They hesitated, looking first at the huge fur-covered attacker then at the fallen Guardsmen strewn about the area. Before they could decide whether or not to attack, the black bear of a man took the initiative and lunged for them. These Guards were slightly better prepared and managed to mount a successful defense at first, but the fur-clad assailant flailed about with his wooden cudgels with such ferocity that the Guards found no opening to counterattack. The savage raider cleared a space around him with wide, swinging blows then suddenly switched tactics and crouched to strike at the legs of the Guardsmen. Two of them fell, clutching their shins and screaming in pain.

The attacker took two steps and came to rest on top of a stone bench. One of the Guards advanced on him with a series of wild swings, but the black bear deftly parried and sent the man tumbling to the ground with a ringing strike to the helmet. Another Guard circled defensively, trying to keep a wide hedge between himself and the imposing figure. With a sharp cry of exertion, the black bear jumped over the hedge and planted both oversized boots in the surprised Guardsman's chest. The Guard struck the ground with terrific force, and the air whooshed from his lungs.

The black-clad attacker landed on the opposite side of the hedge, flat on his back. Sensing a moment of opportunity, yet another Guard stabbed desperately at him, only to have his attack batted aside with ease. The Guard underestimated the reach of the big man, and his legs were swept from underneath him by a sideways kick from the intruder. Quicker than Mekon thought possible, the brute of a man rolled to his feet with swords at the ready.

The remaining Guardsmen, having lost half their number, lost their nerve as well. They turned and fled into the palace, crying out for archers to take the man down from a distance. The black-clad attacker started to pursue them but stopped short, relaxing into a casual stance. He then began to stroll nonchalantly for the entrance leading from the garden to the palace proper.

Something stirred inside Mekon, watching this man walk into the palace unopposed. A sudden inner spark turned into a flame, and he clambered to his feet. His arm still ached from the previous blow, possibly broken, but he gritted his teeth and tightened his grip on the sword.

"Hold!" he said with as much authority as he could muster. "Hold in the name of the king!"

The black-clad figure stopped in his tracks and stiffened visibly then slowly turned his skull mask to look over his shoulder at Mekon, who stood boldly before him, brandishing his sword. After an appraising moment, the bearlike man turned to face Mekon. With a flourish, the savage raider of the palace raised his swords in a formal salute.

Slightly confused but reacting as his training dictated, Mekon returned the salute. The dark warrior attacked with both swords, one swinging high while other swung low. Mekon reacted by ducking beneath the high strike, while making a short cut toward his enemy's midsection. He was rewarded with a slice across the big man's abdomen. Unfortunately, the boiled leather and thick furs protected the large adversary's torso, and the dark warrior suffered but a flesh wound.

Mekon, however, had no defense against the low strike. The powerful blow swept Mekon's legs out from under him, so he landed on his hands and knees with a jolt. His blade spun from his grasp, and the fur-clad man kicked him in the exposed midsection. The blow sent Mekon flying into a bush filled with famously beautiful blooms and notoriously thorny stems. The kick stole the wind from Mekon's lungs despite the breastplate he wore, and the persistent pain he felt at the impact point indicated the breastplate was dented and poking into his flesh as a consequence. Stars danced at the edges of his vision, and his head spun as he gasped for breath.

"That's enough," came a barking voice, one familiar to Mekon. The fur-clad attacker immediately stopped his attack and replaced his two practice blades in his belt. The big man then removed the crude skull mask. Mekon was shocked to see a Midlander and realized he knew the man, at least casually. He was a Guardsman newly reassigned to the palace detail, but Mekon's head swam too much to produce a name.

Another Guardsman entered the garden, sword in hand. Mekon, even through his haze, recognized the markings of the new commander. Mekon had never met Torreg but knew his reputation.

"That went as I expected, for the most part," said Torreg. He took a long, slow look about himself, then sheathed his weapon. Guards littered the entrance to the garden like so many dolls left by children after their play. Mekon wondered what in the world was going on.

The fur-clad Midlander nodded. "It's sad, really. There's not a bad swordsman among them, but they're terribly out of practice. Some of them seem like they haven't sparred since graduating the academy."

Mekon felt a slight pang of guilt. He, himself, never sparred and couldn't frankly remember the last time he had drawn his blade, let alone fought with it. Certainly not since he had joined the palace detail; but then, that was the whole point of joining the palace detail, wasn't it?

At that moment, another black-clad, fur-covered figure with a white mask and pair of practice swords jumped from behind a nearby hedge with a hoarse battle cry. The figure was very much like the first attacker but lacked the imposing stature, closer to average, by Mekon's estimation. His mask was different as well; instead of a skull, it was a plain, featureless face.

"You're late, Bolg," said Torreg. "The exercise is over."

The second raider pulled off the mask and furs covering his head. The man was ugly in the extreme, with craggy features and a bulbous nose with a nasty scar across it. Mekon remembered him as the new captain added to palace detail. The ugly captain cast an annoyed glance at the Midlander.

"You couldn't wait for me, lad?" said Captain Bolg.

The Midlander shrugged in response. "I followed the plan," he said in his defense. "You said 'start the attack just as the sun crests the outer wall.' That's what I did. When I got on the other side, you were nowhere to be seen, and I was in no position to wait. What happened to you?"

"That wall is higher than I expected," said the captain, jerking a thumb over his shoulder. "And I'm not as young as I used to be. Still, I would have thought you'd have left me one or two, out of politeness's sake."

Commander Torreg laughed. "There will be plenty of opportunities for you, old friend," he said "Just wait until next time."

Next time? thought Mekon. He decided he'd had enough of the day and laid his head down in the thorny foliage beneath him. Within moments, blissful sleep claimed him.

Chapter 20

Never underestimate the danger of a hungry dragon or a scorned woman.
--dragon rider's adage

* * *

The leaves of autumn burst upon the landscape with their customary riot of color as the summer wound to a close. Sparrowport had always been most beautiful in the autumn; the variety of trees within and around the town provided an expansive range of hues. Onin contemplated the familiar view afforded by his childhood home. The beauty was different than the Heights, simpler, less grandiose, but all the more pleasing for its unassuming ubiquity.

The Durantis house had hardly changed. He knew most of the servants; the exceptions were the younger ones. Very little changed with the staff over the years, and they seemed to remember many of Onin's habits, falling easily into step during his short stay.

His father, Zorot, had been sleeping fitfully in the bed nearby. The old man had asked for his bed to be moved to better enjoy the view from his window. His illness had progressed steadily until it confined him to his bed, and his servants took great lengths to make him comfortable but with little success.

Zorot awoke with a sputtering cough. Instantly his steward was by his side, holding a cup of bitter tea to his lips. The trade ambassador winced and puckered his lips at the taste.

Onin tried to reconcile the frail man lying before him with the smiling father who raised him. Zorot had always been slight of frame, but the wasting sickness had made him wispy as fog. His entire body rattled with the coughing fit, and he slumped with fatigue once it had subsided.

"Onin?" asked Zorot wearily.

"I'm here," said Onin. He knelt next to the bed. His father grasped his hand tightly.

"I'm glad for your presence. I find it comforting," said the old man. Zorot's face broke into a grin. "How is Yolan?" said the old man, his gaze sharp. "You hardly mention her. Is she all right?"

Onin gave his father a tight-lipped smile. "Yolan is fine, Father. She is as beautiful as ever, and she keeps the household running with no help from Torreg or myself. She is a smart businesswoman."

"But as a wife, she leaves something to be desired?"

Onin stiffened but forced himself to relax before responding. "I . . . don't want to talk about it," he stammered.

"No surprise to me," said Zorot, his smile soft and forgiving. "You've ever been the quiet one where your internal workings are concerned. But you also can't lie to me about this. I can see it written on your face whenever I bring her up."

Onin's shoulders slumped and he hung his head at his father's words. He'd never had much success hiding things from his father.

Zorot placed a reassuring hand on Onin's arm. "Marriage is the greatest challenge a man can undertake," said Zorot. "Say what you will about leading armies and fighting wars; it's the men who know how to talk to their wives who should be immortalized in song. It is a far more rare skill."

Onin chuckled. "I'd rather fight a band of Jaga raiders again than face down Yolan in a bad mood," said the big man. "Her gaze could scorch a dragon's scales."

"Surely she's not always so baleful," said the old man. "She must smile sometimes."

"I'm sure she does," said Onin. "But it seems to stop when I enter the room. I can barely remember what her teeth look like." Onin forced a smile, but his father wasn't fooled by it.

"Oh, my son," said Zorot. "What a lot you've drawn. So much good fortune wrapped around a great misfortune. Forgive me; I did not know your marriage would be so sour. I thought for sure the two of you would come together with time. I'm sorry for the unhappiness you've endured."

Onin placed his other hand on top of his father's where it rested on his forearm. "It's not all bad, Father," said Onin. "You had no idea, as you said yourself. And there is much good fortune in it. I serve as a Guard in the Heights and am part of a Great Family to boot. I see verdant dragons up close almost every day. It's like my boyhood dream come true. If the price is a beautiful but prickly woman, then I can accept that."

Zorot looked at his son with regret and hope. "I still wish you would know love, Onin," said his father. "I loved your mother so much. She's been gone many years now, but I still can't imagine my life without her. I want you to know that kind of happiness, my son. It makes everything else worthwhile."

Zorot's voice grew lower as he spoke until he was muttering. Onin had to lean forward to catch his words before his father lapsed into complete silence. At first Zorot was so still that Onin began to fear the worst, but then the old man emitted a light snore. Onin left him to his sleep and quietly crept from the bedchamber, stopping to converse with the physician on the way.

"Not long now," said the family physician. He had been the old man's most constant companion the past few weeks. "Sometime during the night, I believe."

* * *

Onin decided to take a walk to consider what had passed between them. Just as his father had stated, Onin hoped he and Yolan would grow to love one another as time passed, and he hadn't given up on it yet. Many of the older Guards spoke of early difficulties in marriage, but an improvement as time passed. He hoped things would work that way in his case.

Onin walked familiar paths from years past, taking in the sights his childhood home had to offer. Surprisingly little had changed, save a new coat of paint here and there, and many new faces. Some of the young adults Onin could recognize as children he had once known. They had grown into adolescents, and most of them worked at a trade. He had the sudden sense of age, he mused. Now a father in his own right, he prepared to say farewell to his own. The world around him changed, and he with it.

A piercing scream pulled him to the here and now abruptly. He spun to see the commotion and gave a start as a feral dragon rose into the sky with a woman in its claws. There had been no roar, no sound. The attack caught the town by surprise.

However, screams and shouts could be heard from all directions at varying distances. Other feral dragons swooped and attacked, snatching people and horses from the streets of Sparrowport. Onin counted at least a dozen ferals; rampaging dragons seemed to be everywhere. Onin crouched beneath a nearby oak tree. It wouldn't provide much protection, but he hoped to remain hidden.

The streets of Sparrowport were in chaos. Screams filled the air with unintelligible cacophony. Onin peered around the trunk of a tree to see a dragon swooping in his direction. Several people ran about, and portions of the sky were blotted out by black smoke. The dragons' sudden assault had started fires throughout the city, presumably by knocking over candles and cook fires within the buildings. While the dragons continued to rampage, the city's residents could not mount an effective effort to stop the fires; they would rage unabated, threatening the entire town.

Onin could see a pair of children running through the street in a panic, seemingly unable to decide where to flee. The incoming dragon would have them for sure.

Onin bolted from his hiding place, pushing himself for every ounce of speed he could muster. He felt slow--too slow--and could only watch as the dark figure of fanged death zoomed toward them. His lungs burned with the effort, and he forced himself to focus on his goal instead.

He reached the first child and scooped her up without missing a step. Roughly four years old, she fit neatly under his arm. He spun to grab the second child, an older boy. Onin hoisted the boy onto his shoulder and ran for the nearest cover: a wagon just fifteen feet away. He took three long strides and dived under wagon. Onin rolled over to land on his back, still cradling the children in his arms, and turned over again to shield the children with his body. They were prone and under the wagon when the dragon struck. The world went momentarily dark as the beast's shadow passed over them.

The wagon disappeared in a rush of air above. Onin looked up to see the wagon dangling from the dragon's claws. The contents as well as one of the wheels tumbled down. Onin rose then ran for cover again, keeping the children nestled under his torso as much as possible. He felt several objects strike him as they fled but nothing heavy enough to deter their progress, thank the gods. He came to a sudden stop when a latched trunk landed in his path. The sturdy chest remained unbroken, but the heavy lid flew open with the impact. Onin saw the chest contained a large round object of dark green coloration. Except for the color difference, it looked just like the dragon eggs Onin had seen in the hatchery.

He ducked into the nearest alley between two buildings, hoping the feral didn't have enough interest in them to follow. He stopped near the end of the alley and put the children down. They were surprisingly well composed. Their faces were streaked with dirt and tears, but they watched him attentively.

"Go!" he shouted and pointed down the alley, away from here. "Find a place to hide!"

The children did as instructed and scurried away as fast their legs would carry them. The older boy held the little girl's hand, practically dragging her along. Her voice carried above the noise. "Thank you!"

Onin raced back to the alley to see if his eyes had deceived him or not. He arrived just in time to watch two men carry the trunk into the adjacent building.

The sun disappeared again, and Onin instinctively looked to the sky. He watched as one of the feral dragons landed on the building where the trunk, and presumably the egg, had been taken. A fearful thought took shape in his mind.

He plunged around the corner and ran for the entrance to the building, a warehouse not far from his father's. The feral dragon peered over the edge, its long snout taking deep, probing sniffs. It spied Onin as he made it through the entrance, and it gave an angry screech. The long neck extended down until the scaly snout entered the warehouse. Onin dived to his right and pressed his back against the wall. He looked around desperately for cover or escape, but he could see only a pair of men on the opposite side of the warehouse, holding the trunk between them. One of the men tossed a torch on the floor of the warehouse; the straw strewn about lit quickly. The other smashed a lantern on the ground; the resulting spread of oil turned the warehouse floor into a bonfire.

The feral dragon's snout caught in the first gout of flames, and it jerked back with a sharp cry of pain. Its head disappeared from the warehouse for a few moments; Onin took the opportunity to rush over to the other men. He pressed himself against the wall. Holding a hand in front of his face to ward off the heat, he pushed his way around to where they waited. Both men had swords in their hands.

"Back off now," said one of them. "This crate belongs to us."

"Is that a feral dragon egg?" yelled Onin. "You fools! It's obvious the dragons are here for the egg!"

Proving his statement, the dragon pushed back into the warehouse with an angry roar. With some effort, it pinpointed the three men through the smoke. The dragon roared its fury at them from across the inferno.

"You've put us all in danger!" cried Onin. "Give the egg back!"

"Not a chance," said the first man. He gave a barking laugh. "This egg is worth its weight in gold and more. It stays with me."

Onin drew himself up to his full height and pointed a solitary finger at the man. "I am Onin of the Guard," he pronounced. "In the name of the king, return that egg!"

The first man grimaced and lunged at Onin with his sword. Onin easily sidestepped the attack and drove his elbow into the man's face. He deftly snatched the blade from the man's hand as the egg poacher crumpled to the ground, unconscious. Onin grasped the hilt of the sword firmly and pointed it directly at the other man guarding the trunk.

The second egg poacher had no fight in him and dropped his sword in terror.

"It's all his fault, sir," he said. "There's a guy who hunts in the Jaga who knows where to find 'em, and then he brings 'em to us, and then we sell 'em up high." Having grown up in the Midlands, Onin recognized the term. "Up high" meant selling something to the Heights. He would have pressed for more information, but the dragon's roar to his left reminded him he didn't have the time.

Onin rushed to the trunk and grasped hold of the handles. With a mighty grunt, he hefted it into the air over his head. Turning to face the entrance, Onin took three long steps, striding straight into the knee-deep fire before him, before launching the crate across the rest of the flames to land in the entrance of the warehouse. The dragon watched attentively as it sailed through the air to collide with the ground and tumble out into the street. Once again, the lid flew open, and this time the egg bounced out to roll in the street. Onin stumbled backward to escape the flames and smoke. It took him several long moments to pat the smoldering parts of his pant legs and boots until there was no danger of fire.

By the time he looked back at the entrance, the feral dragon took the egg up in one of its claws. Its mighty wings flapped, taking it aloft, and it disappeared from view above. Onin made his way around the flames, slowly and carefully. He'd been on fire enough for one day.

Reaching the street, Onin turned his gaze to the sky. To the south, dragons flew back to the Jaga. The attack ended as quickly as it began. The cries of the wounded could be heard in every direction, and raging fires burned uncontrolled, like the one in the warehouse behind him. Onin spared no thought for his fatigue or burns; there were others who needed help more, and he would see to them.

A group of men arrived to check on the warehouse, and Onin began trying to organize some effort to control the fire. He found the first man, the one he'd knocked unconscious, still lying in a heap near the back of the warehouse. The other man, the accomplice, had escaped, however. Onin could make sure at least one of them would answer for this act.

But he could also afford no time for those thoughts; instead he focused on the long night ahead of putting out fires, rescuing the wounded, and making sure the dragons were truly gone.

* * *

The news of the dragon attack did not seem to affect Zorot much. He simply took it in stride like most unfortunate events. The following morning, his servants tried to wake him, but the old man could not be roused. They fetched Onin immediately, and he rushed through the halls. With closed eyes and lips turned upward in a wry grin, his father looked peaceful.

It was a good death, Onin decided. It brought him no joy, but at least his father didn't have to suffer much at the end.

Onin spent the next few days settling affairs while awaiting his flight back to the Heights. With his father gone, Sparrowport didn't feel like home anymore. He felt anxious to get back to his family. He intended to keep no holdings in the Midlands and sold everything off as quickly as possible. Money had no real pull for Onin. All of the proceeds from his sales would be put in an account in the Heights.

Onin had taken his father's words to heart. Getting along might be difficult, but he desperately wanted his marriage to be a loving one. He vowed to his father's memory that he would find love, just as his father wanted.

Chapter 21

The Protector shall come before, to prepare the way for his Charge. His symbol is the Shield, and he shall know his calling by it.
--excerpt from *Testament of the Augur*

* * *

Onin had scheduled the necessary time to return by way of Dragonport. He preferred it to the harrowing experience of climbing up the dragon harness. Dragonport had enough altitude that the dragons could hover in place for extended periods. This allowed passengers to embark in a less arduous way. There were about twenty or so seats available on the dragon's back, and despite the significant cost, the seats were usually full on each voyage to or from the Heights. Not many souls could manage the task of negotiating the harness, but the Guard took pride in it. Onin regarded it as an unnecessary risk; several Guards met their end by falling from the harness each year. He had survived too much to risk his skin on pride.

So Onin waited the extra days for a seat on the tierre. Dragonport provided an ample number of cozy and warm inns catering to the travelers. He spent his time with his feet at the fire, sipping ale and remembering Zorot. He toasted each memory silently, raising his tankard to the fire before drinking.

Onin knew he made the right decision when he climbed aboard the dragon's tierre by way of a narrow wooden gangplank with ropes on either side to serve as handrails. Many of the passengers were natives of the Heights and balked at the thin strip of wood they were expected to cross. Onin just smiled in relief and walked calmly across the plank. Knowing the alternative made it easy for him.

The dragon riders waiting in the tierre nodded approvingly at his boldness. Onin guessed pleading and cajoling nervous people to board got tiresome after a while. He thought it ironic so many, wealthy and otherwise, wanted the distinction of flying adragonback but would balk at the danger when the time came to do it. There was no alternative route to return to the Heights, so it was the gangplank or live in the Midlands forever. Onin imagined most would choose to board by way of the harness than stay in the Midlands.

Once the passengers were on board and tied to the hard wooden benches with rough hemp ropes, the gangplank retracted and the dragon riders returned to their respective stations. Two clambered out of the tierre and out of sight. Onin guessed they must be checking the harness that kept the tierre in place. The flight commander, the highest-ranking dragon rider on the flight, surveyed her crew and passengers and, apparently satisfied with the preparations, pulled the horn from her waist.

"Clear!" she cried. She raised the horn to her lips and waited for the response from the dock.

"Clear!" came the reply from the dock master.

The flight commander blew a strong, hollow note from the horn. The dragon lifted its enormous head and hooted in response. The massive wings tilted slightly, and the great beast veered away from the mountain peak faster than Onin would have thought possible. Others were shocked by it; he could tell by the gasps and barely contained yells from the other passengers. The dragon banked steeply to the right, providing all of the occupants of the tierre with a direct view of the ground below. Already the forested mountainside was far beneath them. Onin felt a thrill at the view.

The verdant dragon turned its heading toward the Heights and leveled off, much to the relief of the majority of the passengers. One old woman, from a Great Family judging by her dress, voiced her displeasure to the flight commander in no uncertain terms. The senior dragon rider took it in stride, but Onin detected a hint of a smile. Sensing his gaze, she looked to the left and locked eyes with him. Each could only grin wider, and this sparked a fresh tirade from the aged woman.

Onin could not tear his gaze away from the woman piloting the dragon. While not especially beautiful, she looked at Onin in a way that excited him. Her eyes sparkled at him, and he felt drawn to her. He considered talking to her but had no idea what he would say. He also thought of Yolan and his recent promise to himself. If he sincerely wanted to improve his marriage, then he shouldn't consider talking to this woman. He had seen enough to know it always turned out messy in the end, no matter how innocently it may have begun.

Onin pulled his gaze away from the flight commander and settled in to stare at the landscape as it drifted by far below them. Once again, the majesty of flight took hold of him, and the worries and cares of his life seemed to drop away, falling from the back of the dragon. He could see the grand mountain of the Heights far in the distance.

The wind blew cold and strong due to the altitude, and the dragon riders dispensed blankets to the passengers. Onin took comfort in the briskness of it and leaned back in his bench contentedly. It wasn't long before Onin fell asleep, his head nodding forward onto his chest, even as the wind whipped his hair over his shoulders.

The dream came upon him like a great wave, terrible in its intensity. The sky turned blood red, and the dragons plummeted. His view came upon the egg with the familiar shield-shaped symbol. The urgency of the dream made his heart race. The dream incorporated the old woman of the underbelly who had nursed him back to health. She talked in the same manner as always, never addressing him directly, but he felt everything she said was intended for his ears.

"His heart aches but his pain has only begun. No one can carry the burden for him. It is his to bear alone."

The sky was filled with dragons, graceful, scaled shapes darting across the winds. Dragon fighting dragon, such a terrible battle. Blood fell like raindrops to drench the earth below. The lone nest. The solitary egg. The shield marking. The mismatched eyes.

The egg's shell cracked.

Onin woke with a start. He glanced around but none of the other passengers seemed to notice his discomfort. Most were asleep or gazing idly over the terrain. His mind in turmoil, he grasped for some way to make sense of the strange dreams. Now the images had progressed. For the first time, the egg in his dream had cracked. What could it mean?

Onin pulled the blanket around his shoulders, feeling chilled. He passed the rest of his flight in quiet contemplation. For no reason he could discern, he was very anxious to get home.

* * *

"This is nonsense," said Commander Torreg. "How can the Guard function without proper equipment?"

"The Guard is properly equipped, Commander," said Sensi with a cool tone. Already Sensi could see frustration on the man's face.

Sensi rarely had the opportunity to enjoy the good weather in the palace gardens. He had sought out Torreg at the palace to deal with the requisition and located him in the gardens, drilling the palace guards. The drills were conducted by a scar-faced man new to the palace detail, a subordinate of Torreg's from his time in the Midlands, according to rumor. Sensi indicated the training men with a wave of his hand.

"I see arms and armor on every man present," said Sensi. "I would call that properly equipped."

The air split with the clatter of armor as one of the Guards struck the ground. Sensi thought the sound not unlike an armful of pots and pans dropped down a flight of stone steps. One of the trainers barked out a rebuke and hoisted the fallen man to his feet. The now-risen Guardsman looked shaky on his feet, but the trainer was relentless, shoving him back into the fray.

Torreg motioned to the nearest Guardsman, who dutifully approached him and stood at attention. Torreg grabbed the sword from the Guard's hand. He held it in a steady grip and extended the blade for Sensi to examine. It was brightly polished and clean. The blade was acid-etched with intricate patterns, and the hilt covered with a gold veneer. An emerald was set in the pommel.

"It is fine looking," said Sensi. "Exactly as it should be."

"It's garbage," said Torreg. "Pretty to look at but rubbish in a fight. The balance is completely wrong. The blade is finely decorated, but the steel is substandard and prone to breaking. The additional weight of the gold on the hilt makes the entire weapon slow and cumbersome, not quick and accurate. In short, it's a showpiece, nothing more. No warrior would trust his life to one of these in battle."

"Anticipating a battle at the palace?" asked Sensi. His lips curled into a snide grin. His statement had exactly the effect he had hoped; Torreg reddened visibly.

"Perhaps," said the commander stiffly. Another loud clatter punctuated by a yelp of pain came from the garden. Sensi glanced over to see another Guard lying inside one of the many flowering shrubs that decorated the garden.

"So you would deplete the stores of the king for a battle which may never come?" asked Sensi. "Sounds unwise."

"No," said Torreg. "By law, the king's storehouse is to be held in reserve for emergencies. What I seek is to properly arm and train the men dedicated to his safety."

"Again, the men I see here seem properly equipped," began Sensi.

"Again, these blades are worthless in a real fight," countered Torreg. "But I wouldn't expect you to understand." The commander gave him a smug smile, certain he had the advantage.

"The cost associated with your request is beyond reason," said Sensi without batting an eye. "The amount of iron needed would drain funds from other things equally important to the king's welfare." Sensi fixed him with a sly look before continuing. "But I wouldn't expect you to understand."

The rebuttal hit home. Sensi watched the anger and resentment flash across Torreg's face in an instant. Sensi, however, maintained his composure.

"I can fill your requisition, in part," said Sensi. "But the full order will need to wait until the price is acceptable. Until then, you will use the arms at your disposal."

Torreg looked ready to scream. Secretly Sensi was quite pleased with himself. So many years had been spent being overlooked in favor of the fighting men. Now that he had authority over the treasury, he took great pleasure in pulling the purse strings of men who had constantly condescended to him. It was a trivial thing, really, but he enjoyed it so much.

Torreg composed himself with difficulty and continued with his objections. "The palace detail would be hard pressed to defend against an organized attack with only these at their disposal. What good will it do to equip a third of them?"

"It will keep the financial underpinnings of the kingdom moving instead of wasting capital to prepare for an attack that is not going to happen," said Sensi. "You have failed to convince me this is a vital purchase."

"I'll bring charges against you," said Torreg. His eyes narrowed threateningly. "I'll have you tossed out on your ear for denying the Guard."

Sensi returned his venomous look, but his tone remained calm. "Go ahead. I am interested to see who the lord chancellor thinks is in the right."

Sensi rose to his feet abruptly and gave Commander Torreg a perfunctory bow before withdrawing. As he walked past the drilling guards, one of their number was struck a ringing blow and collapsed in a heap before him. Sensi paused momentarily then nonchalantly stepped over the fallen man and into the palace with Torreg staring daggers at his back.

* * *

Upon returning to the Heights, Onin went to the Manespike hatchery straight away. He did not understand the sense of urgency that gripped him, but since the disturbing dream, Onin had been unable to think of anything else but the clutch of eggs he knew waited there.

The atmosphere at the hatchery was quiet, even somber. There was none of the energetic bustle common when a clutch was being incubated. The lack of excitement worried Onin, and he sought out the master incubator for an update.

His fears were confirmed by the pile of broken shells near the incubation rack. It had been a generous clutch of eggs, more than twenty, but less than half remained. Broken shells had been meticulously gathered into large urns, and the slimy yolks had been gathered as well. As Onin entered the chamber, he witnessed one of the great eggs being cracked open with a small hammer. The viscous fluid flowed out, to be gathered into a bowl. The contents of the bowl were distributed to an array of glass bottles, which were then sealed tightly.

"What is going on here?" Onin exclaimed, his shock palpable. The workers in the room stopped in the middle of their activities to look at him uncertainly. The master incubator approached him, extending his hands in supplication.

"We do as ordered by our mistress," he said. His voice was steady, but his eyes betrayed his anxiety. "She ordered the entire clutch destroyed and the materials salvaged."

"Destroyed? Preposterous!" exclaimed Onin in disbelief. "Those were healthy eggs. The colors were right. The shells were healthy and solid. Why did this happen?"

"The colors turned while you were away, my lord," said the master incubator. The man's expression softened through his anxiety. "If I may, please accept my condolences on your father's illness--"

Onin interrupted him with a wave of the hand. He was normally gracious with the incubator, but he was not inclined toward niceties at the moment. He inspected the remaining eggs for the signs he had learned about. The coloring was indeed dark, but the shells were still strong and supple, not brittle as expected.

"These shells are not ruined," he said. He tapped one with his knuckle, the sound it made reassuringly solid. "Why destroy them already?"

"The mistress has ordered it," repeated the master incubator in a pained voice. "I informed her that the colors had gone dark but the shells were solid. She made the decision to cut our losses early." Onin watched him as he explained and thought he saw recrimination in the man's eyes while explaining Yolan's uncompromising orders.

Onin considered the remaining eggs, turning them about to inspect the shells. It was then he spied a dark splotch on one shell, and the sight of it made his heart skip a beat.

There it was before him, come to life directly from his dreams, the shield-shaped marking plain to his eye. Onin's blood froze as he ran his fingers over the outline of the marking. He cradled it in his hands like a precious jewel.

"This one," said Onin. He turned to look at the master incubator. "You shall leave this one intact. I claim it for myself."

"The mistress gave specific instructions that they should all be destroyed," said the master incubator. He would have continued, but Onin cut him short.

"I will deal with my wife," said Onin. He set his jaw grimly. "But this egg now belongs to me. Move it back to the incubator."

Chapter 22

Duty is an unforgiving mistress. That is why so many fail to heed it.
--Doren, teacher at Scaleback Academy

* * *

Onin tapped the egg lightly at regular intervals as he spun it in its berth. He pressed his ear to the shell, listening for any hint of a flaw in its structure. Despite the poor coloring, the egg grew in a healthy fashion, and the shell remained thick and sturdy. Its berth was heated from coals beneath, making the smooth surface warm to the touch as Onin rotated it continuously, per the master incubator's instructions.

Onin stared at the strange shieldlike marking on the egg. It pulled at him in a way that was comforting and disturbing all at once. He couldn't avoid a feeling of familiarity with it; he had seen it too many times in his dreams. Nonetheless, it was surreal to have his dreams come to life, to hold the egg in his hands. It made him think of other things in his dreams that would not be so wonderful to see in his waking life, such as dragon corpses toppling from the sky by the dozens.

He spent most nights in the hatchery. Only when the egg was under the watchful eye of the master incubator did he dare spend time elsewhere. He feared the egg would be stolen from him, destroyed for its supposed medicinal and cosmetic properties, as had the others in the brood. His encounter in the Midlands had demonstrated the value of dragon eggs, even feral ones, and he refused to allow his dream egg to meet such a fate.

His beard grew long and unkempt over the weeks, and he developed a habit of tugging on it. Whenever he got lost in thought, which was increasingly common, he would grab a handful of the bristles and tug absently. He found it strangely comforting, and sometime during the weeks of watching the egg develop, he decided he would keep it in its bushy state. Long beards were considered uncouth among the Great Families, but Onin felt no particular need to live up to someone else's expectations. All that mattered to him was the egg.

Torreg came to check on him a few times but found him distracted and inattentive. His father-in-law tried to convince him to return to his home and reminded him his wife was waiting for him there. Onin took no notice or simply muttered something about going to see her after the task was finished. No matter how Torreg would protest or plead, Onin would not budge. Hangric also made a point of visiting him in the hatchery but fared no better than Torreg in convincing him to return home. Onin simply would have none of it.

Yolan came to visit him at the hatchery once, after a week had elapsed. She entered the dark heat of the incubation chamber with her usual alluring elegance. Her displeasure became apparent once the smells of sweating humans and rutting dragons assaulted her nostrils. Onin hardly spared her a glance. The egg consumed his attention, even in the face of his wife's ire.

"By the gods, you stink," she said. Her tone implied the unpleasant aroma of the hatchery was solely his responsibility. "When was the last time you bathed?"

Onin didn't answer her question. He knew she didn't really care about that and was only trying to draw him out. He chose silence rather than engage in her game. He knew what she was really about. Sensing his resolve, she went right to the heart of it.

"This egg is sickly," she said, indicating his prize with a vague gesture. "It must be destroyed."

"No," said Onin. "It will hatch."

"You know as well as I do that it will not," she countered. "The striations have covered the entire shell. It even has a huge splotch there." She pointed at the shield-shaped mark. "We waste valuable resources caring for an egg that will never hatch. If we wait any longer, it will lose all value to us. Destroy it now and the remains will help offset our costs."

"No," repeated Onin. "You destroyed the rest of this clutch. You've destroyed every clutch since we've been married. At the slightest imperfection, you're ready to do so. It's no wonder the Manespikes haven't produced a viable dragon in years; you're too focused on selling the eggs for cosmetics and aphrodisiacs."

As was often the case, Yolan's temper flared, and she resorted to violence. Her hand lashed out like a viper, but Onin was prepared. He caught her slim wrist in his beefy hand and held her fast.

"How dare you!" she spit. "You've no idea what it takes to keep our manor afloat. Since our breeders"--she sneered at the shocked attendants-- "lack competence to produce a dragon for sale; I do what I must to bring money to us. If it wasn't for those cosmetics and aphrodisiacs you deride, we would be paupers already."

"What of your family?" asked Onin. "You'll never restore the Manespike reputation without producing good dragons. There's no harm in trying to hatch one egg out of each clutch. Surely the profit lost won't ruin the family estate."

Yolan yanked her arm from his grasp. Her fury so heightened, she seemed on the verge of tears.

"What good is reputation to the poor?" she said. "The Manespikes have a long and notable history as dragon breeders, but maybe that day has passed. We should be looking to new endeavors."

"Dragon breeding has been the family vocation for generations," said

Onin. "Who are you to change that? What would your father say about abandoning such a legacy?"

Yolan gave a bitter laugh. "My father chose to join the Guard because the dragons were not supporting themselves. We needed the money to cover the costs of raising them. When my mother died, father was still stationed in the Midlands, so it was left to me to run the household. Barely more than a girl, I managed a huge pile of debt incurred by my ancestors' *noble* profession." Sarcasm dripped from her tongue.

Onin absently ran his fingers through the bed of warmed sand the egg rested in, the warmth pleasant against his skin. He had no reply for Yolan's words--indeed, he'd never known the difficulties of the family finances. Then he thought back on the squadron of servants who cleaned, cooked, and did all of the work around the manor. Some were frivolous, such as the muscled fan-bearer, but many filled necessary positions. The manor required a full staff, and the resources needed to support so many were increasingly apparent to Onin. Still his stubbornness would not allow him to relent. "One egg will not sink us."

Whatever softening Onin thought he detected in his wife disappeared like a wisp of smoke in a strong breeze. Her expression hardened more than ever, and she spun and fled from the incubation chamber, one hand covering her face.

Onin turned his attention back to the egg. He might be the victor in the moment, but he knew the battle was far from over.

* * *

The dream came and went each time Onin slept, and it interwove itself into his waking life. His days and nights became a string of events surreal in their repetitiveness. He would check the sands, feeling to see if it became too hot or too cold. His fingers wandered the surface of the shell, looking for weaknesses or flaws but finding none. At moments the mismatched eyes appeared to him like a specter left over from his wound-induced fever. His eyes had followed the patterns of the striations so many times, he committed them to memory. In the sporadic moments he would lie down to sleep, invariably next to the egg, even with eyes closed, he was able to reconstruct the patterns in his mind's eye.

The shield he knew best of all. He stared at the strange blotch for untold hours, lost in his own meandering thoughts. Often the child floating on a shield-shaped bed of reeds came to his mind unbidden. He was sure now that he was seeing himself as an infant; it was how he had been found, he knew. The shield was part of him somehow.

The old woman had known about the shield. Indeed, she seemed to know all about the dream. He wondered how she could know the things she did. The idea that the contents of his mind were not private was unnerving. If she knew his dreams, what else might she know? Did the gods grant her preternatural vision? The ancient stories of the Founders were filled with such things.

Onin's musings were interrupted by a sudden movement from the egg. He jumped as it twitched in its berth. The movement was slight at first, but noticeable, and a tapping sound began to emanate from within. The activity became more pronounced, flinging little bits of sand about, and Onin crouched closer, watching with rapt excitement.

"Master Incubator!" he cried. The man rushed to the berth followed by his assistant. They crouched on either side of Onin, anxious to watch the egg wiggle about on the bed of sand.

All three gasped in unison as a crack appeared near the top of the egg's shell. Without thinking, Onin reached out to touch it, but the master incubator placed his own hand in the way.

"Forgive me, my lord," he said in his raspy voice. "But we mustn't disturb the hatching process. If the hatchling is to live, it must escape on its own."

Onin could only nod.

The crack widened and branched further across the surface of the shell until a triangle shape appeared directly over the shield-shaped mark. The piece fluttered in place several times and fell away from the egg. A scaled snout with a minuscule horn on its tip protruded from the hole it left behind. The nostrils flared ever so slightly, and Onin's stomach dropped as the tiny dragon inside took its first breath.

The master incubator let out a burst of happy laughter. "That's a good sign, my lord," said the old man. "It's a small egg, but there's a fighter inside, mark my words."

The cracks spiderwebbing from the hole continued to widen and branch further, and more pieces of the egg began to fall away. Minute wings, soft and wet, unfurled from the sides and flapped to shake away fragments of shell clinging to them. The front of the egg burst open, and the baby dragon plopped face-first into the sand.

Excitement turned to sober concern as the gathered men beheld the misshapen form before them. The creature's spine was malformed, and a distinct hump grew from one shoulder. The general shape of the dragon kept one of its wings at an awkward, ungainly angle.

"Ah, deformed as well as a runt," stated the master incubator with obvious disappointment. "It's doubtful the beast will even be able to fly with that twist in the back."

After a moment, the head rose and shook the sand away. The baby dragon opened its eyes and looked about uncertainly, blinking repeatedly as its eyes adjusted. Onin's heart began to race as he noticed its eyes. One was amber, while the other glittered like a gemstone.

"Can't be." The words escaped from his lips unbidden, barely a whisper.

The tiny dragon lifted its gaze to Onin's. The small eyes burned into his own, and just as in his dream, they superimposed themselves over his vision, as if his dreams had broken free of their confines to be in his waking life. A word came to his mind in that moment, a name, the dragon's name.

Jehregard.

Chapter 23

Sometimes the best things we do are beyond reason and inexplicable even to ourselves. But if my years of experience have taught me anything, it is that our intuition should be heeded. When the heart speaks, listen closely.
--Belond, headmaster at Scaleback Academy

* * *

"Jehregard stays," said Onin. "That's final."

Yolan took his resistance in the usual way: poorly. He watched her face redden, and her eyes flashed with anger. Her hands were at her sides but clenched into fists. Onin was ready to step back if and when she lashed out. However, she stayed her hand and spoke.

"I let you have your egg, and you hatched it just as you wanted," she said. Icicles dripped from her words. "You don't seriously think we're going to keep a deformed runt, do you? So much for restoring the family reputation." Her expression softened and her tone became reasoning, even pleading. Onin was immediately suspicious. "You've tried and I can respect that," she said. Her voice purred soothingly. "But there is no useful purpose for such a thing. We cannot sell it, and for the other breeders to know we've harbored such a pathetic beast would make us the laughingstock of the entire city.

"We gain nothing by letting this pathetic creature live. It must be put down at once, for its own sake as well as ours."

"'Its own sake'?" scoffed Onin. "He has a name: Jehregard. He wants to live as much as you or me. He stays."

Yolan gritted her teeth in frustration. Onin, for his part, was actually beginning to enjoy himself.

"I don't care what you've named him," she grated. "I will not put the household's limited resources to feeding and housing that worthless thing."

Onin merely shrugged in response. "Have it your way," he said. "I'll take care of him myself. He doesn't need your money."

Yolan laughed. "You'll take care of him yourself?" she sneered. "How? Your salary won't even come close to it." He knew there was some truth to that. A growing verdant dragon had a famously voracious appetite. He refused to give her the satisfaction of seeing him worry, so he just shrugged again.

"I'll find a way," he said smoothly. Apparently his continued composure disturbed her, and she gave up in that moment. After throwing up her hands and letting out an exasperated growl, she turned and stormed away. Polgrin's assistant was unfortunate enough to be caught in her path, and she vented her fury on him.

Once Yolan moved out of sight, Onin called back over his shoulder. "She's gone. You can come out now."

A scaled head protruded from one of the hatching berths. A pair of mismatched eyes fixed themselves on Onin with the slightest hint of distrust. Jehregard looked around for a few seconds and sniffed the air. Seemingly satisfied by the lack of scent, he clambered over the floor to Onin. The hump in his back made his movements clumsy and jerky, similar to a lame horse.

"Smart one, he is," said Master Incubator Polgrin. Onin hadn't seen him nearby while Yolan was present. He was fairly sure the old man had been hiding nearby, just like the young dragon. He could see the wisdom in that. "Seems to know exactly what you're saying."

Jehregard rubbed his head against Onin's leg and stared up at him adoringly. It was obviously a ploy for food, but Onin gave in anyway. He pulled some dried beef from his pockets, and the little dragon snatched it with happy greed.

"M'lord, have you considered Lady Manespike might be correct?" asked Polgrin hesitantly. "I'm as happy as anyone to have hatched a dragon, any dragon, after so many failed clutches. But even a small dragon will be expensive to feed. And house. The expenses will only grow as he does and then what? What will you do with him when he is fully grown?"

Onin tugged at his beard as the dragon rolled over and exposed his underside like a puppy. He leaned over and rubbed the belly scales. Jehregard practically purred in happiness.

"I honestly don't know," said Onin. "But I can't just let him be killed after . . . all we've been through."

Onin had no desire to share the private moment of communion between himself and Jehregard. It was far too personal . . . and mysterious.

Jehregard rolled over and pressed his head against Onin's hand. The little creature seemed not to have a care in the world. Onin envied him.

* * *

Hangric came to see him a few days after. The visit surprised Onin; Hangric had a noted distaste for dragons. The big man dressed in his full uniform as a palace Guard. The decorative armor, while not much use in a fight, certainly looked impressive, especially on the bearlike figure of Hangric.

"It looks like palace duty agrees with you," said Onin as the two clasped hands. "I have to admit; you look quite smart."

"The ladies seem to like it," said Hangric with a sly grin, which disappeared after a moment. His eyes broke away from Onin. "I get more attention than I deserve wandering around the city in this getup."

"Well, enjoy it, I say," Onin replied. "We've worked and trained for this kind of opportunity through all those years at the academy. Best not to spoil it."

"Exactly why I'm here," said Hangric. "You haven't reported for duty in quite some time. People are beginning to talk."

"People? Talk?" Onin said, truly puzzled. "Talk about what?"

"You," said Hangric. His tone became matter-of-fact. "The other Guards have noticed your absence, and rumors are flying about regarding your little pet. Some of the rumors imply you've gone soft in the head. Some even say you're planning on keeping the thing." Hangric's distaste at the notion appeared in his voice.

"I am keeping him," answered Onin. "And he's no 'thing.' His name is Jehregard."

Hangric shot a look at Onin. "Why? There's no way you can sell it--him. You'll never recover the feeding costs alone."

"I won't sell him," Onin said. "I'm going to keep him." He had been thinking about this for several days already. Shortly after Jehregard hatched, Onin realized he would never be able to give the dragon up, even if someone wanted to buy him. Once he'd said it out loud, however, he realized how implausible it sounded.

Hangric just opened and shut his mouth several times, searching for something to say. He finally shrugged.

"Well, that makes my words all the more important now," said the big man. "People are beginning to talk. Not just about you but your family."

"What? My family?" Onin shifted back to bafflement.

"You know how the highborn are," Hangric said. He leaned against the stone wall, propped up by his elbow. "Sometimes the smallest thing can give them something to talk about for days. But a palace Guard rearing his own dragon? It's unheard of. People don't like it."

"I'm getting really tired of 'people' already," said Onin. "What does it matter to them what I do?"

"Again, you know how the highborn are," said Hangric. He held his hands up in a helpless gesture. "They're not the kind of people to embrace the unconventional." Hangric's expression shifted to one of disgust. "Although my wife doesn't apply that kind of thinking to fashion trends. By the Founders, that woman goes out of her way to find the most terrible dressmakers."

Onin couldn't help but laugh. He'd had plenty of arguments with his own spouse about the vagaries of courtly fashions. Hangric turned serious again.

"It's time to come back to duty, Onin," said the big Guardsman. "If you seriously intend to keep . . . him, you'll need your salary more than ever. I know you received a tidy sum by selling your family's estate in the

Midlands, but that won't last forever. Plus, some of the other guards are saying you've lost your mind from whatever happened in the underbelly. You've been gone too long, obsessing about first the egg and now a baby dragon."

"Bah, I've only been gone for . . ." Onin trailed off as he furrowed his brow in thought.

"Seven weeks, Onin," said Hangric. "Thank the gods you've got a forgiving commander."

"But Torreg is--" Onin began to protest but Hangric interrupted.

"Your father-in-law, Onin. There are whispers going about regarding him too. You're not only hurting yourself doing this; it hurts your father-in-law, your wife, your entire reputation now. Whether you like it or not, my friend, you are in a Great Family, and the talk of the other Great Families can have a very real effect on your life. It's being said that even the king knows you've been gone. It's time to come back to work. That'll put a stop to the rumors."

Onin couldn't refute his logic. He would most certainly need his salary and more in the days ahead. He regretted selling off the assets from the Durantis estate so cheaply.

"Tomorrow, then," he said with resolution. "I'll be at the palace at dawn."

* * *

The office redefined opulence, even by Sensi's newly heightened standards. Every fixture, from the banisters to the wall sconces to the alcoves containing vases, was carved in the whitest marble. Minor statues occupied out-of-the-way nooks, and colorful blooms overflowed the many vases. Sensi reclined on a couch opposite a large desk with a curved shape not unlike some sort of bean. A single piece of the same white marble formed the desktop. In the inner curve of the bean nestled a chair, resplendent in red velvet, which stood out all the more because of its stark white surroundings. Similar red velvet covered the couch, making it remarkably soft and comfortable on the cold stone frame. Before him sat a divan covered in the same bright red.

Sensi considered resting his feet on the divan but thought better of it. To be found lounging comfortably would seem petulant.

Sensi wondered why the lord chancellor had summoned him. As head of the treasury, Sensi managed to trim quite a bit of fat from the budgets, particularly that of the Royal Guard. Perhaps he was being petty, but he found himself savoring Torreg's little tantrums.

Sensi started slightly as the doors leading into the office opened. Lornavus entered with a brisk step, his white robes billowing about him. He paid no heed to Sensi, even as the fat man scrambled to his feet. Lornavus simply walked around the ovoid desk, his slippered feet making no sound as he stepped lightly across the marble floor. The slender man sat in the chair behind the desk with no hesitation. He motioned for Sensi to sit down once again, which he did with reluctance.

"Are you sure you should be sitting there?" asked the fat man nervously. "The lord chancellor has a notorious temper when it comes to respecting his office."

"I am sure," said the twin calmly. His face held no semblance of emotion, but a slight smile twitched at the corners of his mouth. "This is now my office in all but name."

Sensi looked shocked and impressed all at once. "You mean--" he began, but the thin man interrupted.

"The old fool of a chancellor will be vacating his position soon enough," said Lornavus. "He has been incautious in his dalliances, and they seem to have caught up with him."

"So why am I here?" asked Sensi. It seemed unlikely Lornavus would want to share in his triumph. Sensi knew him better than most but would never delude himself into thinking the two maintained a friendship.

No one had seen Altavus in some time.

"You are here because you have served well and reliably," said the thin man. "I will be assuming the position of lord chancellor. You, in turn, are going to become the chief magistrate."

"Magistrate? But why?" Sensi's asked with confusion. "I've made great strides within the treasury. I have brought the royal expenditures in line with our forecasts. I've even cut the budgets of the palace detail."

"It's true your work in the treasury has been masterful," said Lornavus. "But at each step, the Royal Guard appeals to the magistrate in order to pass the requisitions through. You shall now become a magistrate, all the better to prevent the armed brutes from hamstringing our efforts any further."

Sensi could muster no enthusiasm for the news. He had worked hard--perhaps too hard--to turn the treasury into an efficient operation. It had taken many long days and sleepless nights to accomplish it, but he now had things so well in hand, he could afford some time for himself to rest and relax while his underlings did the bulk of the work. He didn't want to give up the fruits of his labor.

"I don't want to become magistrate," he found himself saying. The words came unbidden from his lips, and though he tried, he could not stop them. "Leave me to run the treasury. Someone else can do your bidding as magistrate."

"Ah, yes," came the thin man's response. "I could find another but none with your acuity, Sensi. You shall become magistrate and leave the counting of coins to those with less imagination."

Sensi folded his arms over his chest like a petulant child. He knew he trod a dangerous line but would not give up easily. "What's in this for me?"

The would-be lord chancellor leaned forward and spoke with an intensity that belied his soft tone. "I'll give you something you've wanted for your entire life." The thin man tossed a paper in front of Sensi. Sensi unrolled it and began to read. The papers represented a prosecution on charges of corruption and negligence. Sensi remained unimpressed until he read the name of the accused. His mouth must have fallen open wordlessly because Lornavus filled in the words for him.

"That's right," said the thin man. "Your father."

Sensi continued to read through the list of charges and smiled widely as he grasped the seriousness of the allegations. Bribery, theft, conspiracy. Sensi had seen men flung from the parapets into the Cloud Forest for less. He imagined watching the smug face that had taunted him from his mother's picture frame as it plummeted into the canopy below them.

"You are correct," Sensi said breathlessly. "I have wanted this my entire life."

"Think of the other things you can accomplish in your new station," said the thin man. "As a magistrate, you'll be in charge of interpreting the law. Laws, after all, are nothing more than words and open to any number of interpretations."

The possibilities inherent in the station began to sink in to Sensi's mind. Beyond his own desire for vengeance on the father who refused to acknowledge him, the ability to set policy on the exact meaning of a particular law would enable as much control over the government as running the treasury. Once again, Sensi found himself impressed by the twins' thinking.

Sensi also began to wonder what had become of the other brother. In their school days, the two could not be found apart from one another. Since then, it had been years since Sensi had seen them both at the same time. Furthermore, his current inability to tell one brother from the other vexed him. He had taken to calling the one filling the role of dealing with him "Lornavus," but in truth it could have been either brother. Sensi was not certain he spoke to the same brother every time. The thought chilled him. Could the brothers be switching places regularly? If so, to what purpose?

Only time would tell.

Chapter 24

Death comes from the embrace of lovers, and it shall be so terrible and far reaching that the sky itself will seek to hide from it.
--excerpt from *Testament of the Augur*

* * *

The next day brought clear skies and singing birds. Onin rose with the sun and arrived at the palace shortly after. He spent the previous evening on proper grooming of himself and his gear. Consequently he looked his most presentable. Hangric's visit prepared him for the sidelong glances and outright stares he received from the Guards on duty. He intended to seek out Torreg, but the matter became moot when a junior Guard approached him with a missive.

"The king summons you, Onin Manespike," said the young Guard. It still felt strange to Onin to use the Manespike name, although it was the accepted custom for the lower-ranked family to assume the name of the higher ranked in marriage. Somehow it felt like a betrayal of the man who had raised him.

The Guard handed Onin a parchment bearing the royal seal and some hastily scrawled writing. "Report to the private chambers."

Shocked into silence, Onin nodded and set off with his mind racing. Like all Guards, Onin knew the way to the private chambers but had never been inside them. Most Guards hadn't unless their duties specifically required it. Onin struggled to think of a reason the king would summon him. His extended absence might be the cause, but it seemed unlikely the king would take a personal interest in such matters. Rumors of his insanity presented another possibility, though Onin loathed admitting it. Anxiety built in him with each step as Onin envisioned horrible consequences for his family. Guards whispered to one another as he passed them in the corridors, which only fed his fears.

Two Guards stood duty at the private chambers. They opened the door without returning his salute. Rich decorations and lush furnishings filled the rooms, along with Hangric, who clasped hands with his friend but did not smile. "The king is on the balcony," he said, his expression showing no surprise at seeing Onin.

Apparently everyone knew about Onin's summoning, which was disconcerting in itself. Squaring his shoulders, he strode to the balcony. No matter what happened next, he resolved to face it with dignity.

A small group occupied the balcony. Torreg was impossible to miss. He grimaced at the sight of Onin. The others were academics Onin recognized from his days at Scaleback and two royal servants. After quickly scanning the assembled, Onin focused on the king for the first time.

A man who appeared to be in his fifties, like Torreg, was adorned in opulent robes. Wearing a jewel-encrusted gold crown, he gazed out from the balcony, a hooded cage beside him. All eyes save the king's turned on Onin as he stepped onto the balcony, blinking in the morning sun. Torreg motioned him forward, his face the unreadable mask of a soldier.

"The man you asked to see has arrived, Your Majesty," said the commander. The king turned to look at him finally. His bearded face showed his age; streaks of silver stood out in his black beard and hair. Bowing his head low, Onin dropped to one knee.

"That's enough, now. Rise, Onin of the Midlands." The king spoke with a smooth confidence that simultaneously soothed fears and commanded respect. As Onin did his bidding, the king used the opportunity to lock eyes with the Guardsman. Being quite a bit shorter, the king craned his neck to maintain the stare, but it did not diminish his intensity or might. One hand rose to hold his crown upon his head as it began to slide off.

The king turned to Torreg. "This is the one I've heard about?"

"He's the one, sire," said Torreg. His tone betrayed no emotion. "He is fairly bright, in my experience. At least most of the time."

"And he's your son-in-law?"

"Yes, sire."

The king stepped back to look Onin up and down. He stroked his long face thoughtfully before addressing Onin. "So what have you got to say for yourself?"

"Your Majesty, um, ah," Onin stammered. "About my absence--"

"Did you work on my behalf and on behalf of the kingdom?"

"Yes, sire."

"Now tell me about the dragon, you fool!"

"The dragon?" Onin found himself repeating.

"Yes, the dragon! You've given it a name, haven't you?"

"Jehregard?" Onin offered.

The king made a sour face and turned to Torreg. "You said he was clever."

"Sometimes, sire," replied Torreg.

The king turned back to Onin. "Jehregard," he said. "That's an interesting name. How did you come up with it?"

"It . . . just sort of came to me, sire."

"It seems wild notions come naturally to you," said the king. "What in the name of the founders makes you want to keep a deformed runt?"

"I . . . it's . . . ." Onin tried to formulate a response that wasn't an outright lie.

"Out with it, man!" snapped the king.

"We . . . I mean, the Manespike family . . ." Onin said in halting words. He nodded toward his father-in-law for emphasis.

"Yes, yes, I understand," said the king. He waved his hand impatiently. "Get on with it."

"We haven't hatched any dragons for several years," said Onin. "It seems wrong to kill him. I can't bring myself to do it. Other than his bent back, he's perfectly healthy."

"Doesn't he have mismatched eyes as well?" asked the king. He squinted at Onin with a slight frown.

"Yes, he does, Your Majesty," replied Onin. "But he sees quite well, I can assure you. Especially when it comes to food."

The king chuckled. "The verdant dragons possess legendary appetites," said the king. "How do you accommodate his?"

"With difficulty, sire," Onin said with a rueful smile. "I'm still working out the details. He has already stretched the estate to the breaking point."

The king turned his squinted gaze back on Torreg.

"You never mentioned your family was in financial straits."

Torreg inclined his head formally. "It didn't feel proper to burden you with my problems, Your Majesty."

"Nonsense," replied the king. "It is unseemly for the commander of my personal guard to be in such a situation. Have a look at the Torreg family finances with due haste, lord chancellor, make a note of it."

A thin man in ornately officious robes bowed slightly. Onin recognized him from Scaleback Academy, but something different nagged at his mind seeing him in the present.

"Of course, Your Majesty," said the lord chancellor. "I must warn you, however, doing so will present considerable logistic problems. The royal treasury lacks sufficient resources already."

"Then find more resources!" snapped the king. "Do I have to think of everything myself?"

"How, Your Majesty?"

"How what?"

"How do we acquire more resources?"

"That's for you to figure out," the king said. He waved his hand dismissively. "You came with a long list of recommendations, all declaring you to be vastly intelligent. It's the only reason I made someone so young lord chancellor. I'm tired of being told why I can't do something. That's all I heard from your predecessor. Instead, I want someone who is going to figure out how to do it."

"As you wish, Your Majesty," the lord chancellor said with a deep bow. "I'll think of a way, but there are certain legal considerations to be discussed with the magistrate here." With a slight nod, he indicated a short, chubby man with wispy hair. Onin also recognized this young magistrate from

Scaleback. He wracked his brain for a name but failed to come up with one. Like most, he had more or less ignored the academic students during those days.

"I am at your disposal, lord chancellor," said the magistrate, also with a deep bow. His voice came across like a well-oiled hinge. "We could start immediately if you like."

"A good suggestion," said the lord chancellor. "With your leave, Your Majesty?"

"Fine, fine, be about it," said the king with another wave of the hand. The two court officials left the balcony. The king turned his attention back to Onin. "Jehregard's hunger will only grow. Thank the founders the adults hunt for themselves in the Cloud Forest. Even I don't want to pay for that. But Jehregard is going to present a problem. He won't be able to fly with a bent back, so I can't see how he'll be able to hunt."

"It does worry me, sire," nodded Onin. "But I am not convinced he cannot fly. His back has straightened considerably since his hatching. As long as the muscles continue to strengthen . . ."

"Willing to risk it all on a dream, eh?" the king said. A mischievous smile crossed his face. "What's so special about this dragon?"

Pent-up feelings poured forth unexpectedly when Onin spoke. "Maybe a smaller dragon is not such a bad thing. Maybe a smaller dragon could land anywhere and be able to take flight again. I'm not certain breeding dragons for size alone has been a wise practice. I'm sorry, sire."

"Continue," the king said in a hard voice.

Before he spoke again, Onin considered his words, knowing they could mean life or death. "I just think a variety of dragons might be better than just a few of the largest beasts possible."

"Excellent," said the king. "Bring him here tomorrow."

Onin jumped. "Your Majesty?" he quailed.

"Bring Jehregard here tomorrow. I know you grew up in the Midlands, but they do speak the same language below, correct? I keep repeating myself to you."

"Sorry, sire," said Onin. "It's just . . . he can be difficult at times. I can't promise he will behave himself."

"Nonsense. I'm the king. He'll show the proper respect. Plus, I have to confess, I'm a bit of an animal lover myself. She's no dragon, but I would be lost without my Duna."

A chirping cry emitted from under the hooded cage. The king lifted the covering to reveal a scaled creature curled into a sleeping ball. The chirping sound came from its lifted head. To Onin, the creature looked like a miniature, wingless dragon.

"Did you hear your name?" said the king. His fingers slipped through the thin bars of the cage and stroked her snout.

"Looks a lot like a dragon, sire," said Onin.

"She is a verduri, my Duna," said the king. He bore a proud smile that set Onin partially at ease. "Rare creatures from the Cloud Forest. They are strict herbivores and spend most of their lives clinging to tree branches. We spend a lot of time in the gardens among the only trees we have in the palace. Isn't that right, Duna?" The miniature dragon trilled excitedly. "She's also nocturnal, so we are awake most nights. Speaking of which, it's about time you went to sleep, my dear." The king returned the cloth cover to the cage.

"Bring Jehregard to the south garden tomorrow morning," said the king. "I'm sure the fresh air will be good for him."

"Are you sure, sire?" asked Onin. He remained doubtful. "Like I said, he is spirited."

"Don't make me tell you again."

* * *

After taking leave of the king, Sensi and the newly appointed lord chancellor reconvened in the royal offices. Once the door closed behind them, the twin described his plan for acquiring additional funds. Sensi could respond with only shock.

"There will be open revolt," said Sensi by way of protest. The other seemed unmoved.

"I imagine so," he replied. "But the king has made his wishes clear. He wants results, so I shall deliver them."

"Aren't you overstepping your authority a bit?" asked Sensi. He was cautious when questioning Lornavus--or Altavus, whichever this happened to be.

"Am I? You're the magistrate. I do believe there is a precedent. The crown has authority to seize the assets of criminals."

"True," said Sensi. "It mostly applies to pickpockets and fences these days, but it is the law. But we're not talking about some petty fence. The Great Families won't possibly stand for it."

"I already have the required evidence. What protest can they possibly offer?"

"So you've selected a target already?"

"Not exactly," said the lord chancellor. "But I have sufficient documentation to implicate any of the Great Families."

"All of them? That must have taken some doing."

"Yes, but not as much as you might think. All of the Families have illicit dealings aplenty, and they are careless in covering their tracks."

Sensi rubbed his chin. "With sufficient evidence, I can make the case. The punishment is draconian, though. And no Great Family has ever been subjected to it."

"No Great Family has been convicted of corruption, either," said the lord chancellor. "We must sometimes blaze a new path."

"But such a risky one?" asked Sensi, worry written plainly on his face. "I understand ambition, Lornavus, but you've achieved so much already. You've acquired vast wealth. You are the youngest lord chancellor ever appointed. Where does it end?"

"We might have risen to positions of prominence, Sensi, but we've not changed anything. Our work is only beginning if we strive to live up to our great heritage."

Sensi made no response. He had always viewed the twins as manipulators and opportunists. He'd never entertained the notion they might be serious about the convictions expressed by the Unknowns. He decided to leave it for now.

"Speaking of such, I have another concern," Sensi said to broach the subject. "Our more militaristic brethren grow impatient and have concocted a plan to take direct action. I fear we are losing control of them."

"What are they planning? They could jeopardize the movement."

"Exactly why I am bringing it to you. They bribed one of the palace Guards recently. Whatever they learned inspired their lunacy. It is some sort of open attack; that I do know."

"I see," said the lord chancellor. He took on a thoughtful countenance. "I shall have to take steps."

Sensi was relieved, certain the resourceful man could somehow defuse the situation.

"I should get started with some research," said Sensi, rising to leave. "I want to make sure our case is on solid legal footing. Perhaps there is some precedent."

Sensi bowed to the twin and turned to leave. As he reached out to open the door, the lord chancellor spoke.

"One other thing, Sensi."

"Yes, Your Excellency?"

"Never again call me by name," said the twin. "From this moment forward, refer to me by my title or not at all."

Chapter 25

Honor and courage go together. In most cases, one requires the other.
--Prendor, teacher at Scaleback Academy

* * *

"Does he bite?" asked the king. Despite the previous day's enthusiasm, the actual presence of a dragon unnerved the monarch. He gripped the arms of the chair tightly but leaned forward to look closer.

"No, Your Majesty," said Onin. He paused and cast Jehregard a sidelong glance. "Well, it actually depends on his mood. He's been very well behaved this morning, though. So far."

Jehregard sat next to Onin, preening his wings. The trip to the palace had been surprisingly uneventful, which had given him plenty of time to think about how terribly things could go wrong. All he had was a piece of thick rope tied about the dragon's neck in case he became rambunctious. Jehregard, however, seemed unperturbed by the situation and napped peacefully in the carriage. Onin knew his dragon to be wily, so he kept a tight grip on the other end of the rope.

"He's bigger than I expected," said the king. "I was told he was a runt."

"Yes, sire," said Onin. "He weighs about as much as me already. But I'm told he's about half the size of other verdants his age." Jehregard raised his head, nuzzling against Onin's hip. The big man absently reached down and gave him an affectionate pat.

"It's true, sire," said Torreg. The commander stood nearby, seemingly ready to leap upon Jehregard at the slightest hint of trouble. "I've seen enough hatchlings in my day. His growth is stunted."

In response to the statement, Jehregard turned a cool gaze on Torreg. The young dragon gave a derisive snort and returned to his preening.

"The eyes are breathtaking," exclaimed the king. "Do other dragons have such jewel-like eyes? I've never seen it before."

"I've not seen or heard of it myself, sire," said Torreg. "It seems to be unique to this dragon."

"Amazing," murmured the king. He leaned forward in his cushioned chair, peering closer at Jehregard. "What causes such a thing?"

"A birth defect, sire," said Torreg. "Like the bent back. He's likely going to develop vision problems with that eye, if he hasn't already."

"You have a bleak outlook, commander," said the king with a frown. "Despite his imperfections, the creature seems healthy."

"That he is, Your Majesty," Onin chimed in. The dragon in question seemed to have concluded his preening and now looked about the palace gardens in curiosity. Birds tweeted from the trees, and Jehregard emitted a honking cry. He loped toward the nearest tree, pulling at the rope in Onin's hand.

"Take the restraint from his neck," said the king. "Give the little fellow some freedom."

The lord chancellor, who had remained silent so far, chose that moment to speak. "I'm not certain that's altogether wise, Your Majesty."

"Nonsense," rebuffed the king. "You can see for yourself he's quite sedate. What's the worst that could happen? It's not as if he's going to fly away."

"True, sire," said Torreg. "He's never going to fly with that hump."

"As I thought," said the king. "Untie the rope."

Onin hesitated for a moment. He leaned down and took the scaly head in his hands. Jehregard met his gaze with mismatched eyes. "You behave yourself," he said. He then loosened the knot in the rope and removed it from the dragon's head.

Suddenly gifted with freedom, Jehregard shot a sidelong glance at Onin, uncertain what to do. The dragon then turned and casually plodded to the king's seat. Torreg bounced tensely on the balls of his feet, ready to leap into action.

Jehregard showed no signs of excitement, however. The tiny dragon stopped before the king, locking his mismatched eyes on the crowned man's. After a long moment, Jehregard took another step forward and gently laid his head in the king's lap. The monarch, grinning from ear to ear, stroked his manicured hands over the scaly snout and head. The dragon closed his eyes in pleasure and nuzzled further into the man's embrace.

"What a delightful creature," pronounced the king. His voice conveyed giddiness.

Jehregard lifted his head to look once again at the king's smiling face. The dragon then casually sank his claws into the robes gathered about the man's legs, shredding delicate fabric with a single rake. The gathered crowd of Guardsmen and officials recoiled, and the magistrate, Onin's old classmate, gasped.

The king, however, laughed uproariously.

Jehregard scampered to the nearest tree, the interaction completely forgotten. Onin followed closely, still nervous about giving his charge free rein. Jehregard spent a few moments sniffing about the base of the tree then sank his claws into the trunk and scaled into the branches overhead. Onin reached out to stop him but ended up with his hands on the dragon's tail. As much as he heaved and pulled, however, Jehregard would not come down from the branches and only squawked his displeasure at all the tugging. The king laughed harder at the display. Torreg and the other Guards snickered, despite their attempts at restraint.

Onin's position provided a splendid view of the garden's western wall. Given his preoccupation with the dragon's tail, he almost didn't notice several black shapes slip over the top of the wall. Onin did a double-take, but his eyes verified the first impression. A stream of black-clad intruders clambered over the wall into the king's garden. Onin absently let go of Jehregard, stunned into disbelief. The intruders covered themselves with black furs and white masks. They appeared just like Onin and Bolg when the two staged an attack on the palace. Onin turned to Torreg for confirmation. The commander, however, displayed nothing but alarm.

"To arms!" Torreg cried. "This is not a drill!"

True to training, the assembled Guardsmen put weapons in hand with due haste. The warriors formed a protective ring about the king as well as the lord chancellor and magistrate. Onin took a place next to Torreg. Still unaware of the intruders, the king fussed. "What is this? How am I supposed to enjoy my garden with you lot blocking the view?"

"We're under attack, Your Majesty," said the lord chancellor. The pasty-looking man seemed calm despite the circumstances. The chubby magistrate beside him shivered uncontrollably, however.

"Nonsense!" decried the king. He rose to his feet, pushing up on his toes to see over the Guards. Very close now, the attackers screamed as they charged. "This must be one of Torreg's exercises. Torreg, is this your fault?"

"I'm about to be very busy, sire!" cried Torreg even as he crossed swords with the first wave of attackers.

Onin met the first of the charging invaders with brute force. He parried the incoming weapon and slammed his shoulder into the man's chest, sending him reeling back into his allies. Several of them tumbled to the ground, but others filled the gap, pressing Onin's defenses with a flurry of blows. He received a stinging wound to his sword arm but delivered a disabling blow in return.

The battle became a chaotic swirl of clashing steel, cycling around the ring of defenders. The Guards, numbering a mere eight, fought hard against the superior numbers. While the attackers lacked skill and training, the few defenders would not hold out for long. Even as the thought crossed Onin's mind, the first Guard fell, mortally wounded. The fur-clad attacker who struck the blow let out a whoop and moved directly for the king, sword aloft.

Not yet finished, the fallen Guard tenaciously wrapped his arms around the attacker's legs, holding him in place. The attacker kicked the dying Guard away, but the delay gave Onin the chance to strike the invader down. He looked toward the king, anxious for the man's safety. Torreg hovered protectively over the king, hauling the monarch about by the arm.

"To the palace!" cried the commander. "Clear a path to the palace!'

Onin and the Guards charged forward with a collective roar. Not focused on inflicting harm but instead on driving opponents aside, they lashed about with fervor. The disorganized rabble melted away before them but filled in the gap left in the wake of the assault.

Another Guard went down, struggling under a pile of black-clad attackers. Onin wanted to help but found himself too hard pressed to cover the distance in time. He fought on, hacking mightily to either side.

Torreg rushed forward, hauling the king beside him. The commander parried a downward slash, felling his opponent with a quick backhand swing. He immediately spun to his right, stabbing another. The entry to the palace drew closer. The enemy pressed into the space between, halting their advance. Another Guardsman fell in the charge, leaving five to protect the king and the lord chancellor. The magistrate had already been lost in the chaos.

Onin thrust his tired arm upward to parry another blow, but his palace-issued blade snapped beneath a superior weapon. Suddenly weaponless, Onin lunged directly at the nearest attacker, wrapping his thick hands around the invader's sword arm. With a wrench of his powerful arms, Onin snapped the man's elbow. Screaming, the man released his blade, which Onin scooped up and used to dispatch him.

The Guards had been scattered in the fighting. Only Torreg remained near the king. Onin fought hard, trying to cut a path to the commander. Torreg fought off three attackers at once, lunging, blocking, and slashing wildly. The poor craftsmanship of their equipment betrayed Torreg in that moment, however. The fancy armor gave under a powerful blow to Torreg's side. Grimacing in pain, Torreg kicked the attacker away. The black-clad invader reeled backward, colliding with the surprised king. The two collapsed in a heap.

With a wrench, Torreg pulled the blade from his side through the rent in his merely decorative armor and launched his own attack. The two attackers fell back before his savagery, blocking clumsily with each stumbling step. Torreg fought with great courage but moved away from the king, leaving him undefended.

Clearing a path before him, Onin feared he was too late. The king was on his back, a fur-clad attacker on top, throttling him. The monarch's face was turning blue while he feebly struggled to remove the hands from his throat.

Jehregard struck.

The young dragon swooped out of the sky, wings unfurled majestically. The scaly form flew low to the ground, colliding with the king's assailant and knocking him away. The dragon clung to his target, landing atop the fur-clad figure. The invader screamed as Jehregard exacted revenge.

Onin covered the remaining distance in a few quick steps. Rather than pull the king to his feet, Onin readied his weapon while standing over the recovering man. A pair of invaders engaged him, and Onin knocked their clumsy strikes aside, searching for an opening. Torreg attacked them from the rear, still clutching his wounded side. He felled one of the attackers and provided Onin the opening he sought. The second invader fell a moment later.

A dozen Guards streamed into the garden from the palace, with Hangric in the lead. Their additional numbers turned the fight in the Guards' favor. The invaders fought tenaciously, however. Onin's lungs heaved for breath as he watched the remaining attackers dispatched one by one.

Reinforcements secured the garden quickly. Jehregard loped to Onin's side, stopping momentarily to nuzzle the stunned king. Suddenly remembering where he stood, Onin stepped aside and helped the king to his feet.

"Are you injured, sire?" asked Onin.

The king dusted himself off. Between the dirt of the skirmish and the shredded robes, thanks to Jehregard, he looked a sight. "I don't think so," said the man. His hand absently went to his head to adjust his crown but it had fallen away in the scuffle. He was regarding Jehregard seriously. "This beast saved my life. He has the soul of a Guard. Smaller dragons, indeed."

Jehregard lifted his snout and released a squawk. The king laughed then looked about at the aftermath. The garden lay in ruins, shrubs had been destroyed, grassy patches churned into mud by tromping boots. Broken weapons, broken masks, and broken men filled the landscape.

Torreg issued orders, already taking charge of the situation. Guards began tending the wounded, Torreg included, and looking for surviving attackers for later interrogation. Several climbed the garden wall to ascertain how the invaders went over the wall. They reported the discovery of crude ladders propped against the garden wall from the adjoining estate.

"Get some men down there," barked Torreg. He held one of the white masks in his hand while a Guard assisted him out of his armor. The objects lay scattered about, many still attached to their wearers. "I want answers. Any prisoners?"

"A few, Commander," said Hangric from nearby. "Not sure how many will survive much longer, though."

"Send for physicians," said Torreg. "We need all the information we can get, so we keep them all alive. For now."

"Why would anyone want to kill me?" asked the king. "Is not the kingdom prosperous?"

"We'll find out," said the commander quickly. "More importantly, you are safe and apparently unharmed. We should have the physicians look you over just in case."

The king waved away his concern. "I'm fine, thanks to this valiant little dragon." The king knelt to stroke Jehregard's head. Almost as an afterthought, he added, "And all of you, of course."

The king suddenly jerked his head about. "Lord Chancellor?"

"Here, Your Majesty," came a call from a nearby hedge. The pale man clambered from the thick branches, his fine robes tattered and ruined. "I took advantage of the confusion to hide. I am unharmed. I have not seen the magistrate, Sensi, however."

"I'm here," came a reply. Sensi limped in their direction, leaning on the arm of a Guardsman.

Torreg looked him up and down. Other than the limp, Sensi appeared intact.

"How did you survive?" asked the commander.

Sensi shrugged. "I played dead," said the magistrate. "I was thankfully overlooked, though stepped on a few times."

"The Guard performed admirably today," said the king solemnly. "But security must be dramatically increased."

"Yes," said Torreg. He scooped a broken Guardsman's swords from the ground. He displayed it to the king and the officials. "The blade, though pretty, snapped during battle, like many others. This is what I feared would happen. I beseech you all, equip the palace detail with quality arms."

"You shall have what you require," said the lord chancellor. He bowed to Torreg. "The danger is now clear to me. I was wrong to question you before, Commander."

Sensi swooned, leaning on a guard for support. Torreg looked equally stunned, like a man who had gone looking for a fight but found no enemy.

"Well, Onin Manespike," exclaimed the king. He gently scratched the ridges along Jehregard's snout, much to the dragon's delight. "We've settled another thing today."

"What's that, sire?" asked Onin.

"Jehregard has proven he can fly!" said the king. "Moreover, he came to the defense of his king in my moment of truest need. His place in the Heights is assured."

The king whirled on the commander. "Torreg Manespike!"

"Sire!" Torreg snapped to attention.

"I wish to purchase this fine dragon."

"Purchase, sire?"

"Not you too," said the king. "Your family sells dragons, correct?"

"Of course, Your Majesty," said Torreg.

"Then I shall purchase Jehregard," said the king. He looked proud of his solution. "Onin shall be his keeper, of course. But he shall be my personal dragon."

Jehregard looked like the cat that caught the bird.

Onin felt all his problems might have just been solved, but a whole new set had just sprung into existence.

* * *

Onin returned home that evening, exhausted physically and emotionally. Torreg had remained at the palace in light of the recent attack but had released Onin on the excuse Jehregard needed to be returned to his enclosure. After getting the young dragon settled in for the night, Onin craved only two things: a hot meal and a warm bed.

To his surprise, Yolan awaited him in the dining hall. She sat demurely at the table, beaming a great smile at Onin. He hesitated and might have turned to leave, but she beckoned him forward.

"Come, sit, my husband. You must be starved after such a day. Howle will have your dinner any moment."

Onin took his seat in resignation. It was rare for Yolan to demand his company, but when she did, there was no suggesting otherwise. Might as well go along with it.

"Tell me all about your meeting with the king." Her eyes flashed at him like gems. One delicate finger traced the outside edge of the goblet in front of her.

"Oh, the meeting? It was all right until . . ."

Horror filled her face. "What happened? Did you embarrass yourself in front of the king?"

"What? No!" he stammered. "Everything was fine until someone tried to kill the king."

"Someone tried to kill the king? What kind of man would do that?"

"It was lots of men, actually. They almost succeeded. Luckily we held them long enough for reinforcements--"

Yolan was suddenly next to him. She gripped his shirt in both hands, pulling her face close to his. "Tell me you saved the king. Tell me you had a hand in that."

"Well, yes, I did. And so did your father."

Her face lit up with glee. She was like the sun rising. "You and father saved the king!" she squealed.

"And so did Jehregard."

She stopped, shocked anew. "The dragon did what?"

"Jehregard saved the king. He flew right into the fighting without hesitation to protect the king."

"The deformed runt *flew?*"

Onin ignored the insult. "Yes, swooped in at the last moment. Now the king wants to buy him."

"Buy him?" Her eyes sparkled again. "You mean to tell me we sold a dragon? To the king?"

Onin gave a nervous laugh. She leaned forward and kissed him deeply.

"The gods surely smile upon us. So many happy things in one day . . . and now another."

"I don't think an attack on the king constitutes a good day, but what do you mean by another?"

She wrapped her slender arms around his neck. Her face nuzzled cheek to cheek so she could whisper in his ear. "I am with child, my husband. You're going to be a father."

Epilogue

* * *

"The dreams change and the Protector along with them," said the ragged old woman. Her domicile reeked of smoke and burning things. "He sees more but understands less than ever."

The slight-figured man in her hut made no response. He had learned from long experience that she didn't really speak to him, at least, not in any way that required a response. On the occasions when he would respond, she would ignore his words or, worse yet, indicate she already knew his words. It unnerved him.

"Of course he is thinking that," said the old woman. "But his comfort is of little importance. He also has his role to serve. He is healthy enough and ready to leave this place."

She spoke truly. He had been nursed to health by the old woman, at least in body. But his spirit still felt sick. Twisted things haunted his own dreams, though he wasn't at all sure what the crone meant. Dark figures and inhuman countenances skirted the edge of his memory when he woke in a sweat.

"Tell me, old woman," said the man. "What did I see? Can you explain these visions that haunt me?"

"He still wonders if they are fever dreams." The hag cackled. "Can't accept the truth of his own sight. How is that supposed to help things?" She absently began to clean the bandage on the man's leg. The wounds had almost completely healed, but three angry red scars ran across his thigh, parallel to one another--just like claw marks.

The man shivered with suppressed memories of horror and pain. Despite the evidence of the scars, he indeed hoped his visions sprang from the fever.

"He has his part to play as well," said the hag. "I know that already. The Crow has one more preparation to make before he goes away." With those words, her gnarled hands pushed a warm cup of foul-smelling broth into his hands. The Crow, as she named him, understood his part and lifted the bitter concoction to his lips to drain the cup. For some reason, he could not bring himself to disobey the old woman.

Then, in a rare moment, the hag looked directly into his eyes. "Go now. Say what you are meant to say," she intoned. "Deliver your message, as it needs to be heard."

JACK MCCARTHY AND BRIAN RATHBONE

With a will not his own, the Crow got to his feet. He could control his legs, and as he walked away, he asked over his shoulder, "What message?"

The old woman had returned to ignoring him, however. His legs carried him out of her hovel and into the tunnels that haunted his dreams.

"What message?" he asked softly, pleading with no one and anyone. The shadows of the tunnels engulfed him.

Be sure to check out *The Dawning of Power* and the rest of the *Godsland* fantasy series. For more information visit BrianRathbone.com.

Made in the USA
Middletown, DE
15 May 2016